The Sea Between

PETER NOYCE

ISBN: 1540352641
ISBN-13: 978-1540352644

DEDICATION

This, my debut novel, was inspired by a night sharing rum and stories on a balcony in Panama City. I hope I've done the emotions justice.
I would like to take this opportunity to thank everyone who has humoured me during the writing process. Also, Mexico. You taught me so much.

1

I was the first to break the silence. 'Can you hear me?' … 'Aurelio, can you hear me?'

'Yeah, I can hear you.'

'Good.'

'Everything OK?'

'Not really.'

'What's up, man?' … 'Simon, what's up?'

'Have you ever tried to get over anything before?'

… 'What do you mean?'

'I mean, have you ever tried to deal with anything really bad?'

'Bad like Club América winning the title?'

'No.'

'Well, how bad do you mean?'

'Pretty much the worst.'

'I don't think so.' … 'You OK, Simon?'

'How do you do it?'

'Do what, man?'

'Get over something.'

'I … I think it depends …'

'On what?'

'I … I don't know. Wanna tell me about it?'

'I always used to worry something like that would happen, Aurelio. It used to scare me to think that nothing tragic had happened to me. I was petrified about what I would do if it did.'

… 'OK.'

'Then it happened. Just like that. A matter of seconds, millimetres, fractions – a near impossibility.'

'I'm so sorry, mate. These things, they … I can't explain why, but they …'

'For a while I ceased to exist; the light disappeared and I stopped caring. I was frozen. Life was something that happened around me, in spite of me. It kept going when I could not.'

'But you're here now, Simon, living life to the full. That counts for something, right?'

'I've always been good at pretending. After it happened, I tried to make everyone think I was fine. Everyone.'

'You've always seemed pretty normal to me, bro. We all have our ups and our downs. We all do.'

'I had a job, I saved some money and to everyone, including my closest friends, I was just another normal guy who'd had his fair share of bad luck and was doing what he could to get on with life.'

'Man, you know, whatever you need to tell me, whatever it is, I'm never gonna judge.'

'I know. It's just, running away is that much easier.'

'Yeah, it is.'

'It's easier to bury something than it is to dig it out. So that's what I did – that's what I've been doing. But I've always known that if I wanted to really *live* again, if I wanted to feel in control, if I wanted to be excited about the future and happy that I'd see it, I'd need to find a way of getting over it. It's just … it's the whole wording of it: get over it.'

'Get over it.'

'Like it's some kind of fixed obstacle I can climb over. As if I could reach the top of it and work my way down the other side.'

'Maybe you just – and I know this is *so* hard – but maybe, somehow, you just need to let go. Maybe you could make a fresh start.'

'What, and leave everything behind?'

'Well, the stuff you could do without.'

'That's the thing, I don't think I'm ready to do that.' … 'Maybe … maybe I'll just have to keep on running – running as far and as fast as I can.'

'What happens when you run out of space?' … 'Simon?'

There, lying on my back, sticking to the sheets of a cheap hotel room in a tropical paradise, looking up at a fan as it whirred above me, each stroke more tired and futile than the last, I felt isolated, alone, washed up on an island between what I could see of my future and what I wanted to remember of my past. I looked over at my bag of dirty clothes and then back to the fan. I knew I had to move on. I knew I'd left home to do exactly that. But right there in the heat and the noise and the stale, turgid space, lost between life's floorboards, I realised my legs might not go much further.

'Simon?'

The sensual beat of Latin music bounded in from the neon-lit darkness of the street below, crawled along the floor and clambered up my bed, through my ears and into my head, banging against everything it found. I reached out to the bedside table, snatched at a bottle and took a swig of warm rum.

'You can get through this,' Aurelio told me, his muffled voice fighting its way through a slender, flaking wall and trickling into the stagnant heat of my room.

I needed to get through it.

The problem was, I was going round in circles. The same thoughts, the same places; I was doing my best to move on, but I'd gone nowhere at all. I looked up again at the ceiling fan trying in vain to take some heat out of the place – the sound of its shark fin blades cutting through my middle. How much longer could I keep it up? Something, or someone, would have to give, surely.

I reached out a trembling hand and flicked a switch. The light went out and the fan ground despairingly to a whimpering halt.

Dead.

2

The plane was inching its way across the endless Atlantic at the speed of a bloated sloth. I tapped on the screen in the headrest in front of me, thinking it must be broken: nothing. It was agonising – like watching a fly trying to escape a bowl of soup. It hadn't moved in at least ten minutes. We were all stuck in the big, wide blue, miles from anywhere we wanted to be.

'You wanna cut that out?' my neighbour spat at me.

'What?' I asked.

'Your goddam foot, stop tapping it!'

'Sorry, I'm just quite keen to get there, that's all.'

'No shit. Have a drink or something, will ya? Relax!'

I sank a couple of mini bottles of wine, pressed my eyelids down hard and waited for sleep. Milliseconds dripped slowly into seconds; seconds drained slowly into minutes – it wasn't working.

'You ever been to Mexico?' I whispered to my neighbour.

'Yeah, sure,' he said, letting me know the conversation was over.

I sat back, rested my head against the window and listened to the low hum of the engines. I closed my eyes again and started to explore the few stories my grandma had told me about Mexico. I drifted across deserts, over mountains and along silver-sand beaches. I felt her hands in mine as I tickled the warm water with my toes. I watched the wind wash through her chestnut hair and rinse the years from her face and hands. She was home and I was finally doing it; I was finally on my way. Slowly, a smile grew across my face and with it the first drops of glorious sunlight. I opened my eyes and looked out the window, down through the gaps in the clouds at the green and brown below.

The plane began to drop as we crossed over snow-capped volcanos, their glossy peaks winking at the plane's skating shadow. Lead smoke drifted out across the valley below, where long, grey lines ran for miles and miles like a ploughed field of concrete – infinite avenues and alleyways dividing perfect square blocks of metropolis. Flat, red roofs and black water butts reproduced for as far as I could see, clinging onto the valley soil, a carpet of choking brown hovering just above.

As we neared the airport, the concrete gave way to glass and steel. Tall buildings stood on tiptoes, peering down at the city below, watching its people charge around chasing tails. Cars screeched brakes and rode bumper to bumper, revving their engines in defiance of the metal inertia that spread out as far as the eye could see. There were no empty spaces.

My heart raced as the plane's wheels thudded against the runway and a thin film of smoke slinked out from under the hot rubber, the engines roaring us to a safe, pedestrian crawl. I clutched my passport firmly as I made my way off the plane towards immigration and the freedom of a new world.

'Have you been to Mexico before?' the immigration lady asked me.

'No, but I've always wanted to come,' I said enthusiastically.

'And how long will you be here?'

'I'm not sure. I'm keeping an open mind …'

'Just say six months.'

'Six months.'

'Welcome to Mexico. I hope you find what you're looking for,' the lady said, giving me a friendly smile. Down came the stamp.

I rushed for my bag and went to the taxi rank, where a toad of a lady sat in a small booth, exhausted by the long lines of English-speaking tourists trying to make their way into town.

'¿Hablas español?' she shot at me.

'Un poco.'

'¿A dónde va mi'jo?' she replied, her thick jaw slowly rising and falling as she worked her way through a pack of gum.

'Errrr, centre? El … centre? ¿Centro?'

She rolled her eyes, a fly settling on the concrete fringe pasted to her heavily-powdered face. 'One hundred fifty.'

I tried to thank her, but she'd already screamed for the next customer as my bag was whisked off to a swish VW saloon taxi with its engine running.

The driver slammed his foot to the floor and barged into a hazy fog of traffic, weaving his way from one lane to the next, around potholes that opened up in the road. I dug my fingers into the seat in a hopeless attempt to control the situation as vehicles swarmed around us like gangs of convict wasps. I closed my eyes but immediately slammed into a wall of angry exhausts, pounding music and the fierce exchanges of drivers so close I could smell the hatred of their words. 'Go fuck your mum!', 'Hey, go fuck yours!' My stomach felt like it was going to fall out of my body at any moment. It was raw. It was exciting. I was far from home.

'I don't believe we've been formally introduced,' I said in my best English, offering a hand to my taxi driver.

'¿Qué?'

'I said … I was just trying to avoid sounding American.'

'¡¿Gringo?!'

'¡No! Yo Inglish. Iiiinglish.'

'Argh, chingón. Ecsillent. Margarit Tacher.'

… 'No, no. Yo gringo. ¡Griiiingo!'

I'd made our introduction needlessly awkward, but I was warming to my driver and for what it's worth, I think he was taking to me too. A short, squat bloke, his driving had something of the theatrical to it. The pronounced slamming down of each pedal was like the violent stroke of a conductor's baton and his erratic movement the twist and turn of a poorly-written soap opera. In fact, I'm sure I had seen him before in one of those telenovelas my grandma used to watch, where every change of mood and each dramatic pause would be indicated by the raising of an eyebrow or the twitching of a moustache. Yeah, I'm sure he must have been Juan Valdovinos, the secret lover of Laura Mendoza and father to more than one illegitimate child.

'What about your children, Juan?' I chanced.

'¿Qué?'

'Errrr, ¿hijos, Juan, hijos?'

'Forrrr … have … I have forrrr.'

'All with the same woman? How do you work holidays?'

'¿Qué?'

'I'm being stupid, ignore me. Why don't we turn the music up? Music up?' I said, poking the air with my finger.

The fragile frame of the car began to shake as Juan gave the music a crank in the right direction – big booming Cumbia: *chun-cha-chun-cha, chun-cha-chun-cha*. Some song about a vampire if I wasn't mistaken. Juan started gyrating and looked across at a lipstick touting señorita in the car next to ours, honking his horn to the beat of the music and giving her the eye.

Looking up and out, I could see flickers of life in between the fumes of the slow-fast moving traffic: houses of every imaginable colour; street vendors clogging up pavements flogging lamp shades, comedy hats and stolen cigarettes to a million different people of all size and shape; shoeshine boys violently whipping the feet of men in ties and suits; juice stands rammed with fruit and vegetables, their blenders feeding off the current of a nearby lamppost.

We came to a standstill by a set of traffic lights and were treated to a show by a couple of juggling clowns. With their makeup streaming under the hazy glare of the sun, they tossed eggs into the air, before hurriedly smashing them on their heads and sprinting from one car to the next, knocking on windows in a desperate plea for charity.

'That's sad,' I said.

'Sad?'

'Yeah, you know, triste.'

'Yis, triste. But they hab money more.'

'They make more money than you?'

'Yis.'

'Really?'

'Yis. You, vacation?'

'Pretty much, Juan. I wanted to escape home life for a while. Sometimes it's nice to go on a bit of an adventure, right?'

'Ahhhh, trabel. Is nice. ¿Primera vez en México?'

'Primera vez … ahhhh, first time. It is, yeah. But I've always planned to come to Mexico. I promised two very special people that I would come here a while back. And I finally made it.'

'Is biutiful. Is beri biutiful. You lub it, beri.'

'I hope so. I'm a bit nervous if truth be told. Life hasn't been so easy of late.'

'Yis.'

'Sorry, you didn't need to know that. So, are we close to the centre? ¿El centro?'

'Yis, is close now.'

It'd taken a full hour to travel just a few miles from the airport, but we finally reached downtown Mexico City. Strong stone buildings stood to attention along every street, a faint whiff of sewage lurking somewhere in the distance. A group of mariachi wedding singers hung out the back of a van just ahead of us, dangling violins, trumpets and empty beer bottles out of the windows, their giant hats forming turrets on their heads. A man decked head to toe in fetching lycra zoomed past on a slender racing bike, disappearing through the cloud of acrid, black fumes churned out by an overcrowded bus.

I stopped the taxi as we reached the finest looking hotel in the centre of the city, The Boutique Hotel Hernán. I'd never stayed in a posh hotel, and since I'd managed to come so far from home, I thought it'd be stupid not to try something a little bit special. Besides, I had a new credit card to break in.

I stepped through an imposing, oak door and into a small courtyard teeming with green plants. A tinny saxophone played over a pair of speakers sat just above the door. A smiling face looked me over from the safety of a marble reception. 'Hello, sir. Do you have a reservation?'

'No, I don't actually. I thought I'd try my luck.'

'Is sir travelling with his parents or guardians?'

'No … just me,' I said, shrugging my shoulders apologetically. 'Do you have any rooms available?'

'Well, we normally require a reservation, but let me see what I can do.' He feigned some clicking and typing, and before I knew it, had come back with an answer. 'Well, sir, it looks like we've got one room free, and I'm pleased to tell you it's the penthouse suite.'

'Is that so?' I muttered. 'Do you take credit card?'

His eyes lit up. 'Naturally, sir. I think sir will find it an excellent choice. If sir would just permit me his card one second, I'll get that all ready for him.' He looked at my card as if he knew it was on its maiden voyage. 'I'm sorry, sir, there appears to be a problem with our terminal. Perhaps we could try again after you've made yourself comfortable,' he said, as an order, rather than a suggestion.

'That'll do.'

I took the lift up to the third floor with a man in a bowtie who insisted on carrying my bag. He then waited, still clutching my bag, until I realised he was due a tip.

'Are you waiting for …?' I asked, reaching for my wallet.

He nodded.

I looked down at the stacks of fresh notes and had no idea how much they were worth, watching his smile grow wider as I moved from red to green.

'Is 200 OK?'

'Is up to you.'

'Here, take these,' I said, shoving a few green notes into his paw and gratefully closing the door to my room.

I danced my eyes across a gigantic wedding cake of a bed and a balcony overlooking the buzz of the city, dumped my bag next to a mahogany writing table and picked up a hand-written menu propped up against a mini bar: forty-year-old whisky, Mexico's finest tequila, Indian gin, organic, free-range snacks.

I sat down on the bed, had a little bounce, led back and listened to the brash sound of horns, exhausts and cracking concrete creeping in from outside. A flat-screen TV the size of a football pitch stared at me from the wall.

'What are you looking at?'

I walked over to the balcony and watched thousands of people scurry like ants across a six-lane road. Buses and cars crawled in angry bursts, inching across the tarmac piano where people crossed. A lady dressed in beige stood slowly turning a music box, its notes crashing against each other and falling to the floor. She held out a hat hoping for appreciation or pity, but most walked past without looking her way.

'Watch out!' I yelled as a small girl with swaying pigtails ran into the road in front of the screaming cars. An irate mother rushed to the girl's side and scooped her up, before carrying her to safety.

I closed the balcony door and sat back down, my hands tapping the side of the bed. I hooked up to the Wi-Fi and opened Kayak: *Mexico City* →

London, £798. My finger hovered and folded back in on itself.

I turned on the TV and immediately started flicking through the channels: a man dressed as a child poking his head out of a barrel; a lady with bleached hair and inflated lips screaming at a terrified member of the public; a man in a cowboy hat and silk shirt singing to the camera. I turned it off, stripped off my clothes and cast them to one corner of the room.

'What the hell am I doing?'

I didn't think I'd miss anything about my life back home. I was pleased to be able to just focus on *me* for a while. But there was something beneath, just below the surface, that made me worry – something that told me I'd sold myself a big fat lie, that I had just closed my eyes and covered everything up because it had got too ugly to bear.

I went and stood under the shower, pounding my head with steaming water. I wanted to make some sense, to relinquish the doubt. I turned off the water and listened to the low hum of alien traffic swirling outside. It was time for a drink.

3

I finally took the plunge and booked my flight the very same day I went to open a savings account. I'd filled out all the forms, made my way into town, got to the counter with a big bundle of cash and was staring at the bank lady on the other side of the gleaming glass by the time I stopped to ask myself why I needed one.

'I suppose since you've got a job at last, you'll be able to save up some money, Simon,' my dad had said, looking down his nose and avoiding my eyes.

'Yeah, I guess so.'

'What you need to do is open up an ISA account. That'll give you the best return on your investment.'

'Best return on my investment? I'm 22, Dad …'

'Which is why you need to wise up and start saving. I'm not talking off-shore banking here, Simon, just a little something to get you started.'

'Get me started? In what?'

I couldn't figure it out. My life wasn't really going anywhere – I wasn't planning on getting married, having a family or getting my life on any kind of track. I was fresh out of uni and living at home with my parents. It'd taken me 10 months to find anything resembling a career ladder and even then it was just an office job at the local bank – something my dad approved of.

'Good, solid job that, Simon,' he said, giving me a reassuring pat on the back. 'Have they got any decent products at the moment?'

'I answer phones in the complaints department.'

'Well, we've all got to start somewhere.'

That somewhere happened to be the Everyman bank – something of a phenomenon in Swindon. There are about a million branches. Swindon bloody loves the place, if only for its indiscriminate goodwill in providing young people with the opportunity to earn an above-average wage for doing very little. Most employees are given a computer and some envelopes and are expected to perform the same mundane function for seven hours a day, with a one-hour break for lunch and two 15-minute breaks in the morning and afternoon for smoking/sleeping/eating/crying. I used to man the phones and speak to people who wanted to moan about how much money they had. I mostly cried.

It was mind-numbing, but I did my best to make the most of it. My friend and I would regularly raid the coffee machine, stacking up our plastic cups with great pride, until they toppled and spilled caramel liquid all over the off-grey carpet. We were keen to prove we weren't a complete waste of space.

There were two big advantages to making the most of the vending machine: firstly, as is the case with many Brits, I felt great pride at abusing the privilege of having something offered to me for free, and secondly, because it meant at least half-hourly trips to the toilet. There is no greater pleasure, and I have always maintained this, than calculating how much you earn at work when in the bathroom. I worked out that due to my often drawn-out encounters with the toilet, I was probably up to about £800 a year taking into account number twos alone. This for me was an enlightening moment. It served to make me aware of two things: that I was robbing Everyman blind (positive feeling) and that my life had hit an all-time low (negative feeling).

It's not like I had always wanted to work for a bank either. I mean, I spent entire days answering the phone to people who wanted to complain about why it was Everyman had let them down. People used to phone up and complain that they thought the bank was moving in the wrong direction. What direction can a bank go in? It takes your money and converts it into a number on a screen. You can then take it back at your will, perhaps with a little more than you had put in. That's it, isn't it? I can't think of anything more boring than spending my time waiting on hold, trying to get in contact with the MD of a bank. Have you ever talked to a banker? I'm sorry to say it, but I've always thought that most of them are just one letter away from revealing their true identity.

But I was worse than all of them. I was sat there taking it, allowing my life to seep away, spending my time wondering whether or not I actually needed the toilet again for a third time that hour. I had almost grown numb to it. I'd got sucked in and did it because … well, what else was I supposed to do? Going on the dole would have meant disappointing my dad and wasting all the money my parents had spent helping me through university, so I elected to get paid just above minimum wage to have people moan at me instead.

In all honesty, it wasn't exactly what I'd imagined of life after university. It's not like I expected to be earning mega bucks, but I thought I might at least be putting my studies to good use. It came as no surprise to my dad, who never thought I should have gone to uni in the first place.

'Those degrees aren't worth the paper they're written on,' he said when I was flicking through prospectuses.

'Uni's not about the qualification, Dad,' I responded. 'It's about so much more than that.'

'You'll be growing your hair and smoking that whacky baccy next! What you need is a proper job, Simon. You don't know a day's work, that's your trouble.'

'Don't listen to your father,' my mum said. 'What would you like to study?'

'Well … I've always been interested in history …'

'History?!' my dad yelled in consternation.

'And I've always been pretty good at it,' I said, appealing to my mum.

'But what would you do after you studied?' she asked.

'I don't know …'

'Bloody youth today,' my dad said, turning on the TV. 'Spoilt for choice.'

We finally settled on business management: a peace offering.

Before I got to uni, I thought I'd spend most of my time reading and debating. I thought I'd make friends with people from across the globe and learn new skills. I thought I might learn to surf or kayak, or perhaps take up plate spinning or live action role-playing. But those illusions dissipated as soon as I was handed a flier by a girl in a school uniform promoting shots for a pound.

Rainbows Tuesday, Smack Thursday, Basement Friday, Wipeout Saturday: I established a routine and challenged myself to stick to it. I devoted so much time to being a complete berk that I almost managed to convince myself that it could be a thing of beauty. I tried to make an art of it by going that much further than my mates. Much like when you see the glee on a sprinter's face when, entering the final straight, they know they're going to pull ahead of the pack, I always knew that shame could never hold me back.

And so I dedicated many an hour to bricking up doorways, turfing dorm rooms, freezing items of clothing and catching my mates out on Facebook. After one girl pulled the best-looking guy on our course, we waited until she'd left her room, snuck in, opened her Facebook and sent the guy a relationship request. She never recovered, but left uni with a First. Turns out she had the last laugh.

I would often wonder if I was making the most of university – if I should make an attempt to actually do some reading, to study perhaps. But inevitably in those moments of reflection, I would be interrupted by someone asking if I wanted to play centurion: 100 shots of beer in 100 minutes. I managed to finish once. I wet the bed. What a pointless game.

That's me though: never one to look too far into the future, never one to push myself or really try hard. I got by just fine without needing to work that much. Besides, I hadn't really found that one thing that I wanted to work for.

Back in Swindon, I became drugged by the safety of familiar retail chains, cosy housing estates and two cars on the drive: one a Honda, the other something a little bit sporty. I allowed myself to become part of the machine. And I was sort of happy with that. I was happy knowing what I liked and sticking to it. I was happy knowing where I would be living and what I would be doing from one day to the next.

But then things changed – everything changed. Everything I'd taken as read, everything I thought would be there forever, disappeared in an instant. In a single moment, an earth-shattering flash, my life was pulled from under my feet.

That day at the bank, just as I was about to open a savings account, I could see her face reflected in the clerk's polished glass.

'What the hell are you doing?' she asked me in disbelief.

She was right.

'Can I help?' the clerk asked.

'Yes, I'd like to withdraw all my funds, please.'

4

It had just rained and Mexico City's squashed streets had turned into fast-flowing rivers, throwing the scent of wet concrete and acid fumes across cold stone walls. Cars charged on regardless, sending tidal waves up towards the pavement, where screaming people clung desperately to each other, fearing they'd be dragged in and under.

I'd got dressed into my second-best shirt and was looking down nervously onto the street from the safety of my window.

'Maybe I'll just call home to let them know I'm OK.'

I went and stood in front of the mirror and gave myself a threatening stare.

'No one can help you now. It's all down to you. This is the last time you can feel like this.'

I gave myself a good shake, practised some breathing exercises and went for the door.

It must have still been early, probably cruising at around late afternoon. The sun was doing its best to be heard above the relentless traffic, burning its way through all remaining clouds and swilling droplets of blue around a sky of frosted glass. With nowhere in particular to go, I picked my way through busy people carrying chairs, bottles and stacks of old newspapers, pulled along the city's pulsating arteries, until I reached the very heart: a giant square guarded by stocky buildings. Bells rang out from the mountainous cathedral, punctuating each beat of my racing heart as I strode towards the centre of the square and stood beneath a flag the size of a swimming pool. I looked around me and breathed in big gulps of Mexico. I could stop dreaming, I'd finally made it.

The smell of damp concrete clung to the mumbling growl of traffic as it echoed off the walls encasing the square. A monster of a bus slipped past, sending fierce tremors through the ground and rattling the church towers. I watched hordes of people pile into the Big Top cathedral – their immense weight pushing it down below the burned volcanic soil, down below the existence of mankind.

Stepping down and inside, I was pulled towards the altar, its gold leaf sending out a beam of blinding light, caught by the setting sun creeping in through the cathedral's enormous doors.

What a monumental effort, I thought as I looked up at the vast caverns carved into the ceiling – years and lives to build a temple the size of a town. It was impressive, mind-blowing, puzzling, intimidating – something I didn't feel I was quite ready to understand.

I walked past gory depictions of Jesus' crucifixion, every moment of his gruesome death captured in harrowing detail – blood everywhere.

I passed a group of people praying in a little side room, surrounded by rich red velvet and shiny figurines. Their gentle prayers echoed up and around the space, each in touch with their own little slice of God. A father and child moved meekly to the altar positioned at the far end of the room beneath a huge tapestry, before lighting a candle, crossing their chests, kissing a crucifix they formed with their fingers, and sending a message to those departed.

'Who's that?' I asked the kid, pointing at the tapestry.

'Es la Virgen de Guadalupe. Es la más bonita.'

'Beautiful, hey? You like her? ¿Te gusta?'

'Sí, es muy buena persona.'

'Es, you know, trustworthy?'

'Eh?'

'¿Es … confiable?'

'Sí, es muy confiable. Es la más confiable.'

'That's good.'

The Mexican Virgin Mary – la Virgen de Guadalupe – looked down at me with a pleading expression, asking me to look deep within. I apologised, quietly telling her that my journey was just beginning and that she might like to come back in a few months to see how I was getting on. She just needed me to believe, she said. I told her to let me come to terms with everything earthbound first, and then I'd give her a look in. She didn't seem too impressed.

I looked over at the cathedral's confession booth. Shoes poked out from underneath the stiffly-drawn curtains. I tried to guess what array of horrendous sins their owners might have committed. I imagined scuffed work boots might have lied to his boss about where he'd been the night before and that sandals and socks had probably dreamed of infidelity.

I turned back to the kid. 'You ever confessed? ¿Ha confesado?'

'No. Soy niño puro pues. ¿Tú?'

'Me? Have I confessed? Errrr … no. No, I haven't. I'm pretty sure the church would close its doors before it'd heard all I had to say.'

'La iglesia perdona a todos.'

'Yeah, well I think we kind of have to forgive ourselves first. You'll understand one day.'

I turned away from the altar and moved back towards the light of the outside world. A crisp breeze swept through my hair and caught the giant Mexican flag in the square's centre, its eagle on cactus flying high overhead.

The day was fast disappearing, the streets maintaining their pace and life. Citrus-neon lights flickered into life, shepherding the metropolis into night, the polished cobble stones beneath our feet still wet from the afternoon rain. Children with outstretched hats darted through the unconscious masses. One kid started pestering a man wearing a Ralph Lauren shirt and a Rolex talking on his mobile phone. Without looking at the child, the man reached into his pocket and fished out some coins, before holding his hand out and waiting for the money to disappear.

I went and bought a hotdog from a corner shop and took it to the kid. He shook his head and said, 'dinero.' I stood, dumbfounded, and tried again to shove the hotdog into his face, but was just met with a plea for hard cash.

'Take it,' I insisted. 'Go on.'

'¡No lo quiero!' he said, batting the sausage to the ground.

'Leave him alone,' Rolex guy said, rushing over and picking up the hot dog, putting it in the bin.

'I wasn't trying to … hey, wait, you know of any bars around here?'

He pointed to a sign: *Cerveza 2 por 1.*

'¡Gracias!'

I took a moment to compose myself and walked in. It was pretty dark inside and there was no bar to speak of – just a dim room with a few tables and chairs. I took a seat and a slick-haired waiter in a tight leather apron came to take my order. I readied myself and took aim, 'Una cerveza por favor.'

'Claro mi jefe, en seguida.'

As I sipped on my first Mexican beer, proud at having successfully completed a transaction in Spanish, something weird started to happen. Food started arriving at the table, plate after plate – everything from rice and beans to a full-on fish.

I stopped the waiter, 'Excuso, yo no … ordeno … food. No comida.'

'No. Gratis,' he said, pointing at the food and giving a thumbs up.

Free food?! I started looking around, wondering if I had caught the imagining eye of a hopeful local – just one guy collapsed against the bar, another table of two sharing a quiet night with a bottle of tequila, and a group of lager-loving students who seemed too immersed in their own egos to care about the gringo in the corner.

No one was taking the slightest notice of me. I shrugged my shoulders and bit into a piping-hot cheese ball just as two of the students came over to my table.

'Can we take your picture?'

'Errrr … what?' I said, blowing hot steam out of my mouth.

'Your picture, can we take it please?'

'Which picture?'

'Picture with you.'

'Oh, right. Yeah, why not.'

So I had my picture taken with the two girls, then flexed my Spanish muscles and ordered them a drink.

'Tres cervezas, por favor.'

The waiter appeared with the beers and even more food.

'Did I just order some food by mistake?' I whispered to the girls.

'Don't worry. You're doing very good,' one of them said. 'It's called botanero. Is a special bar where you drink beer and they give you free food.'

'That's amazing. I love Mexico already!'

'Ha! It have problems, but food is not one of them. So, tell us, why are you here?' they asked.

'Why am I here?'

'Yes, why are you in Mexico?'

'Well, I kind of made a promise.'

'What promise?'

'I promised to one special person together with another special person that I would come here to find an old, abandoned house.'

'Cooool. It sound like a big adventure.'

'Maybe it's a bit more complicated than that, but yeah, why not? I'm pretty excited.'

'Wow. And where is the house?'

'That I don't know. All I've got to guide me is an old photograph. That and a few stories. It could be anywhere.'

'We'd like to go anywhere, wouldn't we Sarita?' one said to the other.

'Yeah, I'm really looking forward to just going wherever life wants to take me,' I said, smiling.

'Cheers to going wherever, whenever!' Sarita said as they both held their bottles in the air. 'Hey, you know what you have to do? Drink mezcal!'

'Nesquik?!'

'Mezcal!'

'What the hell is mezcal?'

'Is like the brother of tequila but maybe like a bit more strong and smoky.'

'Errrr … thanks so much for the offer, but I'm not sure I'm really ready for any mezcal just yet. I'm probably just going to have a quiet one this evening.'

'No, you have to! Is for every occasion. In Mexico we have a phrase: *Para todo mal, mezcal. ¡Para todo bien, también!*

'Meaning …'

'For all the bad times, drink mezcal; for all the good times too.'
'Then I suppose I don't have much choice!'
And that's the last I remember of the evening.

5

I awoke on a sofa in a brightly-decorated lounge, the sun flying through a set of blinds and burning a line across my face – my hair sticky with sweat. I swung my feet round to the floor and brought a shaky hand to my forehead thinking it might stop the pounding. I tried to rinse some saliva around my mouth to dilute the taste of old rum, but there was nothing there. I needed water.

I dragged myself up using the back of a wooden chair and sent an empty bottle skittling across the tiled floor. A photo of an old, smiling man standing next to a dog looked over at me from a coffee table.

'I'm sorry,' I said. 'I know, I know …'

Footsteps. Someone was coming down the stairs.

'Buenos días.' Silence. Laughter. 'Shit, bro, you really went for it last night. Where did you learn to dance like that?'

'I … I don't know. Who … where am I?'

'Shit, you oughta take it easy. You gonna get yourself into a lot of trouble in this city if you keep on drinking like that.'

'I'm sorry … what did I do?'

'I found you lying in the middle of the road, man. Lots of people were just standing there watching. You weighed like a tonne, but I managed to drag you to safety before any cars came along. I took you for some tacos to try and sober you up a bit. Then we went to the club.'

'The club?'

'Then I had to save your ass for a second time. You kept just walking off on your own, bumping into other people's tables. I thought it was kinda funny at first, but then you started hassling this one table of bad guys, proper *cholo* guys. I saw you grab their bottle of whisky and try and walk off with it, so I had to run over to try and persuade them not to show you a bit of a lesson. Lucky for you, I smoothed things over, bought them all a drink and they left you alone.'

'Sorry about that,' I said nervously. 'It's kind of hard to believe it's taken me less than 24 hours to disgrace myself.'

'You only just got here?'

'Well, so long as today is Sunday and I haven't managed to drink myself into a coma, yeah, I've been here 24 hours.'

'Wow. OK so, firstly, welcome. Secondly, you're in good hands.'

'Seriously, I'm so sorry,' I whined.

'Nah, forget about it, man. Just think of me like some kind of angel or something.'

'Right. Sorry, but what's your name?'

'Ha ha, it's Aurelio, man. Wanna go get some breakfast?'

I looked up at Aurelio, his face silhouetted against the sun of a new day, his head shaking at my weak, pallid expression.

'That'd be amazing.'

The sunlight hit me like a wet slap across the face. I was feeling a bit guilty about ruining Aurelio's evening, but he threw an arm round my shoulder and took me to a café set up in someone's garage, where plastic furniture was neatly arranged across the driveway, spilling onto the street outside, and a TV sat on an upended bucket blaring out cartoons. A plump, old lady welcomed us with a big smile and a sweaty brow.

'What are you gonna have, shit head?' Aurelio asked within seconds of receiving the menu.

'Errrr ... I don't really know. I don't recognise anything.'

'Don't tell me you Brits are like the Gringos when it comes to Mexican food: all burritos and fajitas!'

'That's not Mexican food?'

'Psh.'

'I thought if it had anything resembling a bean ...' I said, testing the waters.

'You're an idiot!'

'So what am I having?'

Aurelio whistled to the old lady. '¿Te encargo dos chilaquiles verdes y dos micheladas, por fa'?'

'Ándale joven,' she yelled back, before disappearing into the house.

Aurelio started filling me in on the finer details of the night before. I asked him where the two girls I had met in the bar had got to. Apparently they had left me their number somewhere, but he assured me that he had some above-average cousins that he could introduce me to. I gave a nervous laugh and quickly changed the subject.

My michelada arrived first. A glass full of diarrhoea if ever I'd seen one – certainly a brownish liquid on ice. 'Is this shit, Aurelio?' I asked.

'Ha ha, it's the hangover cure. You won't care what it is once you've drunk it.'

I grimaced at the first sip – tangy, boiled seaweed – but I kept at it and watched my headache slowly disappear.

'Not bad, eh?' Aurelio said as I banged my empty glass on the table.

'You know what? I think everything is going to be alright.'

'Right on. Watch out, here come the chilaquiles.'

A plate arrived: crispy corn triangles drowning beneath a swamp of spicy, green salsa.

'Did you order me a plate of Doritos?!' I exclaimed.

'No I did not, Simon. This is the food of the gods, my friend.'

'Well whatever it is, it tastes amazing,' I said slumping back into my chair, kicking my feet out, sipping on my suds and chewing over the distinct satisfaction of seeing a risk pay off.

'So where were you supposed to be staying before you ended up on my couch?' Aurelio asked.

'The Boutique Hotel Hernán.'

'Wow, I didn't realise I was in the presence of royalty.'

'No, Aurelio, you're not. I'm an idiot. I suddenly felt a reckless urge and got carried away. I didn't even stay there!'

'OK. Don't worry, we can sort this out. Come on,' he said, slamming down a 200-peso note and throwing back his chair.

Aurelio, like most Mexicans I would later discover, was ridiculously generous. He may not have had any plans that day, but still, I'm not sure that I would have been willing to endure hours of traffic to take a hungover foreigner who could barely speak my language to some hotel, no matter how desperate they looked. But that's exactly what he did. In fairness, I was then made to endure his dubious taste in music – high intensity trance trash – but I was so grateful for the ride, I almost began to enjoy it.

'Right, so here's what we're going to do,' Aurelio said, turning the music down. 'You're going to give me your key while you go to the reception desk and hint at staying another night.'

'Cool. The thing is, I wasn't able to pay yesterday because of a dodgy card reader, so they'll probably want some money from me.'

'Perfect! You can ask them where the nearest ATM is and tell them you'll pay in cash.'

'And what are you going to do?'

'I'll go up to your room and pick up your things, leaving a spare set of clothes and a plastic bag. I'll wedge the door open and leave to go get my car. You run upstairs, get changed and leave with your stinky clothes in the plastic bag.'

'Then I go back and pay?'

'No, you idiot. No one's paying nobody. Those rats need a taste of their own medicine.'

'If you say so.'

When we finally reached the luxurious surroundings of the hotel, we felt immediately out of place. The staff shot us disapproving looks as I sidled up to the front desk and Aurelio bolted up the stairs.

'Excuse me …'

'Yes, sir, how can I help?'

'I was just wondering, since I've had such a pleasant stay and you've all made me feel most welcome, if I'd be able to stay another night. Might you know if the penthouse suite is available?'

'Just let me check, sir,' the receptionist said as I watched for Aurelio out of the corner of my eye. 'Sorry sir, the system is being a bit slow. Just one second.'

'Take your time.'

Still no Aurelio.

'Yes, sir, naturally it is available this evening.'

'Oh, what wonderful news,' I said. 'Do you accept cash?'

'Why, yes, of course. The nearest cashpoint is two blocks away, just opposite the Oxxo convenience store.'

'How … convenient,' I said, watching Aurelio glide across the marble floor and towards the exit, giving me a thumbs up. 'I shall just go get changed and I'll get right to it.'

Aurelio already had the car running as I speed-walked my way out of the hotel, slung my bag full of dirty clothes onto the back seat and we pulled away at top speed.

6

Hiya darling,

It's Mum. Obviously you know that, but still.

Simon, I'm just going to come out and say it, we're a little bit worried about you. Well, more than a little bit. I know you've always been determined to live the life you want to lead, and we've always tried to encourage that in you, but it's now been more than a week and we haven't heard anything from you.

My love, yesterday I noticed that there was a photo missing from the lounge, and I think you know which. It sits on the mantelpiece next to William and Kate (long live the King and Queen). The photo of your granny, Si, standing outside her house in Mexico. The photo you always used to say you loved because it looked like it was taken somewhere far away.

Please tell me you haven't gone to Mexico, Simon.

It's not that we don't trust you, love, but, well, I had a little chat with Dr Jayawardene yesterday, and he thinks you might be better off coming home, wherever you are. He's a very nice man, Simon, he wants – we all want – what's best for you. Dr Jayawardene said some space is good for you, my love, but that you also need to be somewhere with lots of support. And we can give that to you here in a safe and loving environment, in your home.

Don't be too proud, my love. I know you can be a stubborn little so-and-so sometimes. Just like your dad you are. But look, sometimes we need help and it's not a bad thing. Even the best people in history have to ask for help. Just think about that nice President Barracks Obama – he's got his right-hand man, you know, the one that looks a bit like a Muppet, the one who's always on the news, the one with Mr Tickle arms. Just think about it, Liam's got Noel, Phillip's got Holly and Messy's got Ronaldo!

Your mum and dad love you very much, Simon, you know that don't you?

Anyway, please, please, please write to let us know you're OK. It's very important. And think about what I've said. Just consider it at least.

Sending you lots of love and hugs,

Mum

PS Swindon lost 3-0. Dad said you'd want to know.

7

'Would you like to go on a boat trip?'

'A boat trip?'

'Well, it's not really a boat, more like a plank of wood with a roof.'

'A plank of wood with a roof?'

'Yeah, but a big plank and it's painted lots of shit-hot colours. You take it out on these canals.'

'Canals?'

'Well, they're not really canals, more bits of water.'

'But the water's nice at least?'

'No, it's disgusting. It's incredibly polluted and it stinks.'

'Right. So, you're inviting me to go out on a colourful plank of wood …'

'With a roof …'

'With a roof, on filthy water, when, knowing me, there's a good chance I'll fall in.'

'If you don't the boat will almost certainly sink.'

'Thanks for the offer, Aurelio, I accept.'

Xochimilco, apparently, was just round the corner from Aurelio's house, but congested roads, poor directions and a driver distracted by a difficult-to-open beer seemed to be slowing us down. Aurelio had his Israeli trance music set to *Xtra Loud* on a sound system he'd picked up at an almost-new market just down the road from the stereo maker's warehouse.

'Are we even close?' I asked, my strained words lost among the airy notes and pumping motifs of Tel Aviv's finest.

'Yeah man,' Aurelio shouted back. 'It's just up here.'

Fifteen minutes later he stopped to ask for directions.

'Go straight. It's aaaall straight, then when you can't go straight ahead anymore, take a left, then keep going straight – straight, straight, straight – until you see a sign that says *puerto*, that's the old docks. You want to take a right there and keep going until you hit the water,' a lady with a wobbly chin told us, before waddling off to a nearby deckchair.

'She didn't know nothing,' Aurelio said.

'Are we lost?'

'Nah man, I totally got this,' he said, opening another bottle of beer on the steering wheel.

We'd been winding our way through Xochimilco's thin, bustling streets for more than half an hour and there was still no sign of any water. We were crawling along, doing our best not to hit anyone, or anything, as people and animals weaved through sprawling market stalls, smashed up TVs, grubby fruit and pig carcasses.

'What's that smell?' I asked.

'That's the water. We must be close.'

Aurelio stopped a man on a bike and asked him where we could rent a boat.

'This way,' he signalled, before racing off down an alleyway.

The boat was a bit more than a plank of wood, but not much more. Her name was Blanquita and she was brightly painted red and yellow, with blue and green seats, and a table running right down her middle. A few of Aurelio's mates turned up to join our expedition.

'We're just going to do the chilled out version today,' Aurelio told me. 'Lots of people like to come here to get drunk, party and escape the eyes of the city. But honestly, you been doing a good job of that anyway. Sometimes you just gotta know when to stop, right?'

'Thanks.'

We stepped delicately onto the boat, which looked for all the world like it would make it less than 10 metres before plunging deep below the pungent, murky water. A lad with a dismal look and a ratty moustache gently punted us forward, looking like he'd rather be anywhere other than escorting us lot.

We soon left the screeching and spitting of the traffic far behind as we slowly ambled forwards, surrounded by blossoming flowers, tall grass and the seductive rippling of water. It was hard to believe we were still in Mexico City.

Other boats began to appear, sliding through a maze of secret drifting parties: floating islands whose guests were living out the night like it was in short supply.

Blanket-covered ladies in boats weighed down by giant vats of steaming corn hovered just above the water, floating alongside the party boats, looking for an empty stomach or two. Next came the candlestick makers, flogging creamy candles as afternoon tumbled into night. Some plucky lad had got his hands on some bonsai trees and was having some success picking off the merrier vessels. Another boat cruised past carrying an entire mariachi band decked out in those oh-so-tight trousers, miniature jackets and embroidered shirts. 'A song, güerito?'

I looked at Aurelio, confused.

'Güerito,' he said, 'it's like a term people use to refer to white people. It's meant affectionately.'

'Ah, gotcha.'

'Well, do you want a freakin' song or what?'

'Why not?'

The musicians strung their boat up to ours and there we were, floating downstream with an entire wedding band, bellowing songs I'd probably never heard, but whose melodies I felt I recognised. Somehow, it all felt so familiar. I felt as if I knew it, as if the notes of the music swam through my blood.

As the light dwindled, the notes of the mariachi bands gave way to boom boxes, marimba and shouting salesmen. The flickering, golden light of the candles bounced across the water top, through a curtain of grey mist that was just starting to settle.

'What do you reckon, mate?' Aurelio asked me, imitating a British accent.

'It's … it's beautiful, man, what can I say? I know you'll think I'm crazy, but I feel like I know all this – it feels familiar.'

'Like you've been here in a dream?'

'Ha ha, not quite, but it just seems like it's been waiting for me, you know? Like my life needed this. I always wanted to come here. My gran was Mexican.'

'Was?! That shit never leaves you, man. If you're born Mexican, you'll always be Mexican. In Spanish there are two words that represent the English *to be*: *ser* and *estar*. *Ser* is all about something that is permanent, something that can't change or be removed, like "*Soy Simon*," or "*Soy mexicano*." *Estar* is about something that can change. "*Estoy vivo*," for example, means "*I'm alive*," and "*Está muerto*" means "*She's dead*." Some Mexicans think we're never fully alive nor dead. Funny, right?'

'I don't know about you, but once I'm dead, I'll very much be dead. That's the end, I'm afraid. Curtains.'

'Open your eyes, man. Body, spirit, memory, they're all you, bro.'

'Right, so when it rains at a barbecue and everyone says, "That was Grandma that was. She loved a bit of rain at a barbecue," it actually was Grandma?'

'Like, it wasn't her in person, obviously. But her spirit, her memory – what or who she was – for sure. Why not, man? Someone's image and energy might change over time – just look at Stalin, there are some people now who celebrate his life, despite the fact that he killed millions of people – but that energy will always be there.'

'Right.'

'It changes man, but it'll last forever, trust me. Anyway, what about you? What's your story?'

'Errrr, yeah, my story … it's a complicated one … maybe quite a sad one, I guess. There was this girl … she, she was pretty special … I'll tell you about it sometime. There are a few things I'm not that proud of hiding back there, but I know I've got to get over it.'

'Yeah, we all got that shit, man. We all got it. Only idiots got no shame. You tell me when you're ready.'

'That's kind of the reason I'm here, I guess – to move on a little bit … oh, and I'm going to try to find my grandma's old house.'

'No shit! Where the hell is it?'

'I don't know, really. All I've got is an old photograph.'

'Where there's a will, man. I might know one or two people who can help. Just leave it with me.'

And at that we kept on drifting, moving along the ancient waterways that had transported thousands of people for thousands of years, the sun hanging around for last orders, casting deep, elongated shadows across the water.

Peering over the edge of the boat, I looked down, deep down into the water, trying to find its bottom. I wanted to see its bed, to quantify its depths and see for myself that trace of those that had passed before me. But the dark, mouldy water just stared back, revealing nothing but thick, black glass.

'Hey Simon, look!' Aurelio said, pointing at a load of old dolls hanging from a tree, as if from the gallows. The dolls looked down at us through missing eyes, their coarse, scraggly hair raising like flames from their muddied heads. 'Pretty fuckin' freaky or what?'

'Yeah, I mean … why?!'

'That's Mexico, man. You never know what you gonna see next!'

8

When I think about my abuela, I'm immediately dragged under by the rich, fruity smell of the hibiscus flower. Its overpowering scent draws out patchy memories of a poky London flat with a bath in the kitchen and such little furniture that I always used to wonder if she'd just had the bailiffs round. It's funny how our minds attach sensory information to loose images that then come together to make complicated jigsaw puzzles, like those jumbled pictures you get in Christmas crackers, whose pieces you have to slide around for it all to make sense. I can't explain why hibiscus flowers conjure the select images and emotions they do, but I'm always cautious to delve too deeply into nostalgia in case I begin to alter those memories that I treasure as being what makes me *me*.

So, like it or not, my grandma shares the same space in my memory bank as the smell of a wild, tropical flower. Sat there in a Mexico City *fonda* with a cup of deep-red hibiscus tea, I was carried off with each sip back to my grandma's side, where I could hear her shrill cries of, 'No mi'jito, no comas tan rápido o te conviertes en vaca.' In the way that only grandmas can, my abuela had managed to convince me that by eating too quickly, I would turn into a cow. I distinctly remember imagining myself waking up one morning to find an udder sticking out from under my duvet and a couple of horns trying to escape my head. Adults really ought to be careful what they tell kids sometimes. I was once told that if I ate the crusts of my sandwiches, I would have curly hair. Now, that may have worked in the 1970s (though as far as I'm aware, the afro can't exclusively be attributed to crust intake), but growing up in the 90s, all I was interested in was making sure that my hair was combed forward in perfectly straight furrows, before it swept up into a stiff slope of a quiff. So began my total exodus of crusts. Not sure why anyone bothered with that one anyway – it's a crust for Pete's sake – but the point is that if you tell kids that by eating chocolate they'll go to hell, they'll sooner binge on Brussels sprouts than go anywhere near the stuff. Actually, that might not be such a bad idea. Anyway, I never did stop eating quickly, but I put that down to the fact that I've always quite admired cows.

Besides warning me against sprint-eating, my abuela was a proud woman whose nascent desire to care for all the world and its dog meant she had arms the size of Big Ben and a heart as warm as a winter fire. As a kid, it seemed perfectly natural to me that someone could have so much love to give without it running out, but these days it all seems a lot more complicated. Abuela used to say, 'Life means nothing at all if you grow up scared of giving up all you have and all you are.' I used to wonder if she meant giving up my Transformers or my Super Soaker, but it turns out she might have been talking about something a little more profound. She must have given up a lot because she was always incredibly happy.

Reading at Grandma's funeral, Mum said that Abuela had always been satisfied with her lot, telling the story of the time she demonstrated her well-honed but little-exploited clairvoyance skills.

Sat around the dinner table on a warm summer's evening, enjoying Dad's infamous Fireman's Risotto, Abuela suddenly revealed that she had come upon the winning lottery numbers.

'Impossible!' my father exploded. 'If you're that in touch with the future, what am I about to do now?'

'I'm no mind reader,' Abuela replied as my dad, reminiscent of a pelican diving for fish in the ocean, plunged his face into what remained of his dinner.

He has always been prone to a bizarre turn, my dad.

I later approached Abuela, just as she settled down for her evening snooze in front of the snooker. Unable to wait even a minute longer, I asked her for the secret code.

In the back of her eyes I could see the brightest of glitters: an indication, a clue, a portal to a world where doors opened to other doors and time moved sideways, not forwards; a world of parallel possibilities where everything you could have done was done, each choice taken – a glimpse of the infinite.

'6, 8, 19, 22, 27, 44,' she whispered out of the corner of her mouth as Steve Davis executed a textbook safety.

I tried to buy that ticket, believe me I tried, but as a 12-year-old who was long overdue a growth spurt, it was never going to be easy. That week, I couldn't sleep thinking about how blind my dad seemed. What better feeling than to cheat the system, to profit from powers greater than anything we could possibly comprehend, to close our eyes, jump and dive without knowing how close we were to the bottom? I have a feeling that my dad would have leapt once upon a time, but that through the belief that one day he would lose everything he knew, including his memory, he had been drained of every last shred of hope.

'Just you wait till you start losing your hair,' he would bellow as he hunted desperately for his keys, my mum reeling off a detailed checklist of places he should have looked.

That weekend we huddled around the TV, just as we always had done on Saturday evenings. I was determined to prove my dad wrong, determined to prove to him that there was life beyond the immediate – that magic well and truly existed.

The drum roll began as the independent adjudicator gave the all clear. I felt like I was going to burst with excitement. I couldn't wait any longer to see the results, my parents sat next to me with their blank expressions, having forgotten that the conversation had ever taken place. All of a sudden the numbers appeared on the screen. They could have been any numbers in the world and somehow they would have been the same that Abuela had picked out for me, but there they were, right in front of my eyes: 6, 8, 19, 22, 27, 44. I jumped up screaming, waving my arms above my head, 'You see! You see!'

But of course, they didn't see. My parents remained entranced by the television, numbed to my wild dances. Abuela sat and gently rocked in her chair, pretending to be asleep. I wanted her to wake up and pull out the winning lottery ticket from the sleeve of her cardigan (where she normally kept anything of any importance), before the walls fell and a marching band came and celebrated our victory to the emphatic whistles of thousands of screaming fans. But no, she remained faithful to her plays of ignorance, at peace with herself.

The story had remained forgotten for years until that dreary day when the heavens opened. We remembered my abuela with stories and songs, so many keen for the world to know what a wonderful lady it had lost, as if it hadn't felt it already. I knew that the rain that day was just nature's way of saying, 'Me too.'

I've always loved that story. It reminds me of how impervious my abuela was to life's imperfections and how at peace she was with everything. She simply believed that life had a course for everyone to run and that if we put obstacles in its way, we put it off balance. Why try and change your life through earthquakes and tsunamis if you're already happy with what you've got? I think my dad might have seen it as a lack of ambition, but I've come to see it as a profound understanding of nature's forces and the careful balance of life and death. It's something that we can blind ourselves to when we become so occupied by our own ends, I think, forgetting that we are just players in a drama without a script.

I've tried to follow my abuela's example, but it's not easy. After her death, I confused myself asking too many questions about whether she had lost belief or whether her passing fitted with every fable and tale she had ever told me.

As time moves on, I'm still trying to figure out how she achieved life's greatest trick of *true* happiness. Walking around from day to day, you see so many people who think they've made it, who think they've won the race to life's most coveted prizes: an attractive spouse, a massive car, a beautiful home. I've never had any of these, but I can't say that they would make me that happy – not truly happy anyway. I wouldn't be that disappointed with those things either, but I reckon they're an accessory to happiness, not its cause. I think the only thing that ever made me truly happy was the one *real* relationship I have ever forged. With Carla, I never felt anything alone, I never suffered anything on my own. She was there when my grandma passed away. She was there to hold my hand, to give it a squeeze whenever she felt me sinking. She was there to tell me a joke when I needed it and cry with me when I didn't. My grandma loved her so much. Abuela whispered to me just before she passed away, 'Don't let that one go. She makes you happier than you know.'

I felt a little lost after my abuela died. I knew it would happen – she had been ill for a while – but it didn't make it any easier. The dots were left floating while I was forced to try and join them together again. But eventually I did get over it. Or at least I learned to live again.

Just before she passed away she gave me a letter that she said I should only read when I felt I was ready. 'Why not take it with you to Mexico someday?' she said.

It was always my plan to do just that. Carla and I used to spend hours looking through photos of Mexican landscapes, plotting on a giant map exactly where we planned to go and when. We used to talk about every beach we would visit and the people we would meet. We wanted, more than anything else, to go find my grandma's old home. We'd promised Abuela we were going to go and find what she'd left behind. There was never any doubt. Carla and I made that promise as Abuela slowly faded from this world into the next. It was *our* promise.

Sometimes life has other ideas I suppose.

9

Aurelio was pretty good at twisting my arm. I hadn't planned to stay too long in Mexico City, but he managed to convince me that I couldn't leave without going to the *Feria del Caballo*. My trip of a lifetime was still in its infancy, but I had already been roped into an agricultural event, a horse fair to be precise.

He came to pick me up in his '88 Beetle – a rusty orange number with boy-racer hubcaps and an aerial the length of an industrial fishing rod. About eight of us were crammed in, the bottom of the car scraping along dishevelled roads. 'We're going to pass through some of the most beautiful places in the city,' Aurelio told me.

Angry dogs snarled down from the flat rooftops of half-finished, concrete houses, where curtains substituted doors and cardboard replaced broken windows, the surrounding walls still awaiting the splash of paint that would lift them from construction to home. Empty water tanks perched on every rooftop, wondering when they would next get to see some action. People peered out of their houses, watching horse and carts heave sacks of rubbish from one street to the next, piled high with plastic and furniture and plastic furniture, being pursued by opportunistic individuals looking to salvage anything of value.

'So, these parts are pretty poor, right, Aurelio?'

'Yeah, man. This ain't the kinda place you wanna get lost in late at night, if you know what I mean.'

'Looks pretty tough.'

'Yeah, but these guys have it good compared to others.'

'Everyone looks happy enough, I guess.'

'Why wouldn't they be?'

… 'So what's this *feria* we're going to?'

'It's a horse fair.'

'A horse fair?!'

Now in Britain, a fair is quite a civilised event. There's the see-how-abnormally-large-you-can-grow-a-vegetable-for-no-other-reason-than-the-competition competition, a game where you have to stick your head in a bucket and pick out an apple with your teeth, and a fire engine you can have your picture taken in. About the craziest it gets is an overly-competitive uncle trying to win his nephew a toy car by *splatting the rat*. I doubt many other nations would find hitting a vermin-shaped sock as it drops down a drainpipe quite so entertaining, but that is what we deem *fun* – that's as far as it goes. No guns, no drunks, just fairy cakes and people trying to get rid of old VHS players and wicker chairs. And ridiculously, that's what I expected of the Texcoco horse fair. It was a long time before I saw any horses.

Arriving at the feria was a bit like falling in love; it was overwhelming, all consuming, and I knew that at some point, somewhere down the line, it was going to hurt. A great ocean of cowboy hats and plaid shirts stretched out for as far as I could see as a suffocating flock of country folk pushed us along, further into the crowd of bodies. Wherever they went, we went.

The blokes were dressed in full cowboy garb: pointy something-skin boots, dirtied jeans, a belt the size of my head, tucked-in shirt, a 'tash, a hat and a scowl. The ladies were more or less the same, but with everything that bit shorter and, in most cases, minus the facial furniture.

The men would form predatory packs that hunted alcohol, sex and fighting in equal measure. Loose fingers tickled the triggers of faithful pistols strapped to the hip of all but the untouchable. Gents, who looked like they would kill you if you had the temerity to breathe, swigged on giant beer bottles or straight tequila. The aim was to get more drunk, more quickly. Above those of us stuck in the crowds, an aerial runway flew the most daring overhead, spilling frothy beer over everyone below. Fireworks were flying off everywhere – rockets and Catherine wheels exploding in people's faces. It was absolute carnage.

Deafening oompah-pah bands, somehow squashed into the moving mass, provided live music on foot, doing their best to chase custom. It seemed an odd choice for the swathes of blokey blokes, but that's what made it all the better; they lapped it up, feverishly waving their bottles in the air and sporadically belting out high-pitched yelps. I couldn't tell if they were ecstatic, or on the verge of tears. Most were probably both. We just kept shuffling round – part because we were intrigued as to what lay ahead and part because we had no other choice, pushed by the hundreds of people falling over behind us.

We stopped at a couple of fair games on the way: the bucking bronco, or crazy donkey as it's known in Mexico, and some shooting game, where we had to knock down targets with an air rifle that for some reason would cue a giant mechanical gorilla to vomit water all over us. Everyone was in fits of laughter. I was a bit freaked out.

Out of nowhere came a group of complete twonks, their shirts half-unbuttoned, their chests shaved and their sleeves rolled up once so that their cuffs looked like a pair of '70s flares.

'Watch out for these guys. They're classic *mirreyes*,' Aurelio said.

'*Mirreyes*?'

'Yes, my-kings.'

'Why my-kings? Are they related to royals or something?'

'Don't be ridiculous. It's because they call everyone *mi rey*. It's like their calling card, a way of trying to make everyone else feel better about their miserable lives. They're people with a lot of money who walk around like they own the world, when in fact, they're bigger losers than you or me.'

'You or I,' I corrected him. 'Point taken.'

They might have been losers, but they seemed like they knew how to have a good time. Together with a guy dressed up as Zorro, they were going around grabbing unsuspecting victims and holding them upside down, before pouring shots into their mouth and over their faces, all the while shouting, 'Happy birthday' in really Hispanicised English, 'Haaaappeeee biiiirrrrdeeeeiiii.'

The *mirreyes* would giggle high-pitched squeals, before pulling off the same manoeuvre on each other and moving on to the next victim. They seemed to want to screw me over in particular. Rum and tequila, direct from the bottle, cascaded over my face and into my eyes. I felt like a Year 7 all over again – a prime cut for the local bullies.

'Maybe we should go and hang out with the *mirreyes*,' I suggested to Aurelio.

'Are you kidding me? A bunch of jumped-up rich kids? Don't worry, I got plans for us. Follow me.'

Clattering our way through the bumbling herds, knocking bottles out of hands and drunks to the floor, we seemed to be in a bit of a hurry.

'Aurelio, where are we going?'

'We're going to the *palenque* my friend.'

'Should I be worried?'

'Chill, Simon. You're going to absolutely love it,' he said.

We soon reached an arena that sank into the ground, steep terraces threatening to throw us down into a bottomless pit – a salacious den of illicit activity – smoke and sweat weighing down heavily on the air. Stocky body guards dressed all in black shot nervous looks around the building, occasionally reaching into their jacket pockets as if to scratch an insufferable itch. After everything I'd seen, I was slightly on edge.

'Now for the cock fight,' Aurelio said.

At first I thought he was challenging me to a duel, but I soon realised he was actually referring to a couple of birds.

Two proud men brought their prized assets to the ring below us as moment-building music accompanied dramatic orange and purple lights sweeping over the audience's faces. A huge anticipation circled above the crowd – expectant and waiting – each member chewing on a cigarette, baying for blood. Neighbours shared expert analysis through the dense smoke and the pitch black, their voices rising, one after the other shouting about which cock would come out on top. And then, as the birds were released, everyone jumped to their feet, screaming empty words charged with emotion, building a wall of high-pitched, angry sound. One cock, Aurelio's tip, began to stumble around as the other flapped furiously in the air, the beating of its wings resonating up and around the concrete hole in the ground, whipping the crowd's fervour. Our bird was soon blinded, its eyes scratched out in a fierce battle to the death, before its satin-stained corpse was dragged away by a despondent owner. Half the audience shrieked and hugged while the rest sank into despair claiming an unfair fight, that somehow nature had been reversed and trembled at man's more powerful hand. The winning cock, itself bloodied by the fight, looked on in disbelief before it was scooped up and held high above the ring to more jubilant scenes from parts of the crowd.

'Thanks for bringing me to see this, Aurelio.'

'Just wait, shit head.'

The blood was quickly washed away by a couple of surly old bats in trench coats and all thoughts of feathered fratricide were soon forgotten. Out stepped Vicente Fernández, Mexican singer and charmer, to a great roar from the crowd. Aurelio pulled out a bottle of tequila and we all began to feel more Mexican than a donkey-riding cactus. I bloody loved it. The big hat, the tight trousers, the sighing ladies, the manly whoops – this was about me, the tequila and an old man with a winning cock.

Fernández pulled out all his best numbers, enticing most of the women to throw their underwear down into the pit – he the matador and we the bull, charging his seductive moves. This guy knew he was hot and he wasn't about to let anybody forget it. With just a twirl of his moustache, the crowd began to swoon. What a way to live. The Mexican Tom Jones.

Leaving the arena, we eventually saw some horses. I, of course, slightly worse for wear, had my picture taken with one that had a giant penis. I think I thought it'd be hilarious. It's the only photo I took of the night. For a horse fair though, they were pretty well tucked away. The horses, I mean.

It was time to leave Mexico City. I'd had an amazing time with Aurelio and all his friends, but it was time to make up some miles. I didn't want to get settled on the trip and I needed to track down my grandma's house. I was feeling good about life, about myself, for the first time in a while. It's not that I hadn't been at all happy, but that feeling – happiness, with nothing underneath, no preconditions or limits – I hadn't felt that for some time. I wanted to do everything I could to preserve it. And I knew just the person who could help.

'Hey Aurelio, are you going to join me on my trip then? I could do with someone who knows the place.'

'Yeah, you could. From what I seen so far of you, Simon, you gonna need all the help you can get.'

'Cruel. Cruel but fair.'

'So listen, I gotta sort some things out here, but I'm gonna hook you up with this girl in Cholula. It's about two hours from here. She's travelled from north to south, so should be able to help you out with that photo of yours. Go there, have fun and I'll catch you up. How's that sound?'

'Sounds perfect.'

10

Thanks so much for your email, Mum, and sorry it's taken me so long to reply. I really appreciate you taking the time to get in touch. It's great to know you're all thinking about me.

Please don't be offended or upset by the way I left. I never meant it as any kind of message – it wasn't anything personal, but I understand how you could see it like that.

Lots of things have happened since I left uni, Mum. Many incredible things, but loads of things that have made me feel a bit rubbish too, as you know. If I'm being honest, I'd been stuck in a bit of a rut for a while. My life wasn't what I imagined it would be. I felt like I was never truly in control, like I was sort of a spectator.

My job and everything, it all felt a bit superficial. When I finally took stock, I couldn't really justify to myself why I was doing what I was doing, beyond the fact that I hadn't thought of anything better to do. We've only got one shot at this life, Mum and it can all be snatched from us so quickly. I really had no reason to hang around any longer. I needed to get some perspective, to really shock myself into doing something different and awaken myself to the world around me. So that's why I left. That's why I went on this trip. Like I said, nothing personal.

You were right, by the way, the photo of Abuela is with me. I just saw it sat on the mantelpiece and knew immediately what I needed to do. You know I've always wanted to come to Mexico.

You'll be pleased to hear I've kept myself out of trouble so far. I behave a bit differently when I haven't got my idiot mates around me. That might not surprise you actually. I've been visiting museums as much as I've been puking in bars, so it could be an all-round new, improved me.

I met this guy called Aurelio. He seems pretty decent. Actually, everyone here is really nice. I'm not used to it. You can look at people straight in the eyes without them wanting to head butt you. You can sort of go up to people and say, 'Hi, nice to meet you' and, rather than wanting to chop your legs off, they say it back. Everyone seems genuinely happy to meet you. It's weird. Weird but nice.

Please don't worry about me, Mum. I'm in a positive place for the first time in a long while. I've still got a long way to go, but I do feel like this trip is doing me the world of good. It's the space I needed – the time to get to know *me* again. I'm tired of being the miserable one, Mum. I don't want anyone to feel sorry for me anymore.

Sending you and Dad lots of love. Keep the old man in line.

Simon

11

Escaping Mexico City was like wearing a washing machine while trying to swim up the Niagara Falls – a cascade of cars, coaches and carts, making it almost impossible to leave.

I looked out the window of the bus and across the city. Formulaic scenes of weathered grey trundled past in the vain hope of reaching some place different, piling up one on top of another, each crumbling façade repeating itself for mile upon mile, occasionally interrupted by a shiny glass motel or a brand-new shopping mall.

An old couple led a donkey along a busy street, just off the one road out of town. The lady wore a frayed floral dress, its once-bright colours faded for having spent so many hours in the sun. The man, his arm linked through the lady's, walked slowly but purposefully, his trousers held up by a pair of prominent braces, his waist somewhat thinner than it had once been. The donkey plodded on behind them, carrying thick canvas bags on its back, occasionally whipping its hind with a straggly tail in a pointless attempt to ward off the swarms of flies gnawing at a couple of bright-red sores. A yellow sports car charged past them, spewing out a plume of dirt, before getting snared by a pothole. Enraged, the driver got out, cursed his luck and ripped a mobile phone from his pocket. He kicked the flat tyre and began screaming down the phone as the donkey and its owners shuffled back past the car and up the hill in front of them.

'Life can be funny, can't it?' I said to my neighbour.

'Eh?!'

'Never mind. Hey, how far do you think we've gone? You think we're nearly out of the city yet?'

'How the hell would I know? Looks kind of dangerous round here though. Just one colony of rats after another,' she said, her eyes painted with fear.

It could have been two hours, maybe three, before we were finally free of the city, the bland necessity-driven designs of cost-effective living making way for dense forest – grey to green – as the bus dragged itself slowly up and out of Mexico's central valley. Rich pine trees rocketed up out of the ground, concrete giving way to more organic flavours. People in coats, hats and scarfs stood by the side of the steep, winding road waving red rags in an effort to entice passing traffic into their cabin-style restaurants, where smoke poured out of chimneys and freshly-caught rabbit roasted over open fires. The bus kept on climbing, the tireless pursuits of one of the Western world's largest cities now a distant memory.

I was heading for Cholula, a town on the outskirts of Puebla, Mexico's fourth largest city and infamous among Mexicans for its expensive tastes, Lebanese influence and just a pinch of arrogance. A lot of people I had met in Mexico City referred to the Pueblan people as *pipopes*, or *pinches-poblanos-pendejos* (fucking-Pueblan-bastards). I was really looking forward to my stay.

As we sailed down the other side of the mountain pass, the sun fell out of the sky and back down to Earth, night taking its place. A constellation of land-bound stars scattered themselves across the distance, a community of sparkling street lights illuminating the dark. Puebla had little of the high rise of Mexico City, but it was just as sprawling – low-lying, one-storey buildings spilling out for block upon block, distance impossible to judge. It took a while to reach the station.

As I stepped off the bus, I choked on a sudden rush of cool air, my spluttering breath spiralling as thick smoke up towards the black, imitating the Popocatépetl volcano that lay somewhere in the distance. Voices rang around the giant bus terminal. It was late, but no one seemed to notice. Taxi drivers shouted, offering above-price journeys; luggage men scuttled from one place to the next, piled high with other people's possessions; undecipherable announcements squawked out of tinny speakers, and the smell of freshly-baked churros wafted from one nose to the next, inviting us to huddle with a warm drink and a sweet tooth.

To one side of the terminal, I found a public phone, picked up the metal receiver and with a healthy serving of nerves, dialled the number Aurelio had given me.

12

I'd done it again. Sure, I wasn't expecting radical change, nothing too drastic too quickly, but I thought I'd at least keep it chilled for a while. Sadly, a betting man would have put his money on me finding a way to keep myself at the bottom of the barrel and that's exactly what happened.

I didn't want to roll over; I was scared. I knew I'd done something wrong. Even before I'd opened my eyes, I knew I'd messed up. I tried to press rewind, but the tape was all chewed up. I had absolutely no idea where I was.

I tried to picture the girl. I looked from bottom to top, laying one piece of the puzzle at a time. She was short – about half my size – had little trotter feet strapped up in massive heels and robust sausage legs wrapped in plastic leggings. Then came the turtle neck – a tight violet number, the neck piece stained tan after her makeup fell victim to her lack of fitness and an overly-enthused dance routine. Then, the face. A pretty face but painted like a circus clown, pink and blue eyeshadow, DRAWN-ON eyebrows and big, purple lips. She didn't look great but she'd made me laugh and offered to buy me a drink, which, in that moment, was more than enough to seal the deal. Besides, I'm pretty far from Prince Charming myself. Having mentally prepared myself for an uncomfortable confrontation, I opened my eyes and rolled over: an empty bed.

I could hear the pots and pans banging downstairs as I carefully dropped my feet to the floor, trying for some reason not to make a single sound, as if she had no idea I was there. I inched my way towards the conflict zone, pausing between each step, painting increasingly vivid pictures of what awaited me downstairs – pictures of an entire family sat around a breakfast table, patiently sharpening knives. The smell of fresh coriander escaped upstairs. I could hear a juicer going. Fresh OJ – a nice touch.

And there she was, Elena, Aurelio's uni mate, liquidiser on, eggs in the pan, washing up as she went along. You would make the perfect girl for some lucky guy, I thought. If only I wasn't such an idiot, I'd probably realise a good thing.

'Thanks so much for doing this,' I said.

'No problem. I do this anyway,' she said, smiling at me.

So began an excruciatingly awkward half hour: two hungover strangers who had been thrust together, pretty much against their will, making their way through a three-course breakfast. Our attention was focused on the food in front of us – energy and finesse applied to each chew as we made an art out of eating so we didn't have to make an arse out of conversation. We exchanged the odd smile and nasal chuckle just to prove that this, despite however much it seemed to be the case, wasn't awkward.

Man it was awkward.

'Thanks so much for breakfast,' I said. 'Do you cook often?'

'I try. I like. But I no cook so good.'

'Well, you certainly look like you enjoy your food.'

'Really?'

'Yeah. I mean, it looks like you know what you're doing in the kitchen. Not that you should, of course. Just that, when I was watching you, you looked like you were doing a great job.'

'It no taste good?'

'Oh yeah, it tastes great.'

'OK, I go shower.'

'Do you want me to help out with something?'

'Help with my shower?'

'No, I mean, like cleaning or something. You know, help out.'

'Cleaning! Ha ha ha ha. You so funny. I come back very soon.'

I briefly considered making a break for it, running away as fast as I could. But I couldn't bring myself to do it.

I moved to a window by the front door, resigned to the fact that I'd have to face up to what I'd done. I looked out, struggling to recall anything of the town I had arrived to the night before. A couple of kids ran up and down the street, laughing out loud at the freedom of childhood. This, I was told, was the real Mexico – postcard stuff, earthy colours and 'tashes the size of slippery eels. This was it now. No more wondering, no more *ifs* nor *whens* nor *hows*, just a glorious invitation to live closer to life's edges, away from its sagging middle. I could get down with that.

Elena came downstairs. 'So, you like go explore?'

'Yeah, that sounds great.'

We left her house with no idea of where we might be heading. We just wanted to walk around and enjoy the still air of a clear afternoon, refreshed and enlivened by an unexpected bout of rain. As the tapestry of intricate paving passed beneath my feet, I felt invigorated without really knowing why. At 2,000 metres closer to the sun, the air felt purer, more precious. The rain, with its healing touch, had settled the restless dust of the midday sun, washing down the earth and laying out a blank canvas for the world to enjoy. An excitement rushed through me – the feeling that this was it, that this was truly the start of my journey. No turning back. Every opportunity would be accepted, every barrier withdrawn.

A huge shadow dissected the street ahead of us, reducing the world to black and white, disturbed only by the fluttering tail of a defiant kite overhead, its owner lost somewhere among the warm colours and crumbling plasterwork of stuccoed houses all too familiar with the sun's charm.

Directly in front of us, some 200 metres away, a proud, yellow church stood on top of a giant mound.

'That hill used to be the most big pyramid in the world,' Elena told me. 'Then the conquistadores turn up, kill all the local people and put great big Catholic church there.'

'Mexicans sure love their churches,' I said.

'Oh yes, 'specially here in Cholula. Here we have 365 churches. One for each day of the year.'

'That's mad. Does anywhere need that many churches?'

'Probably no. We have saint for every church. Every day we celebrate a different saint!'

'That's a lot of parties.'

'Is why you always listen the fireworks.'

A faint pop hummed in the distance.

'I guess some people just love the idea of god,' I said, raising my eyebrows.

'Is easy answer,' Elena responded, drawing her hand across the Popocatépetl volcano sat on the horizon, so spectacular as if it were painted on, watching with indifference and smoking contently, its glistening white cap framing the towers of the church in perfect symmetry.

As we approached the foot of the mound, bright colours fluttered overhead, more kites dancing freestyle, led by the odd gust of wind. Children looked up with glee, hoping to be carried away by these mythical creatures, understanding at once their desire to fly freely. Their parents sat close by, exchanging words in a dialect I couldn't recognise as Spanish, the ladies in woven dresses and tightly-plaited hair. It was an incredible sight to behold. I wondered which world this was all taking place in – one I partly recognised as being my own but which at the same time resigned me to the status of foreigner, washed up, coughing and spluttering, on an island of ignorance.

We began to climb up one side of the pyramid, drawn in by the beacon above, my breathing now deeper, more concerted and regulated – my lungs doing their best to work with the lack of oxygen in the elevated air.

'I race you!' Elena shouted, leaping up the stairs for no other reason than the sense of liberty it entailed.

Out of breath as I reached the top, I propped myself up against a stone wall and absorbed the view. Stretching out below was Cholula, Puebla, Huejotzingo, Atlixco – thousands of spires and roofs, farmers' fields with glistening flowers and sandy corn. Paper flags, strung from every lamp post, tap danced across the breeze, sending beams of translucent, rainbow light over the low-lying houses that stretched down straight and earth-bitten streets. Churches, houses, homes huddled together, and there, in Puebla – the city – modern office blocks shimmered and swayed, overawed by the incredible distance they enjoyed. I don't think I expected to see so much space – miles and miles, life in all its preoccupations, every last inch of it. Ours was a bird's-eye view, God's view.

'Can you hear that?' Elena asked. The gentle beating of a ceremonial drum began to circle above the busy people at the foot of the pyramid, lifting the kites higher and higher. 'Ooooh. They going to fly,' Elena said. 'Come!'

We raced over to the opposite side of the pyramid, where down below a group of four men dressed all in white perched on a wooden square attached to the top of a 30-metre pole, their eyes closed, captivated by the movement of air around them and the steady rhythm of the drum. The square began to rotate, spinning the four elements around and around, their feet bound by a length of rope attached to the frame. A fifth man stood on the pole itself, playing a wooden flute.

Like a diver returning to the water, a simple lean back was all it took for the men to begin a beautiful journey back down to earth. Held by the ropes, they floated head first back to reality, continuing their rotating pilgrimage, like the earth round the sun, each in their own space, falling further hypnotised, lost to some other time than now. Round and round they span until suddenly the moment arrived to let go, complete a half-somersault and put feet back on solid ground. Life was secure for another day.

I let out a long sigh as the sun, by now just a fiery red dot, fled behind the mountains. The world was at rest. My mind was at rest.

'OK,' Elena said. 'Philosophy too much. You can't feed it the spirit if you don't feed it the body.'

'I couldn't agree more.'

The thick smile stayed on my face as we left the pyramid and descended on the streets, enjoying the parade of daily life around us. Elderly ladies carried on their heads baskets laden with grasshoppers, chilli and mango spilling out at impossible angles, while gents sat outside their favourite cantinas, numb to the trivial concerns of daily life – the sun and its shadows slowly moving across their faces as another day slipped out of view.

We went to one of the famous *cocinas económicas* that adorn street corners in every town and are all worked by stout, old ladies in pinafores, who strut about their territory with freshly-pressed tortillas in one hand and a bag of change in the other.

We sat down at a table with a sticky, plastic sheet glued to its top.

'Cuatro molotes de tinga por favor,' Elena cried out.

'What's that?' I asked.

'Is like a fried tortilla with different things folded in it.'

Elena ordered me *tinga*, which was, as far as I could tell, spicy tomato chicken. Then there was *huitlacoche*, or for us English speakers, corn fungus.

'I think they've forgotten our cutlery,' I said, frantically padding down the table.

'Ha ha, you funny. You have to use your hands,' Elena chuckled.

'It's going to get pretty messy then,' I said, a dollop of cream and salsa clinging to my nose.

'Don't worry! Maybe just go slowly. The animals, they eat better than you!'

'Sorry.'

'Ha ha. In London, they always use knife and fork?'

'Pretty much. I'm starting to realise we're a bit standoffish when it comes to food. It's all pretty prim and proper – you know, skirting round the edges and doing what you can to avoid confrontation.'

'Here is very tactile. We make it simple: hands and mouth, mouth and stomach, stomach and … what the word … rectum?'

'What a lovely image,' I said, placing my *molote* back on its plate.

'OK, you order next round,' Elena demanded.

'No … don't do that. My Spanish isn't all that just yet.'

'Well, they not Spanish words. Is Mexican and you have to start or you never going to learn.'

'But the words, they're so hard. Why make it that complicated? Chips, for example, one syllable. Boom. Or roast dinner. That second word's got two, but still, it rolls off the tongue …'

'Just try it!'

Elena signalled for the waitress.

I gulped.

'Dos molotes who .. it … la … coach … ey, please,' I said, fumbling my words.

'Try again: wheat – la – cochay.'

'Dos wheat … la … cochay, por favor.'

'Perfecto!' Elena said with a gleaming smile.

I'd passed. Just.

'What now?' I asked.

A wicked smile spread across Elena's face.

*

The following day was a bit of a write off.

Lying back, stretched out on Elena's sofa, I followed the lines of the cracks that were just starting to tunnel through the paint of the lounge ceiling. It might have just been the hangover, but I was starting to feel increasingly self-conscious. I knew I wasn't technically doing anything wrong by staying at Elena's house – not by most people's standards anyway. I knew it was OK, being in a girl's house, yet I could feel a dull ache creeping somewhere within me – a few drops, a leak that I had tried to seal. Somewhere it began to drip. Small insignificant drops, but I could feel each and every one.

I'd wanted to leave my home behind and hit the road. I'd wanted to put comfort to one side and open up to new experiences. I'd wanted to give myself a bit of a break. But something, somewhere within me, kept trying to take me back.

I wondered what to do about that.

Elena eventually surfaced, all showered and spruced up. She looked carefree, young and happy.

'How you wake up?' she asked.

'Well, I sort of just opened my eyes and that was that.'

'No, silly! How you rest?'

'Yeah, great thanks. It's always amazing to wake up and see bright, blue skies. Believe it or not, that doesn't happen everywhere in the world.'

'Yes. Is nice, but I prefer the cold.'

'That's ridiculous.'

'You want go for walk?'

'Yeah, I could do that.'

And so we were back out walking among the vivacious colours and embalming heat of the Mexican afternoon, the sound of 365 bells ringing through the air, carried on the back of a cooling breeze. We walked in silence mostly, allowing our senses to do the talking.

We ended up at Bar Reforma, an unassuming kind of a place with a flickering pea-green neon light above the entrance – windowless and with a set of pugnacious wooden swing doors.

We sat down with a couple of sangrias poured nice and strong. Black and white photographs of old film stars were plastered all over the walls and ceiling. In one corner of the bar was a large waist-high sink with a big plug hole and a hose in place of a tap. A note attached above it read *vomitatorio*. The name seemed like a bit of a giveaway, but I thought I'd ask.

'Is for when you have drink too much,' Elena confirmed.

Innovative.

'So Elena,' I said, tossing a bar mat in my hands, 'Aurelio said you know Mexico pretty well.'

'Yes, I visit so many places. I never get bored.'

'Amazing. Have you ever been here?' I asked, whipping the photo of my grandma from my pocket.

'What's this?'

'It's my grandma when she was a little kid.'

'Wow, that's your abuela?'

'Yeah, it is.'

'I have to say, she really look not like you!'

'Ha ha. Yeah, the good genes stopped with her.'

'Well, to answer your question, she can be anywhere.'

'Right …'

'That kind of architecture is very typical of lots of city in Mexico.'

'I see …'

'But, I don't know, it can be Oaxaca. Is a city close to here.'

'Oaxaca? Look, there's an address on the back: Guadalupe #42, esquina Tonalá, RDC.'

'What's RDC?'

'I'm ashamed to say I don't know. I was hoping you might be able to tell me.'

'I sorry. I really not know, but it can be Oaxaca maybe. There are a lot of places that looks like that there. Is also a very nice place. You have to go!'

'Sounds amazing.'

There was a moment's silence between us and then she came out with it: POW, like an angry bullet from a smoking gun, 'Why you no sleep with me last night?'

'Good question.'

'Yes, is a good question.' … 'And?'

'Listen, you seem really nice, you really do. I'm not sure things like this happen elsewhere in the world, I mean, just meeting someone and spending time with them. I've enjoyed it, I really have. I think I needed it even, but I sort of have this girlfriend.'

'Sort of?'

'Well, we're not actually together. It's kind of complicated. I'm not sure I should talk about it.'

'OK, Simon.'

'I'm really sorry, but …'

'But …'

'But I think I have to go.'

'Where?'

'I have to meet a … a friend in … Mérida in a few weeks, so I really need to get going,' I said uncomfortably, clutching at the only place name I could remember.

'Is it serious?'

'Very. I love Puebla, but I just have to keep travelling south.'

'It's sad.'

'Very.'

'I see you again?'

'Yep' – bit of a porky.

'When?'

'I'm sure destiny will cross our paths once more.'

'Yes, I'm sure.'

'But for now, I must continue. This country won't explore itself.'

'Who explore it?'

… 'Me, I was referring to me.'

'Yes, you!'

Looking into her wide, trembling eyes, I felt like an absolute shit. She clearly felt she'd done something wrong. I couldn't think of a way to make it right.

We walked back to her house, I picked up my stuff and I was gone. Just like that.

13

Simon my love,

Thanks for the email and believe me, we want what's best for you. We always have. It is hard as a parent to separate the two sometimes – I mean, what you think is best for you and what you think is best for your child, but that's what we have to try to do; we're giving it our best shot.

It's taken me a while to write this email. I tried to write it yesterday but ended up deleting it this morning. There's no point in us being mad or upset, I've decided. We have to just let you get on with it. At some point, you just have to hold your hands up and say, 'I've done all I can,' right?

Still, I wish you'd have just come out and told us, Si. It's enough to give me a bloody heart attack knowing you've flown off halfway around the world. I know that you're fine and that you're fully capable of taking care of yourself, but it's not you I worry about. There are plenty of crazy people and psychos out there.

Mary, you know Mary next-door-but-one, she comes round yesterday to tell me that someone has been killed up in town, Simon. Some Polish bloke she reckons, murdered, in broad daylight! Madness it is, Simon, madness! And that could happen absolutely anywhere in the world, my love, it's not just Swindon.

Sorry, you probably don't want to hear about that, but I don't know what this town is coming to. I bet he was involved in all that mafia rubbish – the Polish bloke, I mean. Me and your dad are watching this programme at the moment. It's called Very Bad, or something like that. Everyone's watching it. It's about these drugs people in America who keep having to kill each other and fill barrels with dead bodies, but the main drugs guy is the brother-in-law of the main police chief, except the meat head doesn't notice. Anyway, it's very good. Ironical really, but it does make you think, it really does. This big drugs man was a school teacher. A school teacher! Really, you can't trust anyone these days.

It's been ever so quiet since you left. I know you've not been gone long, but the house seems so empty. Dad says he doesn't seem to notice, but I know he does. We don't play music when we're eating anymore, I can tell you that much for free. Pure silence. Mr Collins is just gathering dust! ... But seriously, dinner times are such a dismal affair. They really, well and truly are. Your dad does this chewing thing, where water builds up in the front of his mouth and sort of sticks and unsticks. It makes me sick just thinking about it. I know he doesn't do it on purpose, but it's like he's just given up on decency. He's given up, Si! I know that he's thinking, 'Oh it's alright, she's been with me so long now that she's not going to care.' Disgusting. At least when you were here I could argue with someone, or tell someone off. He just ignores me. Most nights I've just been getting the wine out, Simon. I have to. That spices things up a little bit. We've just been watching whatever's on the box. But even that's a trial. His Highness apparently doesn't like Graham Norton. He says he's a loveable poof and that he makes him ask some uneasy questions. But what's better than a loveable homosexual, Simon? Honestly, there were a few years when I thought you were ... well, you proved me wrong. But I just want you to know I would love you the same, man or woman, single or married.

Anyway, please do take care over there and let me know how you're getting on. I want daily updates as much as possible. I don't want to hear any of this rubbish about you not having the Internet or anything. This world is very much a global one these days. Everyone's got everything the same, haven't they? Maybe you could send us some pictures with that bloody camera we bought you for your birthday. Just a thought.

We love you ever so much, Si. We always will.

Mum

PS Your dad says Swindon lost again. Goalkeeper scored an ogger. Ogger – that's right, isn't it?

14

In my ignorance, I imagined Mexican buses to be paltry things made out of cardboard with a bucket for a toilet and all the charm of a dirty old man loitering outside the local library. I thought I might be forced to endure the kind of gruelling encounters that were school ski trips: 17 straight hours crammed into a bus designed for transporting inmates between high-security prisons. Unbearable they were, but we didn't help ourselves. We'd often try to see how much Fanta we could drink between toilet stops and there was always some kid loaded with the most sugary treats known to man. Once, on a Year 8 French exchange, a friend and I were amazed to find a turd on a bus. That's right, a poo. A proper, full-blown poo. In some kind of ridiculous face off that we were always destined to lose, we decided to see how long we could last sitting next to the thing. I had been sick all over my brand new kappa tracksuit before the end of the trip.

Anyway, to my delight, the Mexicans were happy to prove me wrong – comfy, reclining seats, flat-screen TVs, flushing toilets and coffee machines. I even got a plasticky sandwich thrown in for my buck.

I was excited to be back on the move, the road stretching out for miles in front of me as life presented me with one path and one path only. Watching the inky blue of the sky and the singed copper of endless plains, I felt lifted by the vastness of it all, the empty road feeding my journeying imagination. Strong mountains emerged as if from the underworlds, like giant pyramids of a mirror life. Reaching through the glass, I pushed my cheek against their cold surfaces, my blood passing through the stone down deep below. I could have looked at them for hours. Those giant pieces imposed themselves upon the map of existence as ultimate survivors, infinitely more knowledgeable than any human being. There was something about their stubbornness that I admired. I could see a determination in their expressions, the faces of centuries of struggle etched into their surfaces: torrential rain, blistering sun, earthquakes and the destructive desires of man – they had seen it all and were still standing. They had seen millions of lives pass by and fade away – year upon year of challenges – yet nothing had brought them down. I could have learned a thing or two.

The whole bus held its breath as we crept over the rocky mountain passes. Small, white crosses peppered every bend, presiding over a sharp precipice, a deadly drop, urging us to slow down and think about all those who hadn't made it. I kept myself busy with my sandwich. Then, as we started to descend back towards civilisation, prickly cactuses giving way to blossoming, molten trees, golden Oaxaca dropped into view.

I gasped when I got off the bus, shocked by the sticky, stolid heat of a tropical world. I jumped straight into a taxi and opened my window to let the intoxicating midday sun sweep through its melted plastic and rug-covered seats. The driver drove with one hand firmly on the wheel and the other dangling over the side of the car, protected against the rays by a cut-off leg of a pair of jeans. We slinked gradually from one corner to the next, the straight and cobbled roads channelling us towards the emerald green mountains in the distance. People plodded along the street, their faces soothed by the colours of the slow-passing time, ushered on by packs of sitting crows squawking another afternoon into view. The soft, persistent whistle of a mechanical tortilla press drifted out of an open doorway as it pumped out thousands of warm corn plates ready to be whisked off in the safe grasp of a loving tea towel to every lunch table in the city.

'What do you think of Oaxaca?' my taxi driver asked me with a huge grin on his face.

'It looks amazing,' I said as we sailed passed crumbling colonial buildings.

'Where am I taking you, sir?'

'I don't know, really. Wherever you think I should visit.'

The taxi driver dropped me off smack bang in the middle of the city, where I stepped right into a crowd of angry people: men and women crying with rage, trying to batter their way past an old oak door – the presidential palace – held back by a sturdy metal gate and a small group of armed guards.

The mob waved homemade cardboard signs with fluorescent slogans, shouting obscenities at the guards, who looked totally unmoved by the commotion. One or two were being held back by friends fearing the unrest might get out of control. Some had fallen to the floor, paralysed with rage.

A group of nuns scuttled past, taking no notice of the mayhem.

I stopped them and asked what was going on.

'Argh, it's the teachers again. Just ignore them. Shame on them. Shame on you!' they shouted, spraying irate stares over the mob. 'Bless those poor children left all on their own in empty schools.'

'The teachers are just fed up with getting paid a miserable wage, angry at all the broken promises,' the taxi driver shot back, counting his change, before slamming into first gear and driving off.

'How long have the teachers been protesting?' I asked the nuns.

'From the day they start until the day they retire. They're all the same,' they replied, tutting their way past the protests.

I wandered over to the other side of the square to get away from the noise, only to be welcomed by the deafening embrace of musicians competing with each other for the public's attention: a child in a huge hat with an eyeliner moustache belting out Mexican classics in a piercing, high-pitched falsetto; a full brass band honking their way around la cucaracha, and a lonely-looking old fella pounding a single drum.

Kids danced about, waving miniature hands in the air and trailing bubbling armies of balloons behind them. Some had got their hands on giant inflatable sausages and threw them against the floor, bouncing them high into the air, their glowing eyes momentarily fixated, until they ran for cover as the bratwursts came crashing back down to earth. It was chaos, but the kind of madness I was growing to love.

I went and bought some beers, before making for the centre of the square and plonking myself below a giant broccoli tree. A thin wall of sunlight gently warmed my feet as the protesters left and the kids all tuckered out. I could hear the breeze running its fingers through the lime-green trees.

Outside the cathedral a couple of priests flirted harmlessly with old ladies. Two old men dressed in cloth shirts and cowboy hats started playing a marimba, their faces moving to the well-honed notes of the few tunes they both knew how to play off by heart. Their mellow, exotic melodies permeated every corner of the Zócalo, offering themselves up to the foot-tapping clientele sat in its cafés and bars, whose faces were buried in food, books or the lips of a loved one. Across from me, suited gents sat for half an hour or so to have their shoes shined and enjoy the weightlessness of sitting, flicking through yesterday's newspapers to see if they'd missed anything important. At the far end of the square a barber sat in his chair, a sheet draped over his three-piece suit, pretending to read a tatty magazine when really he was peering at the ice cream lady behind her cart, who in turn had her eye on Tacos Tony.

I caught the eye of an old lady sat on a bench opposite mine. She smiled at me, comforted by the fact that someone else had come to join the people-watching party. She wore a mauve sleeveless dress with a broach that added a little sparkle to her appearance. I fancied her to be a bit of a goer in her day. I reckoned she probably worked as a dressmaker, raising a family as a single mother, reliant on the favours of others to make ends meet. She looked happy, content just to have a group of people she loved to spend her life with. I reckoned she was Oaxaca born and raised and would know its streets inside out.

'Excuse me,' I said, walking over to her, photograph in hand. 'Do you recognise this house?'

She didn't respond.

'Excuse me,' I repeated, tapping her on the shoulder.

'Oh, I'm sorry,' she said, snapping into action. 'Are you talking to me?'

'Yes. Do you recognise this house?'

'Which house?'

'The house in the picture.'

'I'm afraid I'm blind, child. Why don't you describe it to me?'

'OK, it's a small, white house with a stained-glass window above a big, iron door. There are flowerpots in front of the windows and a young family are stood outside ...'

'Is there a cat?'

'I can't see one.'

'Then no, I don't recognise the house. It sounds like a nice place though.'

'Sure ... what about this address: Guadalupe #42, esquina Tonalá, RDC? Do you know it?'

'Guadalupe #42?' she repeated, intrigued.

'Yes! Have you ...'

'Never heard of it. Are you new to Oaxaca?'

'I am.'

'You'll love it. It's a truly magical place. Make sure you try all the food. Here, take my arm. I'll take you to the market,' she commanded, pulling herself up and ambling across the square.

'How do you know where you're going?' I asked.

'You can't smell it?' she said incredulously. 'No mistaking it. It's just up here.'

Plump ladies with stocky shoulders and skin the colour of bitter chocolate welcomed us with stern expressions, each bearing the market uniform of pinafore and blouse. Ear-breaking announcements sporadically informed us of the one product they were selling that particular day. Most were hidden behind giant stacks of small, crispy, blood-red bites that hungry punters bought up by the bag load. Dragon smoke wafted across from one side of the market to the other as dogged chefs fried animals and vegetables of every shape, size and disposition. One lady wandered around with a couple of lizards slung across her back, its bulbous eyes nervously scanning the room. A meaty old dear waddled up and ran her finger over their thighs, giving a nod of approval, parting with a couple of sweaty bills and slapping the reptiles next to a red-hot grill.

A slight and wheezy man ushered us across to his stall, where he promised us the finest food in Oaxaca along with a free straw hat. It was an opportunity I couldn't miss. Trying not to choke on the dense smoke that bounced off the low market roof, I raised my voice to be heard over the chaos and asked the man what he recommended.

'You cannot leave Oaxaca if you no try the *mole*,' he replied in a sort of Italian English.

'What? They even eat moles here?'

'No, *mole* is a special dish made with the chicken and the chocolate,' the blind lady said.

Surely not, I thought. They must be having me on.

But they weren't. True to her word, the *mole* was made from the chicken and the chocolate; succulent pieces of meat arrived before me bathed in a sauce so rich it laughed at the poverty of flavour surrounding it. The chef, Miguel, watched me devour every last piece of *mole* with excited eyes.

'I've never had *mole*, Miguel – I've not even had mole – but that was spectacular. So where did you learn to cook it?' I asked.

'It was my mother's recipe. Each family it have its recipe. It have its way of cooking the *mole*. For us, cooking the *mole* is like a way of communicating with our past, with our ancestors.'

'Wow, it certainly seems popular,' I said.

'Yes, is probably the most popular dish. And mine is the best!'

'So, how do you make it?'

Miguel laughed and shook his head. 'I cannot say. Is a secret. But I can say it takes hours, days sometimes. You have to crush everything, hundreds of ingredients.'

'Well, it's a far cry from my mum's turkey twizzlers, which, on their day, are hard to beat, Miguel. But I think even she would balk at a *mole*, and she's been known to knock out a pavlova or two in her time.'

'Pavlova?'

'A dessert with lots of cream. Apparently it gets quite tricky. Anyway, what are those big mountains of fried, red things that I see everywhere?'

'Is the grasshopper.'

'Grasshopper?! Why?'

'Something like a local delicacy. Very tasty. You have to try.'

'Maybe later. Hey, you're a man in the know, what do you think I should see here in Oaxaca?'

'There's too much to see,' the Mexican-Italian chef replied.

'Too m …' I managed, before he butted in.

'Yes, too much, but one place you have to see is the Saint Sunday church. Is beautiful, really.'

'You really have to go,' the blind lady said. 'It's just the other side of the Zócalo. I'll take you there myself!'

It took some time for us to find our path through the crowds, but we made it just as the sun was falling from its perch, silhouetting the pensive mountains enclosing the city and turning the church's vast stone walls a cooling peppermint green. A newly-wed couple posed for photos with the church's two bell towers in the background, the bride straddled atop an ice cream cart in a sea of white. A number of young couples circled the church, enjoying every minute of youth beneath the shade of tall palm trees, sheltered from the dwindling glare of the sun and the unwanted attention of their parents.

'Will you come in with me?' I asked the lady.

'You're on your own, kid,' she said. 'I'm a devout communist, you see.'

'Wow! I never would have thought. How did you become a communist?'

'That's a story for another time. I've got a drum lesson to teach in 20 minutes,' she said, hobbling off down the street.

'Well it was nice to meet you!'

Inside, the church was delicate and beautiful. A spider's web of intricate, resplendent gold leaf clambered its way up the chalk-white walls, in and around the earthly depictions of saints and deities. A tangerine light infiltrated from above, seeping in through a stained-glass window, lending an extra shade of calm to an already-peaceful space. Devotees sat or knelt in perfect silence, their gazes fixed on the cold stone floor, or straight ahead to Jesus on the cross and the ever-present Virgen de Guadalupe – both sending sombre expressions out to a hopeful crowd.

As I swept my eyes across the grandeur of the temple, they fell upon a blind man begging in the doorway, his trembling hands outstretched in hope, pulling at the feet of those who came to pray. I started to walk in his direction just as a side door opened and those of the elderly congregation that could stand did so. A nervous priest emerged, hiding his face, almost as if he was embarrassed to be there. He walked hesitantly to the front of the church and took centre stage, where he began to lead the attendance in prayer. Faces of conviction bowed towards the Earth's centre, eyes lost to an inner space.

'Hail Mary, full of grace. The Lord is with thee. Blessed art thou amongst women, and blessed is the fruit of thy womb, for thou hast given birth to the Saviour of our souls.

'Holy Mary, Mother of God, pray for us sinners, now and for the hour of death. Amen.'

A tall statue of Mary stood on a plinth to one side of the priest, her pallid, sorrowful face indifferent to the repeated words of the priest's prayer.

I looked around the church, feeling the tangible hope rumbling through those present, the shame for what they had done, and the belief that salvation awaited them in a timeless, limitless clemency. No matter what, that door would be open. A beautiful finale awaited – a promise of peace.

'What about us non-believers?' I asked Mary. 'Are we supposed to carry our sins with us to the grave, left to battle against the things we wish we'd done differently? Are we supposed to just live through the struggle of doubt and regret? What if we wish we'd done things differently?'

A fragile old man moved slowly down the central aisle on his knees, quietly mumbling prayers all the way, his soul leaving body behind, in search of a reassuring and steadying presence – a painfully true display of faith. One awkward shuffle after another he moved, completely won over by the art of devotion.

I closed my eyes hoping to mirror the old man's journey, hoping to overcome my pride and cynicism. I sat and waited, delving deeper into the silent black of consciousness. I swam deeper, further in, hoping to find some secret at the bottom, waiting for some kind of message to appear, and trying to figure out what it might look like if I did find it. I was torn between the doubt that had underpinned my life from day one and the hope of finding something more immediate than the present, my will to uncover some hidden world beyond that of the mortal, somewhere good souls could meet and rediscover each other. I kept digging; desperately, painstakingly, I kept trying. But I just became more frustrated and fearful. I realised that with every second that passed, I was moving further away from where I actually wanted to be. There was nothing. Just black. Just infinite silence. Dark space for as far as I could see. When I opened my swollen eyes, I dried my cheeks and turned to walk out of the church.

'I'll be fine,' I said to la Virgen, before climbing back into the real world.

The sky had turned a thick red. A flock of big, sinister birds were coming into nest, their shrill cries ringing around the city. Turning around for one final look at Santo Domingo, I realised that someone had spray-painted a stencil of a masked man to one side of the entrance. The man, a steely look in his eyes, proclaimed, 'Long live the revolution! It's time for change.'

15

Aurelio had asked me to meet him at what turned out to be a bit of a hippy hostel where there were more bongos than guests. When I turned up, he was led in a hammock chewing the fat with some guy carrying a guitar and a yoga mat.

'Well look who it isn't!' he shouted over at me. 'Don't I at least get a hug?'

It was good to see him.

'Hey, you smell that?' he asked, inhaling heavily. 'That's the smell of freedom, my friend.'

'Or illegal substances,' I said.

'Hey!' Aurelio belted at a po-faced hostel worker. 'So are we allowed to just blaze up in here?'

'Well, I wouldn't say "blaze up," but we see nothing wrong with anything that comes from Mother Earth.'

'Amen, brother! So you do know how to have fun!'

'Just remember, gentlemen, there is strictly no noise after 10 pm. We believe sleep is a vital component of holistic living.'

'No drinking after 10 pm, got it.'

'Certainly no drinking.'

'What's this?' I said, holding up a laminated sheet.

'It's our menu of yoga and spiritual cleansing sessions. What exactly are you looking for?'

'Good question. Does the spiritual healing stuff really work? Do you actually feel better after it?'

'Of course.'

'And what do they actually do to heal you?'

'We use local shamans who practise techniques used for thousands of years. They use their medicinal knowledge of local herbs and flowers to select the precise remedy for each particular ailment.'

'So do you have to confess to them before hand?'

'You don't have to, but the shamans we use *do* encourage it. Would you like me to book you in for a taster session so you can try it out?'

'I don't know if …'

'I don't know if we can,' Aurelio butted in, snatching the menu from my hands and edging me towards the front door. 'We arranged to meet someone this afternoon. Maybe we'll give it a go tomorrow.'

'Well, I'd need to book you in …' the hostel worker said, his voice trailing off as we hit the street.

Aurelio let go of my arm as soon as we were clear of the hostel and proudly said, 'You're welcome, Simon! Trust me, I just saved your ass a lot of money. I mean, you don't believe in all that bullshit do you?'

'Well … I try to stay open-minded.'

'Forget open-minded, man. All they're interested in is how open your wallet is.'

'I think there's a little more too it … where are we going, Aurelio?'

'Don't you worry about that. There's more important things to chat about. How was your time with Elena?'

'Errrr … it was good, I guess.'

'Good?'

'Well, something happened between us.'

'I know, she said.'

'She did?'

'Yeah, I think you've got yourself a bit of a fan.'

'Really? Shit, she probably thinks I'm a right bastard.'

'Ha ha, not even close. I think she's a little bit in love.'

'Don't say that, Aurelio. I don't feel great about it.'

'Nah, no worries. Mexican people love falling in love. We do it all the time. Just be careful, I think I remember her being a bit of a … what was that thing I learned? … A bit of a cooked rabbit?'

'A bunny boiler?'

'Yeah, that's it!'

'Great.'

'Ha ha, chill, man. We're in Oaxaca. We're going to have a great time. I'm here to protect you now,' Aurelio said, giving me a firm pat on the back. 'You can tell me all about it over a tequila.'

El Gusanito bar was a hole of a place, packed to its flaky rafters with drinkers both young and old. The locals stared suspiciously at us as we grabbed a table next to the jukebox and ordered a round of mezcal and beers. 'It doesn't look like we're that welcome here,' I said, necking my beer. 'Shall we just drink up and leave?'

'Relax!' Aurelio said 'These guys are gentle giants really.' … 'So, I don't want to pry, but what's the problem with the girl, Simon? I don't get it. Most people are happy when they meet someone.'

'I know … the thing is, there's this girl that I haven't told you about … this other girl.'

'Ahhhh, now it's starting to make sense. And would this other girl be annoyed if she found out?'

'Yeah … I mean, she's unlikely to find out, you know …'

'Right. You're over here, she's over there …'

… 'Right.'

'Listen man, I've not seen much of this world, but if there's anything I've learned so far, it's that it doesn't matter if you mess up, cos we all do that, it's how you react that matters. Just never stop trying to do the right thing.'

'You think?'

'Of course! We all do stupid stuff – we all hurt each other from time to time. That doesn't make it right, but nor does it make you a bad person. Sometimes we mess up. What's important is making sure you don't make the same mistake twice. Like I say, it's how you react that matters.'

'I hope you're right, Aurelio.'

We sat there talking through life and sharing stupid stories for hours. I didn't really notice at the time, but we'd managed to get through a bottle of tequila between us. At some point Aurelio disappeared and I was left alone at the table, trying to avoid eye contact with everyone around me. Suddenly I saw him walking away from the jukebox and an upbeat, brass band music came on. Everyone got up and started dancing – Aurelio was twirling around at breakneck speed, spinning a girl twice his size into increasingly complicated knots. There were just a few sullen looking men like me sat around the edges, either nervously hoping they wouldn't get asked to dance or else too shy to approach a partner. I decided to go and talk to a guy who looked like a proper local – a giant of a man dressed in dusty denim and pointy cowboy boots – to see if he knew anything about my grandma's house.

I staggered over to his table and sat down with a thud, placing the photograph in front of him.

'What the fuck is that?' he exclaimed.

'It's a photo.'

'I don't give a shit what it is. Get the fuck out of here gringo.'

I got up to leave, but something within me glued me back down to my seat. 'Look at it,' I said with determination.

'I thought I told you to get the fuck out of here.'

'Just look at the photo.'

'You must be fucking stupid.'

'Probably.'

He got up, pushed his chest out and turned to make his way to the toilet, just as I stood up and knocked over his drink.

'Fucking gringo, I'm gonna kill you,' the giant said, his eyes searing with disdain.

'Back the fuck up big man!' Aurelio shouted from the other side of the bar.

'I'm gonna kill that son of a bitch,' he yelled again, his eyes filling with blood.

The giant marched over to me and took a swing. I tried to duck and fell back, away from his bulldozer fist. He looked down at me, drew the tip of his boot across the sawdust on the floor and prepared to charge. If it weren't for the bottle, the hand, the arm and the landlady's ongoing feud over an unsettled tab, I would have been well and truly cooked. As it happens, he fell to the floor like a dynamite-loaded skyscraper.

I looked at the body and then up to the landlady, her face emotionless. 'Thanks.'

'I think you better leave,' she said calmly, before turning and looking at the gathered audience of stunned faces. 'Back to your drinks!'

Aurelio grabbed my arm and tried to drag me out of the bar before the giant stirred. 'Hang on – the photo!' I shouted, reaching out and swiping it from the table before we fled at top speed.

Oaxaca had grown beautifully peaceful as night settled in. The main square was occupied by just a handful of guardians responsible for shepherding the darkness through to light. In one corner, a mariachi quintet serenaded the cool night air with laments of lost love, waiting to be whisked away by a repentant boyfriend who, having betrayed his lover, would seek to apologise through the medium of song. By their side, a slight, old lady wrapped in arctic attire kept warm by the glow of her wood-burning stove – a giant pot of corn broth simmering on top. A drunk stumbled out of a nearby bar. Struggling to stay on two feet, he finally slumped against the giant oak doors of the cathedral, where he would wait until morning to confess his sins and start life afresh. For a few precious seconds there was silence.

'Hey Simon, you want a corn cob or what?' Aurelio bellowed. He'd managed to borrow a trumpet from the mariachi band and started tanking it full blast.

I feigned an apology to corn lady, who was either deaf or else taking no notice, and dragged Aurelio off to the mariachi band to give them their instrument back.

We ended up drinking tequila out of the back of the mariachi group's van and taking pictures of ourselves in their outfits. It was there that I met Don Marco, a wise, old man who'd been crooning mariachi hits for some 50 years. He was leader of the group and personally claimed to have saved more than 1000 rocky relationships over the years. I remember asking him why he thought Mariachi music was so popular in Mexico. His answer was simple, 'Everyone loves a good cry.' I asked if Don Marco had spent as much time maintaining his own relationship as he had saving others.

'Been married 50 years, my boy,' he said putting me in my place. 'I must have found true love.'

'And what's that?' I asked.

'I think it's waking up one day and saying, 'Fifty years, wow that went by quickly, how about another 50?''

'But what if it doesn't last 50 years? What if she goes?'

'You have to enjoy it while it lasts, my friend. That's all you have to do.'

'I guess so. Can I tempt you to a tequila Don Marco?'

'Haven't drunk for 20 years. No sense starting again now.'

We left Don Marco and his merry men as a blacked-out car pulled up and the call came in for a damsel in distress.

It was a long walk back to the hostel.

The following morning, having been kicked out our hostel for breaking the *no-noise-after-10* rule, I suddenly remembered Don Marco had invited us for lunch. I slipped my hand into my pocket and found the torn shreds of a cigarette packet containing Don Marco's name and number, along with a poorly drawn map that I could only assume must have made sense the night before. *Turn right by the big cactus plant then left by the barn.* Aurelio and I grabbed our things and head out of town in a taxi.

Don Marco's house was everything my spoiled imagination wanted it to be. A half-rotten gate swung back to reveal a dusty yard full of kids playing tag. Turkeys waltzed behind a blanket screen at the back of the garden, enjoying their final bows before the brutal axe of mankind turned its attention their way. The kids played freely by a well that had famously been carved out by one of Don Marco's 10 brothers, who, having been in search of gold, ironically found greater value in striking water. A bucket was lifted and sunk with great delight, the discovered treasure splashed about by little Juanito. Don Marco looked around with pleasure. It was his – all his.

Don Marco's house was spartan: the main living space occupied by a table and some purple plastic chairs along with a shrine to la Virgen de Guadalupe. A grey, concrete floor juxtaposed the brightly-painted salmon walls and the warm light of a collection of candles. An old Victorian-style family portrait looked out over the lounge, the classically glum faces belying the wealth of affection that lay within. Mother at centre, father behind and a bevy of bright children – it was a beautiful sight. Vicente Fernández LPs rang out from an old record player in one corner, *Por tu maldito amor* and *La diferencia* hitting us all with that sense of shared nostalgia you find in classic Mexican boleros.

We had arrived just in time for lunch. 'Just wait, shithead,' Aurelio said to me, tucking a huge flag of a napkin into his creased shirt. 'This'll be one of the best meals of your life.'

What followed was an embarrassingly rich display of hospitality –

course after course carted out and delicately placed before us by Don Marco's wife, Fatima, a plaintive smile written across her face as the entire table waited nervously to see if it met our approval. Rice, chicken soup, black beans, pipián, fish stuffed with fish, coconut flan, and buckets of mezcal. Double thumbs up. Sigh of relief.

We must have spent hours sat at that table. No one thought to look at the time; no one thought to leave. We just sat, and talked, and drank, and ate.

'So, next weekend at your place, right Simon?' Don Marco said.

'You'd have to sell a kidney just for the airfare,' Fatima joked.

'I wish I could take you all with me,' I said. 'I really do.'

I imagined Don Marco's family around my kitchen table at home. It was all so improbable. There would be no clucking turkeys in the background, no open windows or doors and no virtuoso tuba playing – Don Marco was an amateur tuba player and no night was complete without him piping out some absolute bangers. The food would be carted out at high speed and my mum would be worried that there wouldn't be enough to go round. Yet there, in Don Marco's small, squat house with an outdoor toilet, concrete floors and a failing electricity supply, there always seemed to be more than enough. Whatever was there was shared. No one wanted more than there was in front of them.

Don Marco's home was what I'd been looking for since I left the UK: something completely different, totally original, spontaneous and all about love.

I could feel a small change within myself. I was relaxing, letting my guard down, a guard I had honed and employed as soon as I was ever left alone, as if I expected to be under constant attack. I was hugging old men and spinning Salsa with their wives. I was taking the time to learn about someone else, to share and release. I liked it. It felt healthy and closer than I had been for a long while to what really matters.

Fatima and I stayed up till about three in the morning talking through life in a rough, broken Spanish-English. She told me all about growing up in Oaxaca, about the life you are expected to lead. She told me about her children and what she hoped for each of them. Getting them through school would be the first step. She counted herself lucky if she managed that much. Some kids, she told me, drop out before they can finish primary school and help their parents at home or at work. She told me of her pride at little Marco Junior's 10 goals so far this season and the way Hermania looked after her baby sister, Valeria. She hoped they would go to university and maybe, someday, set up their own businesses.

'There's no way of improving your situation here without being your own boss,' she said.

I asked her if she could see them one day visiting me in the UK.

'We'll start saving.'

I felt like I wanted that moment to last forever. I felt I needed to shield myself from the reality of a shallow world to which I was accomplice and facilitator. I saw in Fatima a lot of what I aspired to be, a lot of what I doubted I could ever reach. She was peace, harmony and goodness. She was wholesome. She was beautiful.

Fatima asked me about my life, but not with any ulterior motive, just the preoccupation of a mum who always knows when there is a book missing from the case by the stairs, or if a single mug is astray from the kitchen cabinet.

'So, why are you here?' she asked me.

'You know, a lot of people ask me that. There's a short answer – an easy one – and there's a longer answer too.'

'What's the short answer?'

'That I came here because I was bored of home and because I'd promised my dying Mexican grandma that I'd try to find her old house, the life she'd left behind.'

'Well that seems like a good enough reason to me. Time will sort the rest of it out.'

'You know what? I think it will. Actually there's something I was meaning to ask you,' I said, slipping the crumpled photo in front of her. 'Do you have any idea where this might be?'

'Is that your grandmother? She's very pretty. She even looks like you a little.'

'Ha! You're a good liar, Fatima. She's standing outside her childhood home. Could it be here in Oaxaca?'

'It could, Simon … but I don't think it is. It's something about the way your grandma is dressed – I don't think she's from here in Oaxaca. Mexico is such a big country and each place has a different identity. She could be from Chiapas, I guess. Is that the address?' she said, turning the photo over.

'I think so.'

'What's RDC?'

'I don't know … but you think my grandma could be from Chiapas?'

'Yes. It's quite far from here, but you should go there anyway if you have time.'

'Time I've got. Thank you, Fatima. I guess you and Don Marco can't take any time off to join me on my trip …'

'Aiiii muchacho! In spirit, Simon, in spirit.'

That night Aurelio and I stayed at Don Marco's in the presidential suite. DM took the sofa and Fatima bunked up with one of the kids. They wouldn't take no for an answer.

We snuck out early in the morning, gone as quickly as we had arrived, Don Marco still snoring with a mariachi hat perched safely on his belly. I left a note on the doormat: *Until next time.*

16

Mum,

I'm sorry I didn't tell you about coming to Mexico, or about taking the photo. Really, it was all completely last minute. It didn't take much for me to realise Swindon was a dead end.

It was the right decision, I think. I've seen so much already and feel like I've learned a hell of a lot. You know I always had a special connection with Abuela, Mum. When she was dying, she made Carla and I promise we'd come out here and explore. She wanted us to come and find out a little bit about the country she grew up in. The plan is to try and find where Grandma used to live. It's a bit of a wild goose chase, but I think the journey will do me some good.

Mexico's been amazing so far. I don't want to get too flowery about it, but it's been a bit like Déjà vu. It sounds weird, but it feels like I've seen it all before in a dream. I'm convinced I've seen, smelt and felt it somewhere before, Mum. Abuela, she was Mexico. All of this was in her eyes and her skin, in the way she moved and spoke, in the way she looked on life.

I think it was important for me to see it in the flesh, for me to live it and breathe it for a while. I think I'll come back a better person for having been here and that you'll notice some positive changes in me – changes that if we're being honest, were a long time coming.

I'm doing fine, Mum, really. Please don't worry.

I promise to keep you updated with it all. I'll even try to take some pictures.

Love,

Si

17

We caught the first bus out of Oaxaca heading for the beach – a mammoth twelve hours of sitting, gently sweating and watching poorly-dubbed films. It was downhill almost the entire way, the bus rolling down the mountainside like a run-away boulder. Few found the words to speak and for those who did, it was more to stave off the growing fear that our driver had left our fate to the gods as he eased off the brakes and clung to a rosary bead dangling from the rear-view mirror, appealing to a large stencil of Christ that obscured half the windscreen.

'You OK?' Aurelio asked me. 'You look kinda green.'

'Just trying to find my special place.'

'Just think, the mountainside is so steep, it'd only be a matter of seconds before it was all over. I can think of much worse …'

'Yeah, yeah.'

'I mean, some people find horrible ways to die and you're in a beautiful country on your way to some of the finest beaches in the world. What's not to like?' … 'Simon …'

'Please just watch the film, Aurelio.'

The bus eventually came to a screeching halt outside a small concrete hole of a restaurant.

'Lunch!' the driver yelled.

It was unbelievably hot outside the coach and the restaurant did a good job of keeping the heat in.

'Simon, sit by the fan before your freaking face falls off,' Aurelio said to me with a kindly tone of concern.

Motorbike taxis buzzed up and down the street outside, ferrying school kids home for lunch. A thick black box of a TV sat in one corner of the restaurant, its volume turned up to max. A man with a painted-white face, fluffy, lime-green hair and a big, red nose read out the news: Ten Dead in Michoacán Shootout; Local Mayor Arrested for Money Laundering; Teachers Planning One-Month Strike.

An old couple sat across from us drank it all in, their eyes pressed against the screen.

'Why's a clown reading the news?' I asked Aurelio.

'Apt, don't you think?'

'Is there always so much blood?'

'I'm sorry, Simon. Do they only show good news in your country?'

Our beers arrived first, then the tlayudas – a giant spaceship of a tortilla, spread with a field of beans, juicy meat and an icing of cheese.

When the weather came on the telly, I perked up immediately at the thought of unadulterated sunburn. A heavily-made-up weather lady in a miniskirt broke the bad news. There was a real possibility of storms along the coastline. My heart sank.

'Are you heading to the beach, son?' one half of the old couple asked me.

'Yep.'

'Just be careful. The waves can be awful big this time of year.'

'Thanks.'

'Don't worry about him,' Aurelio chuckled to the old lady. 'He's stronger than he looks. Balls of steel.'

I smiled and sank my beer.

18

I awoke to the sound of heavy sea air weaving its way through palm leaves, gently rocking my hammock along to the soothing rhythm of the waves crashing below me. I reached up and grabbed at my matted hair; I had sweated the whole night through. Turning over and looking out to sea, I watched as a giant white rock of a ship slowly inched its way across the horizon, oblivious to the parcel of perfection I'd found myself. A lone fisherman chugged into shore, content with the meagre catch he brought with him. He jumped out, plunging into the sparkling blue glass beneath him, breaking its still surface and splashing rich liquid over his face and back. The day's work was done. He stopped to talk awhile with a young lady with long, plaited hair and a green dress rolled up to just above the knee, a basket of crisp crab tacos resting on her head that shielded her from the endless sunshine pouring down from above. They shared a joke and she continued along the mouth of the sea, leaving a trail of squashed peanuts imprinted in the wet sand behind her.

I was in Puerto Escondido in Oaxaca, on Mexico's southern coast, contemplating the vast Pacific Ocean and the smell of salt water and coconut flowing freely around me. I may have gone out drinking the night before, but the world was showing me forgiveness. I was out on bail, my trial suspended. The heat would sweat it all out of me before too long.

As I looked across the beach and water, the wooden decking of the floor beneath me began to shake, rattled by the off-balance footwork of a drunk – a slack-faced man looking lost to the world, stumbling around in a vacant mind. I recognised him from the night before: some slimeball who went from girl to girl at this Salsa joint trying to convince them that he was anything but a complete mess of a man. He'd carried a bottle of tequila with him and administered routine shots to anyone who wouldn't run away. It was likely his fault my head hurt quite as much as it did. I can never say no.

Listening to one heavy step after another, I turned over in my hammock in the hope he would ignore me and leave. I pricked up my ears, straining to pick up the slightest movement. Silence. Had he left? Then, the faint patter of liquid splashing onto hardwood floor. I turned back expecting to see him relieving himself on all of my possessions, but saw him tipping the remains of a half-finished bottle of tequila out onto the floor as he tried to see if there was any left. He stopped, looked up and shouted, 'Culos a mí,' before downing what remained of the bottle, stripping off and zigzagging down the beach and into the ocean.

'That's one classy guy!' Aurelio said from the safety of his hammock as we watched the slimeball's bare buttocks dive beneath the glistening surface of the ocean.

'Not sure we're the ones to call him out on it,' I said, planting my feet on the deck. 'Breakfast?'

It was while attempting to tuck away a plate of fresh papaya that we met Patrice, a smooth-looking French lad with beach-perfect hair and an immaculately shaved chest. Obviously, the first thing I did was to ask why he owned one of the most girly names ever to be bestowed upon a man, but once we'd all gotten over my awkwardness, we got on like a maison on fire.

Patrice had come to Mexico on a whim. A friend of his had recently visited le Mexique, returning with tales abundant in Latin lust and a love so hot that Patrice declared there and then that he just had to go. Patrice's friend put pin to map by giving him the name and phone number of one of his most lively conquests. Exercising his limited Spanish, together with a serious overdose of Gallic charm, Patrice phoned the girl, asking quite bluntly if she might be after some more French stick. 'No, but my sister's looking for a boyfriend,' came the reply. 'Zat iz gud h'enuff for mi h'I tell 'err. H'iiiit waz fuckin' craaaayzy mayt,' Patrice told us with big, glowing eyes.

'I'm guessing it didn't quite go to plan,' I said.

'H'arrrr you kiddin'? It waz ze best h'ever, but she make me suffair.'

Patrice had arrived with little more than a faint idea of what he believed this girl might look like – no home address, no phone number, just a distant memory of a Facebook stalk 6000 miles away in a shabby, Parisian apartment.

'I just know she work in ze university of zis town by ze bitch. I don't know nuffin h'else.'

So Patrice took a taxi to the Universidad Tecnológica Costeña on the sleepy Oaxacan coast.

'I h'arrive and explain to ze guard zat I luk for ze girl, but my Spanish iz soooo bad. 'Eeee says, "You work 'ere?" I tell 'im zat I'm a visiting professeur from one of ze best university in France. 'Eeee h'understand zat.'

Patrice, worried he might be turned away, told a big fat lie. It seemed to work though – well, sort of. He was whisked off to the rector's office where he was treated to a briskly opened bottle of warm white wine and a shot of tequila.

'Zey culd not believe it. H'I mean, a French docteur visiting from Parie. It waz a big shock for zem!'

Such a shock in fact that the rector called for all the teachers to abandon their classes and meet in the courtyard, where a now half-cut Patrice was presented in front of the entire university. Spotting his opportunity, Patrice went around and greeted each and every teacher until he found his prey. She didn't look as good as her profile picture, he was quick to tell me. Needless to say, what had to happen, happened.

'We 'av jus ze incredibul sex. You 'av no h'idea. She want it zis way and zat. H'upstairs, downstairs, h'on every bitch and at ze back of h'every bus. She crayzy.'

Patrice and his lady would meet every day after he finished work, the town now a little confused that a visiting professor had got a job serving lethal cocktails at a local bar. They would eat long lunches, before succumbing to their insatiable passion and falling in love all over again.

All was going swimmingly, until her boyfriend showed up.

It's the kind of event that normally cuts things short, but the situation was made worse by the fact that the boyfriend was 'somesing h'of eeeey local drug baron.' Yet Patrice was not one to let a good thing die young. Oh no. In fact, Patrice saw no reason at all why he should make a dash for the nearest exit.

'Iz just, she 'ad zis body zat I swear, she drive me crayzy. She – what iz zat word h'I learn – she, she mesmerise me.'

'Continue.'

And he did, sneaking around among the shadows, stealing moments from the impossible afternoon heat, when the rest of the world would admit defeat and sink into a heady abyss of siesta. Patrice's work was conducted in silence – a crime he claimed was inferior to that of calling time on a love so true.

It all worked perfectly, he told us, until something that began as mildly irritating soon escalated into something more severe and Patrice had to pay a visit to the local doctor.

'She give me ze syphilis. I couldn't believe h'it. I'm sure h'it waz 'im, but h'I still go back for more.'

And about one week later the inevitable came to pass, though not without a grand finale. The boyfriend of course found out and of course he was less than happy. He quickly rounded up his mates to go and give the French lad a pounding – or worse – and he knew exactly where to find the Gallic charmer.

Patrice ran out of the bar, flip-flopping his way down the street, deep into the night's darkness. Heading down a side road, he took refuge in a random house whose owner seemed only too glad of the company.

'I'm only *too* glad of the company,' an old American expat told Patrice, sweating into a glass of Rioja.

'I can see zat,' Patrice replied.

'Take your clothes off.'

'Pardon?'

'Take your clothes off.'

Things had somehow got worse for Patrice. He needed to think and think fast. He decided to up the ante and play the drunk American at his own game, outwitting him in a battle to out-scare his opponent.

'H'it will cost you 200 dolleeeeuuuur,' he said, his syphilis-ridden phallus now hanging loose in the stiff evening air.

'What?'

'Come h'on, 200 dolleur.'

'I ... I ... no, get out of here!'

'You loze.'

By this point Patrice reckoned that the path was clear. He went for his things and left town, moving a safe distance along the coast, no less enamoured than when he arrived.

'I just love ze sex. What can h'I say?'

Aurelio and I looked at each other in awe.

'That's one of the best stories I've ever heard,' Aurelio said, offering his hand to Patrice.

'Nah, iz nosing. Sometimes h'in life, you just 'az to turn off zat voice in your 'ead zat try to stop you from enjoying sings and just live for ze moment.'

'Amen,' Aurelio said. 'So, Patrice, tell us, where are you going to next?'

'I don't know. Normally h'I go back to France, but maybe zis 'ol sing 'az changed my mind. I love ze Latin women. H'I luuuurve zem.'

And with that, Patrice got up from the table and followed the waitress into the kitchen.

'Man, I love that guy,' Aurelio said, opening another beer.

'Yeah, he looks a lot of fun. He's making life look pretty easy.'

'It *should* be easy, man.' ... 'It makes you wonder, doesn't it? I think sometimes we don't know how scared we are.'

'Scared of what?' I said.

'You know, most of us just seem to walk through our lives covering our ears and eyes. We never really realise how scared we are.'

'I guess.'

'Yeah, we're all scared of losing. That's it. We keep ourselves and everything we own locked up, locked away somewhere safe. We all got this belief that loss is avoidable, you know? That if we are in control then we're kinda untouchable. But we're not. We're so far from untouchable. And there are people like Patrice who get that. Why fear the inevitable? Why be scared of losing things, of losing pride or money? Why be scared of losing people? Patrice, he's truly *living*. That guy is alive!'

'I think we're *living* too though, mate. We're on this trip aren't we?' I said hopefully.

'We are. I just wonder if we're both still running away from something.'

'You saying you're scared?'

'I don't know. Maybe …'

'Of what?!'

'I think maybe I'm scared of failure.'

'Shit, really?'

'Yeah, man. Like I don't want to be found out, you know?'

'You seem like you're doing alright to me.'

'Ha! Thanks, Simon. Big praise. So, how about you? What scares you?'

'Nothing, mate. You know me. Solid as a rock.'

'Nah, come on. You can tell your ol' pal Aurelio. We're all scared of something.'

I laughed, but Aurelio kept looking at me expectantly. 'Come on, Aurelio. Shall we just enjoy the beach?'

'There you go, you're doing it again. Running away!'

'I'm not …'

'Come on, man. That's why we're travelling, after all, to find a little more out about ourselves.'

'I … sometimes …'

'Sometimes what?'

'Sometimes … this is stupid, mate.'

'Of course it's not. You trust me, right?'

'Sometimes … sometimes I feel like maybe I'm scared of never getting a chance to make amends.'

'Make amends for what?'

'I …'

'Come on, man, make amends for what? You're not talking about what happened with Elena again, are you?'

'No! … Aurelio, I … I'm sorry, mate. I shouldn't have said anything.'

'Simon, man, you know it's none of my business, but maybe it would help to talk about it.'

…

'What do you need to make amends for?' Aurelio asked again, looking me right in the eyes.

'Listen, I'm doing my best to deal with it, believe me. I'm doing my best. Who the hell cares if I'm running away?!'

'Simon …'

'Who cares if I'm running away? Why would it matter?! What if that's just what I need to do?'

I turned away and looked out to sea, where a cloud was parking itself in front of the sun.

'You'll get there, mate,' Aurelio told me. 'Wherever it is you want to get to.'

'I'm not sure you really get it.'

'Sorry, man. I'm trying. Come on, let's finish these beers and go for a surf. Girls love guys who surf!'

'I've never been surfing before.'

'All the more reason to go! Isn't this trip about doing new things?'

'Right.' ... 'The waves look pretty big though. Do you reckon I'll be alright?'

'You'll be fine. We'll just tell the rental guy you've been before. Then I'll show you exactly what to do when we're out in the water. You can swim, right?'

'I'm good at the breast stroke.'

'That's the spirit. Now, drink up!'

The board was enormous, way taller than me and I'm not small. I bounded down to the water, and launched myself into the waves.

'Just do what I do,' Aurelio said.

The sea was beautifully cool, the waves coming in as if in a desperate hurry to reach the shoreline, a powerful antidote to any worries washing around inside me. I looked back at the guy from the rental place and he gave me a reassuring thumbs up. How hard could surfing be anyway?

I managed to follow Aurelio beyond the waves and out where the sea was calm enough to gently lull my board to sleep. I climbed up on top and sat, floating away from human existence, the sun on my back, its golden rays glinting off the brilliant azure of the Pacific. Aurelio picked out wave after wave, cruising them back to the adulation of the beach.

I must have been out there watching him for a good 20 minutes when he came swimming over to me. 'Hey, Simon. I know I told you to watch the first few, but don't you want to give this shit a go? It's amazing mate. You'll love it.'

'It looks incredible. I'll have a go in a minute, mate.'

'What's wrong, you scared?'

'Ha ha. Nah, it's just so beautiful out here, you know?'

'Look up man. Looks like it's going to rain pretty soon. There's some pretty mean clouds coming in.'

And with that he was gone again, gliding back into shore, one wave after another.

I could see the surf rental guy, hand on hip, shielding his eyes from what was left of the sun as he looked out to where I was sat. He started waving at me and pointing up at the fierce black clouds that had started to paper over the careless blue. A lively wind whipped over the surface of the water. That storm was rushing in.

I looked behind me and could see a wave I thought was big enough to surf coming in.

I got flat down on the board like Aurelio had told me and began to splash about in a way I thought would get me some momentum. I checked back and the wave, now roaring just metres from me, was the size of a big double decker, its headlights blaring. I had about a second to realise that I was in trouble before a three-storey tonne of water collapsed on top of me, dragging me down – deep down – to the ocean floor.

My face hit the bottom first, the strength of the wave pinning me down and scraping my head against the rough sand beneath me, dragging me rushing back up and sending me crashing back down again. I struggled at first and tried to find my way out, but it was hopeless, pointless. So I just lay loose against the sand, watching a beam of light shining down from above – the world of the living now an insurmountable distance from where my body lay. As the crushing water kept coming down on top of me, I tried to breathe in, but just inhaled a gallon of salty water, a further weight holding me to the bottom.

I felt pathetic and weak knowing how helpless I was to do anything to stop it. I could feel myself slowly giving up, giving in, accepting that life – my future – was out of my hands, that I was simply disposable, worth little more than the bones and flesh that held me together. Was this how it would end? Was this how I would be erased? Was it my destiny? Strangely, I began to feel calm. I started to feel at peace. The fighting had stopped and the war was over. I could no longer hurt anyone; I was no longer a threat. I would die there and the world would move on, my existence banished from the world map. It was just my time to leave. And probably for the best.

19

Hello my little soldier!

You've always been my little soldier. You wouldn't like me to say that mind, but I don't care a sausage.

You know, I'm starting to warm to the idea of you being out there in Mexico, my love. As the months get colder and darker over here, I can't help but feel that I might rather be with you in the hot places with the tanned people and nice smells. Not that I don't like it here in Swindon, of course – you've got retail outlets, job security and now, finally, a Nandos. I've heard there's some good food in Mexico, Simon, but honestly, give me chicken, chips and a refill any day of the week. Still, it's the dark days that get me, Simon. I can't do it. I feel like the whole world is coming to an end. You know that's why all those people in Scamdanavia get depression, don't you? It's the bloody dark! And what with energy prices going through the roof, it's enough to drive anyone mad.

Your grandma would be so happy you went, Simon. She was a 100% Mexican lady, and proud, Si. And like you, she'd left her home behind to go somewhere new (rainy old England). As she always used to tell it, she'd met my dad at a dance under a starlit sky in her small mountain town. He had gone over there as an engineer looking for oil – El bloody Dorado more like. Just as we British do best, his company got its filthy little nose right in there. Though I reckon my dad actually just went across for some fun in the sun, but I 'spose I can't really say that about my dad, can I?

Anyway, they met when Dad had his first little trip away from where he was living in Mexico City. He went somewhere to see some friends from Cornwall and it was there that he fell in love.

They met at a birthday party and my dad gave up oil there and then. He said he'd spent his entire life searching for gold miles underground, but that he'd never found anything as precious as he did at that dance. 'You had tequila in your eyes,' my mum would say. 'I had it in my legs as well,' he always replied with a sparkle in his eye. A proper old romantic was my dad.

But Mexico was going through a difficult patch because of the evolution or something, and it wasn't that easy for foreigners there. Your grandad had to come home – 1958 I think it was. He would never have left her behind.

It was a strange old place, England, your abuela used to say. Everything in its place, mid-morning tea and people always talking about the weather. She used to think that everything was so organised. She loved it, though I think ol' Blighty beat the fun out of her a bit. It can't have been easy moving from being so close to the sun to the dark evenings and endless rain. 'It's not even like it really rains. It just sits in the air and hits you in the face,' Mum said.

But she loved it really. She used to enjoy the simplest of things: getting the bus into town; sitting and having a good old gossip about the neighbours. They were a bit of a mystery to her, the neighbours were. She used to try and talk to them, normally using local phrases in an effort to fit in, phrases that seemed out of place alongside her Mexican accent. 'It's bloody raining cats and dogs again. I can't believe my mince pies.'

No one tried harder than my mum, but the neighbours, in that classic British arrogance, just thought she was a bit strange. She never stopped trying though. She would try and do good deeds for everybody, like she had some kind of debt to pay back for having come over in the first place. She said she didn't miss home, but you could see in her eyes, Si, in her determination, in how she did things the hard way – you could see she thought about it often. I would beg her to take us to Mexico, but she always used to say I wouldn't like it.

'It's all guns and lies,' she would say.

'Tell me about it, please Mum. Tell me everything.'

'What can I tell you, my love? Anything I tell you will not be true anymore. I lose my memories years ago. It would all be fairy tale nonsense.'

One time I spent all day begging her. 'Pleaaaase.'

'Really?!'

'Yes! Just close your eyes and tell me what you see.'

So she closed her eyes and began to speak.

'Brown, green, blue, never-ending blue. It never ends my dear; the colours they never end, neither the stories and contradictions. You can explore every day for the rest of your life and never truly understand the place. Every question have another. No answers my dear, just a story with no end. From one city to the next, a different world of traditions, culture, music and food. Desert, jungle, sea, sky, mountain and romance. Yes, romance is everywhere, my dear. You fall in and out of love every day. You love and you hate. You hate and you love. You are lost to a story of love, a downhill that takes you further, deep into a rich valley, with no road out of there. I read you Pedro Páramo, my dear, Pedro Páramo and his questions, his search through what he know and what he don't know. The deep valley, the heat on the horizon, a dust storm where every piece is a different story …'

She paused, biting her lip.

'Why did you stop?' I said.

'This … it's silly, my love.'

'It's not to me. I want to hear more.'

I ran to the front door and picked up a telephone notepad, rushing it back to Mum. She closed her eyes again and started writing.

'I go north through dry, cactus lands. The smell of angry dust and heavy silence fills my nose. I'm going home, I think. We're in my dad's old car, looking for my old town, but is not there anymore. It's been left behind, forgotten, throw to that dark space of my mind where I can find the things I lose along the way. It's there, somewhere, but I can't see it

yet. We find a town where my home needs to be, but the streets, they don't look or feel the same. Nothing is where it has to be. And then the ground it starts to shake, like big thunder, and mountains appear in front of my eyes. The years start to go back, carry by a strong and insistent wind. I'm moving backwards too, backwards but higher on a big hill. The wind it pulls me along. Far off churches ring their bells as the volcano, Don Goyo, explodes with a frightening roar. The earth has moved, it's not where I or it thought it was. I'm high up, lost among the mountains, volcanos and forest. The sky is a thin blue-grey, hiding behind the mist. Deep green stands both sides of me, a dark but interesting character. Then I begin to fall, down, back down to life. A calm gold wraps me, together with the happy glow of the evening. Is a different space now: bugambilias, jacarandas, orange flamboyan trees, ancient and old worlds, cracked and falling walls, past histories, distant, covered treasures. The cold mist and thick fog slowly lifts up like a venetian blind, giving way to hot, hot heat, desert land and brown, dry earth. I look forward and I can see great, blue oceans, palm trees and hairy coconuts just wait to fall, grass green, green, green, it spread out and into the water – the timeless, infinite water. Mexico is the world in one country: mountains, beaches, towns, cities, forest, and rainforest, ancient and new. Is poetry and prose, bright and dark – the whole of human existence from rich to poor, the most beautiful and the most ugly. Is everything or nothing. Is part of who I am and what I am.'

'Aren't there lots of donkeys?' I remember asking.

'More than you can shake sticks at,' she replied in her unique way.

My mum hardly spoke about it after that and whenever she heard Mexico, she would always meet it with a sigh. She was resigned to the fact that it was all a distant dream, Simon. Whatever she did, she'd be stuck in the middle: never quite here, never quite there.

She told me that she always hoped you'd go, Si. She used to say that she thought you would understand it best. I'm not totally sure what she meant by that, but that's what she said. Maybe you'll get it better than I do.

She also used to say you were a *sun baby*. Now, I have no idea where the hell she was going with that one because you were born in the gloomy wing of The Princess Margaret Hospital in Swindon. A grotty, grey day if I remember rightly, the rain hammering it down outside and your dad asleep in the empty bed across the way. There was nothing remotely sunny about the occasion. I needed 10 stitches! Apart, of course, from the fact that my very own soldier had been born.

Your abuelita was sat in the corner in a high-backed armchair. It was the only time I ever saw her pray. She was quiet, concentrating deeply on something, her fingers moving carefully from one bead to the next. I'd never seen her use her rosary before. Like every good Catholic, she never went to church.

She'd be really proud of you, Simon. Your abuela would be very proud of you going and finding her roots. You needed a bit of a break didn't you? Maybe now's the right time to start a new chapter, or turn the page at least. Travelling is the best for that, I reckon.

I would have loved to have done something similar myself when I was your age. But I never did. I never got lost. I always knew the path that I was supposed to take. In school they used to tell us to be a secretary or a nurse. I didn't really want to be either so I became a housewife instead, but how I would have liked to travel the world, to have seen the Pacific Ocean, to have been to palm tree beaches and crystal-clear waters. I always wanted to see China, I don't know why.

I'm too old for all that nonsense now, of course. I'm too set in my ways. I'm too convinced about what makes me happy. Maybe I'm too scared to be truly happy, I don't know. It shouldn't be such a risk, Simon, but it is. When you get comfortable, all the foreign stuff … it just feels like a big hole that you can't see the bottom of …

Right, I better go. Your dad's just got home with a Chinese and I can smell the prawn crackers from here. He better have got my extra portion!

Speak soon my love,

Mum

20

I woke up in a bit of a bad mood, it has to be said. Gone were the swaying palms and lapping water of the Pacific Ocean. Now I was in the cold and grey, led on my back studying the tangled, black-wire framework of a bunk above my head. I didn't feel much like getting up.

I could hear Aurelio talking loudly to some girls outside our dorm room. I knew he was trying to coax me out of bed, but I just needed to be alone. I closed my eyes.

A determined rustling floated across from the other side of the room: the zipping and unlocking of vacuum-packed clothes bags, a busy body.

'Hey you,' a Dutch guy called over.

I breathed out heavily, 'Yes?'

'Want to go get some breakfast? You can't lie in bed all day you big lazy bones. It's beautiful outside.'

His tone grated on me. As did the fact that he was probably right; I shouldn't have still been tucked up in bed. 'Give me 10,' I told him, dangling my feet over the side of the bed and pulling on a T-shirt.

The Chiapas mountain town of San Cristóbal de las Casas spread out beneath us – an earthy blanket of terracotta roofs. The wind chimed gently through the pin-cushion trees that peppered the surrounding hills, guiding the smoke that rose from homely chimneys, the earth breathing beneath our feet. A stubborn dampness saddled the air, trapping the piercing scent of burning wood and wet pine.

'Wow, it's like another country,' Aurelio said.

'What, you mean you never been here before?' Hans chipped in.

'No. It's pretty far from Mexico City.'

'Yeah, but this is like the real Mexico, no?' Hans said.

'I guess so,' Aurelio blurted. 'I'm just glad I'm finally seeing it.'

The wind picked up as we headed downhill into town, battering the sails of all the unlucky vessels caught in its wake. We squeezed past intrepid ships, their bows stooped low as they tried to make it to their destination before the storm took hold. Some had their coats fastened tight and thick scarfs wrapped around their necks like anacondas; others were sandaled, or barefoot, with just a hand-woven dress or shirt to keep in what little warmth they could salvage from the narrow streets. Corners were dotted with beggars – indigenous Maya people. We, the tourists, looked like clumsy idiots in our flip-flops, cargo shorts and creased T-shirts. I'd never felt more like an outsider. Nervous eyes looked at us with a measure of suspicion as some held their hands outstretched, rattling old tin cans of loose change. I was just another gringo; I was there to gawp, gasp, take a picture and move on. I kept my head down, blowing hot air into my icy hands.

We pulled up at a café offering organic food that looked like it had been lifted straight off the streets of trendy London – exposed brickwork, naked lighting and hidden costs. Bob Marley did his best to welcome us in. I looked across at Hans, who was filled with joy, a big rosy smile pasted across his face. We the aliens were heading home to the mothership. Our fate had already been sealed.

We were greeted by happy-looking waitresses, dressed in some kind of hipster-Maya attire. Camera-toting tourists spilled from one table to the next, getting drunk off the warm smell of brewing coffee emanating from a stove at the back of the café.

Hans looked at the menu and frowned.

'What's up?' I asked him.

'I don't see any omelettes,' he replied.

'I think it's all meant to be regional cuisine, or at least Mexican,' Aurelio said.

'Yes, but I want a cheesy omelette. I always eat some kind of cheese for breakfast.'

'OK, well maybe you could try asking them to grate you some cheese onto a side dish,' I suggested, shrugging my shoulders.

'Don't be stupid. I'll just ask for whatever. Not even a fuckin sausage,' he said, batting the menu away.

I was starting to regret getting out of bed.

'So what do the Dutch eat for breakfast?' Aurelio asked.

'Maybe some cheese, maybe a sandwich. Hell, maybe even a cheese sandwich. Better than the crappy English breakfast,' Hans said, pointing his fork at me. Then he started lecturing us on how beautiful Dutch women are. He was talking pretty loudly and attracting a lot of attention.

'Mate, I'm sure you're right, but maybe keep it down a bit,' I said.

'You guys, your women are disgusting. But then, so are your men, so it's quite a good match actually,' he said, nose-diving into a pool of laughter.

I buried my face in my breakfast, hoping Hans might not be there when I looked back up.

A pretty looking child in a grubby dress and bare feet crept up to our table, a wicker basket of trinkets under her arm. With her eyes bigger than the moon, she pleaded with us to buy something, anything. Hans didn't look happy.

'No thanks,' he said abruptly. 'Now go away.'

The girl looked at us both, clearly still fancying her chances.

'Look girl, I told you to fuck off,' Hans said, shooing the girl away with his spider hands. 'Get the fuck out of here. I don't want anything.'

The girl's eyes hit the floor as she scurried off to the next table.

I wanted to tell Hans I thought he was out of line, but I didn't have the guts. I kept my mouth shut and just waited for the bill to arrive.

'I fucking hate it when people do that,' he continued. 'It's like the only thing that matters about me is my money. It's like racial discrimination or something.'

We paid up and left.

'Hey, you want to go check out this museum with me?' Hans asked as we left the restaurant.

'I think I'm just going to have a little walk about Hans,' I said, glancing over at Aurelio, who was drawing a line across his throat.

I wasn't much in the mood for socialising, or going to museums for that matter. I wasn't much in the mood for anything, if truth be told. It took all I could muster not to go running back to the safety of my bed.

'Ha ha. Walk about. You crazy Brits. You crack me up. What about you Mexican boy?'

'I think I'm going to accompany this miserable one,' Aurelio said, giving me a pitying slap on the back.

'Your loss boys. Chiapas is all about the culture don't you know,' Hans said, raising an eyebrow. 'So long!'

Aurelio and I began to walk, our bodies recoiling at the spirals of cotton-white mist seeping out of our mouths and up into the freezing air.

'I thought Mexico was just going to be uncomfortable sweating and peeling skin,' I said to Aurelio.

'You come from somewhere it snows. This must be like a nice summer day for you.'

'Look at them all!' I said, pointing at the men and women shrinking behind giant shawls.

I zipped my jacket right up to my chin and put my hands firmly in my pockets. 'Mate, I know this is going to sound weird, but sometimes I wonder if I deserve to be here.'

'In Mexico?' Aurelio said.

'Yeah. I mean, I've done nothing in life. I've never really done anything for anybody but myself. Some of the people here, they haven't even got a pair of shoes between them. They have to beg for a living. They have to beg to keep their families alive, to keep themselves from falling through the trapdoor.'

'Right, but …'

'I'm not a bad person. I mean, I've done some bad things, but at heart I don't think I'm a bad person. It's just that, I think I'm about as far from deserving as you could imagine.'

'But who is? Who decides that?'

'Despite everything that's happened, despite everything I've messed up … I'm able to enjoy all this. Here I am swanning in and out of these incredible places. I haven't earned it. I've nothing to give. I'm just a lucky guy with a pocket full of cash and the right passport.'

'Man, I just don't know if we're the right people to be asking those questions. Sometimes I think you can ask *too many* questions. Listen, why don't we go get a drink or something?'

'Thanks, Aurelio, seriously, but I'm feeling a bit crap. I think maybe I just need to be on my own for a second. Can we meet up later?'

'Sure, man. You know me. I'll just be chasing some tail around. Let's hook up later.'

He walked off and rounded the corner, leaving me alone to battle the bruising cold.

I rounded the corner and sought refuge in a small, anonymous-looking café – bland, boring, safe. Approaching the counter, I decided to have a go at acting Mexican. I'm not sure why, it could have been for entertainment's sake, or my effort to fit in, but that's what I decided to do. I rehearsed my lines, invented a new walk and before I knew it, was at the counter asking for a macchiato in my most Mexican Spanish.

'Yeah sure, coming right up,' the lady answered in perfect English.

Slightly deflated and with my macchiato in hand, I took a seat by the window. I looked around me at everyone enjoying their coffees and tried to catch the eye of a few of the more lonely types, but no one seemed to be interested.

Staring deep down into the immense, bitter-black ocean beneath me, I slowly drifted back to the beach, the sand and the sea. I floated to the water's edge, held in the arms of an unknown man who carried me, spluttering, choking beneath the surface of the water and further out to sea, where I lay nailed to the seabed, battered by a ram of liquid force that guided me to life's emergency exit. I went back to that empty space between consciousness and dream, where my weightless body floated in a non-existence, a shapeless area, a waiting room. Lying there, water rushing past me, over me, through me, I felt safe. The sleepless nights, guilt, doubt, shame and resignation washed out of me, leaving me empty in a dark, forgotten world. 'You crazy, you wanna kill yourself?' the lifeguard screamed. Kill myself? It'd never crossed my mind. But maybe I did, in a way. Maybe I was hoping to kill myself, or part of me – the part I didn't like, the bits I wanted to leave behind. People had encouraged me to blame it on circumstance – the cards I had been dealt. They wanted me to believe that fate had played its part, and that was that. I was encouraged to look for excuses, a scapegoat, a way to blame my failings on a sort of depressing fatalism that had suddenly and unexpectedly chosen to tighten its grip. How can you be to blame if you're never truly in control? I didn't buy it. My decisions had forced my actions and the situation I'd found myself in. There is no destiny, nothing is written. We *are* responsible, we *are* the end part. And that part of me, that momentary me that had made that decision, that life-changing decision, I wanted rid of it. I wanted out. I wanted to leave my past to the ocean where that which doesn't float sinks down far below, where it lies way out of the reach of living memory. But there was a chance that those memories – those decisions – would drag the rest of me down with them. Down, to the very bottom, the darkest place on Earth …

BANG! BANG!

I jumped way out of my chair, spilling half my posh coffee down my leg and onto the floor. As if I hadn't looked stupid enough ordering it in the first place, I was then made to suffer the indignity of looking as though I didn't know how to handle it. Like a farmer trying to mix it up in a Ferrari, I should have just known my limits.

I turned around expecting to see Bigfoot or some towering grizzly bear of a creature, but what I saw was a small grinning child with a snotty nose pressed playfully up against the glass. He was laughing about the coffee incident. I just shrugged my shoulders. The kid kept laughing. Then everyone else started to laugh – a shy giggle that slowly broke out into more of a hearty bellow.

I left.

The kid ran up to me as I closed the café door behind me, keen for some recognition – praise even – for his hilarious prank. I couldn't even bring myself to look at him. Poor little mite – he wanted Krusty, but he found Scrooge.

The sky had grown a dark, charcoal grey and the wind was riding through the town like a gang of snarling bandits looking for a stagecoach to hijack. Startled people started retiring to their houses, warned off by the dense, cotton-wool clouds that started dive-bombing the town. Everyone around me had some place other to go. Everyone but me. The sound of my footsteps echoed around the fast-emptying streets as I began to follow the only human sound left in the town, 'Tamaaaaleeees.' I followed its wiry, high-pitched call from one street to the next, until I saw a thick-skinned lady sat under a blanket next to a huge steaming pot.

It was there I had my first tamal – a corn-dough barge stuffed with spicy chicken and wrapped in a banana leaf. The lady squawked at me when I tried to eat it like a sandwich, leaf and all. 'Noooo güero, hay que abrirlo primero. ¡Sácalo!'

I couldn't help but feel that once again I was the butt of the joke as the lady grabbed the tamal from my frozen hands, forcefully unwrapping the banana leaf and releasing a plume of steam from its hot belly. Exasperated, she shoved it back towards me. My abuela would have been disappointed.

'What is there to see here in San Cristóbal?' I asked the lady.

She slowly shrugged her shoulders and then, after a few seconds of thought, pointed to a church on a hill on the opposite side of town.

The church was open, a fearsome silence escaping from within. A lady knelt awkwardly in one corner, a lone candle warding her through the empty space. Tears rolled down her face as she tugged at the sleeves of her muddied sweater, her sobbing cutting through a dead hope that had once filled the building. The candle flickered and went out, sending a slender trail of smoke towards the ceiling.

I couldn't take it.

The dark, haunting grey of the sky had turned almost black, the ominous clouds sinking down further and further. The wind had grown violent, ripping chunks of plaster from the church walls and sending them rushing past me and up into the darkness above. The steps piling up to the church creaked, ached and sighed – just another day sat on the edge. I tried to make out anything I recognised of San Cristóbal below, but as the clouds flocked beneath me, I was slowly but surely cut off, isolated from the land of the living.

There was only one thing for it.

I passed from one building to the next, past doorways that were boarded up or shut. A sniffling rat poked its head out from underneath an abandoned bucket, took a whiff of the outside world and pulled back. I was well and truly alone.

I must have lapped the entire town before I found Arturo's Bar, a suitably unimpressive place – dank, crumbling and with little on offer other than dirt-cheap mezcal poured from a jerrycan. I picked a magazine from a bookcase by the toilets – any old thing – and sat myself in one corner, hoping to disappear for a while.

I was reading an old National Geographic from the 1970s on the Tarahumara Indian community living in Chihuahua, North Mexico. The guy had written it like it was some major trek into the unknown, as if he were reporting back from the dark reaches to the civilised world. He was amazed that the Tarahumara could run marathon distances in a pair of flimsy sandals. There were these amazing pictures of men dressed in baggy shirts and white skirts sprinting up mountainsides, framed in the wide-eyed naivety of the photographer. The reporter appeared dumbfounded to find people doing exactly the same thing other people do in different parts of the world, only in different attire. Maybe the sandals were a little sturdier than he thought.

I was struck by one picture in particular: the now-faded portrait of a Tarahumara family. The photographer had gathered Mum, Dad and five children on the precipice of a canyon, as if perched on the edge of a skyscraper, each in a different coloured top, but all with the same solemn expression on their face, staring out further than they could see, beyond the horizon.

This picture had lasted forty years and would outlive anyone in the room around me. I looked at the family and they looked back at me, the stern look in their eyes piercing my finite frame. Was this was how they wanted to be remembered?

I flicked through the rest of the magazine, before abandoning it in favour of the heart-breaking ballads the bar owner was pumping out over the stereo. There were only a few of us in there and all of us were on our own — loneliness our shared currency. I called the owner over and got him to pour me another.

'Hey, kid, you reckon you ought to slow down? You'll end up like those guys,' he said, pointing at a couple of men asleep in the corner opposite mine, their faces stained with self-abuse.

'I'm OK, really. You'll know when I've had enough. Hey, barman …'

'My name's Lalo.'

'Yeah, Lalo. Listen, have you seen this lady?' I said, pointing at the photo of my grandma.

'Have I seen the lady?'

'I mean the house. Have you seen the house? Is it here in San Cristóbal?'

'Errrr, I don't think so.'

'You don't think so, or you don't know?'

'I don't think so. It looks too dry to be down here in Chiapas. Everything is very green down here.'

'Do you have any idea, any idea at all, where it might be? There's an address on the back.'

'Kid, I have to be honest, it could be …'

'Anywhere … yeah, I know. But if you had to guess, what would you say?'

'It looks to me like it could be in the north.'

'The north?'

'Yeah, I mean, it could be in Guanajuato or somewhere like that. Or … maybe it's Mérida … I don't know. Mérida's not too far from here. Who's the lady anyway?'

'She's my grandma, alright? She's Mexican. I promised her I would find her house,' I said, downing my mezcal, folding the photo and returning it to my pocket. 'So that's what I'm going to do.'

'Sometimes it's more about the journey, right kid?'

'Huh? Hey, how about another shot?'

Weak street lights began to appear outside, illuminating our eerie paths to nothingness. Luck-lost men would come in from time to time, look around and nod at those still conscious, before taking a table to themselves and starting the process of forgetting. Lalo had seen it all before. Life, love, loss, death – all were welcome. Some came more than others.

21

When people ask me about Carla, it's always the same question: how did you guys meet? Perhaps they expect a romantic tale of overblown gestures, fate and chance, or a conquest of hearts spanning years, but they couldn't be further from the truth. The fact is – and I take great pleasure in telling everyone – I met Carla when she was near choking on her own vomit somewhere in Swindon town centre. Just outside Yates's if I remember rightly.

I had been on one of those infamous lads' night out when the aim is to drink so much that you're sick by about 1 am and the doner kebab on the way home tastes nice by comparison. Sometimes you might get the timing wrong and end up seeing dinner before it's been properly digested, or far, far worse, it doesn't happen until the following morning, at which point you are reminded of every bad decision you made the previous evening. Sprawled over the toilet bowl, you promise never to drink again – vowing never to so much as sniff a Smirnoff Ice. That's it, it's over – you're fully prepared to hand your life over to salads, spinning and box sets.

It's not that I was much of a lad about town, but you know what it's like – the pressure, the pressure to pull, the pressure piled on by mates who act like they're on day release from the world's most conservative seminary college. And I'm no oil painting, if you catch my gist. Get what you can sort of thing.

On this particular lads' night out, I had actually managed to behave quite well. I hadn't been sick, I hadn't dropped my phone in the toilet, and I think I'd even got my penis out fewer times than my wallet, which by anyone's book is a fairly major achievement. Someone had stitched me up at the start of the night by reaching over my shoulder when we were at the cash point and pressing the £100 button. I seem to remember deciding that if I got as drunk as I normally do, it would be adios 100 quid, so I got sensible instead.

We started at the bottom of town doing the ol' pub crawl thing. Drinks were downed and shots were chased. Dan managed to get his face in a pair of breasts by about 10 pm and Umar had his picture taken with a truncheon being shoved up his arse by about 10:15 – hen night. I remember being asked if I wanted a kiss or a shag by a member of the same party, but I politely refused, citing old-school issues of respect and not wanting to displace my mother as the focal point of female attention in my life. I was promptly and fairly told to, 'Fuck off and get a life.'

We ended the night in The Tavern, the local gay bar. Someone had heard somewhere along the way that it would really get going later on. So there we were, a group of lads heading off to the local gay bar in search of a good time. Decision made. Part of me worried that this particular group of friends might try to make up for their insecurities with bravado and offend people who really didn't deserve to be offended, while another part of me wondered if we might just weed out a number of closet curious types and all have a good laugh the following morning, before swearing never to mention the event ever again. As far as I'm aware, nothing happened, though there was one incident involving a slightly confused Chris, who walked into the toilet with a pool cue and started poking it through holes. He surprised a number of people and received a good few invitations, but swears he politely turned them all down.

It was when leaving The Tavern, which allegedly would still not get *really* going until much later, that I first saw Carla. Some people reckon that when you meet the love of your life for the first time you are overcome by emotion, showered with colour and light as if the skies had opened and a supernatural being had floated down from above – a divine gift. I suppose you could say that was the case for me, only my angel had not so much drifted down, as tripped, wobbled and fallen flat on her arse.

A conscientious friend had kindly placed her in what she thought was the recovery position, but which looked more like someone trying to imitate a slug. I don't know what it was about me as a passer-by that made her friends believe I might be of any use, nor what it was about the slug that made me take pity, but pity I did take. I found a taxi and then carried Carla to the car as she vomited down the shirt my mum had so carefully ironed earlier that evening. I even then, in a moment of complete madness, gave the driver 25 quid, telling him she was going to make a complete mess of his car. 'I'm gonna get his number!' one of Carla's mates screamed. I put my number in her phone and saved it under *Phil Anthropist*, presuming, like the arrogant turd that I am, that she would never figure it out.

The next day, while I was still trying to come to terms with the fact that I was feeling quite so fresh on a Sunday, my phone vibrated: message. 'I don't remember you, Phil, but I thought I'd say thanks.' It took me about a month to tell her that my name wasn't actually Phil and that it was just my idea of a joke. I can be really awkward sometimes.

And so began the most innocent and beautiful relationship I've ever had. I find it difficult to describe what I felt when I was with Carla. I've tried, but the words never seem to come together in a way that does it justice. I suppose I felt secure and safe, which at the time scared me a bit. I think there are many people who saw us together and thought that I was the useless other half and that I would never be able to survive on my own. That always kind of annoyed me. But now that she's been away for a while, I have to say that I feel completely lost without her. Carla is perhaps – and some people might think it's quite sad to say it – but she might be the only person I have ever *truly* loved. I love my mum and my family, of course. They've done so much for me. They've sacrificed so much. I'll be forever grateful. But Abuela used to say that true love is knowing someone better than you know yourself. Maybe I'm just naive, but I can honestly say that Carla reached a part deeper than I am capable of finding myself.

It was an innocent love, a love that asked no questions and required no answers; it just *was*. Carla and I never celebrated anniversaries because we didn't think it was any great challenge to be together. We didn't see the need to congratulate ourselves on surviving another year. Each morning was just another chance to live our lives together, happy in the knowledge that we'd be seeing each other come the end of the day. Every second away from the grind of work was spent planning our free moments together, our future – a time that we'd almost lived already, moments we'd already touched and smelt in our collective dream. Everything was in place; we just had to live it.

That was all there was left to do.

After I got to Mexico, there were times I would find myself just wandering from one street to the next for no particular reason, and I would see Carla in people, in faces that passed by. That annoyed me a bit too. Even if I'd wanted to escape her, I couldn't. My trip was about getting some distance. It was about trying to find myself again. It was about trying to find my place in the world. And, as Aurelio rightly recognised, I was trying to do that by running away.

22

I'm not sure how I got back to the hostel if I'm honest. I woke up fully clothed and, luckily, in my own bed. My body felt like it'd run a marathon backwards. Energetic, busy people buzzed around me, happy to be alive. Yet again, I just felt like drawing the curtains, wedging a chair against the door, and spending the day in bed. I guess I would have done just that, had I not had to make a dash for the toilet. It was at that point, slumped over the basin, my mouth swamped with hot, bitter saliva, that I heard the commotion.

'Oh my God! Someone has broken the mirror. It's smashed. I can't see a thing!'

'Shit, look! There's blood!'

'Oh my God. What kind of a psycho prick would do that? Do you think there was a fight or something?'

'Nah, probably just some drunk-ass loser.'

Curled up at the foot of the toilet, I had that sinking feeling. I looked down at my cracked hand, mottled red, and my head dropped even lower.

I grabbed at chunks of my hair, pulling hard, trying to find something that I could recognise. Is this as low as it gets, Simon? Is this as low as you'll go? I couldn't find an explanation. Nothing made sense.

'God, why the fuck would anyone do that? Why the fuck would anyone break a mirror?! Don't people know it's bad luck?'

I didn't want to think on that too long. I didn't have to.

A voice came from the corridor outside, 'Can all those booked on the *Day in the life of a Maya* tour meet in reception in five minutes?'

I'd arranged to head out of San Cristóbal and into the surrounding hills – a mass tourism job. I only agreed to go on it because I thought the receptionist would break down in tears if I knocked him back. I deeply regretted it.

I waited in the toilet until the coast was clear, before making a dash for the bedroom.

'What's up with you, man? Out late last night?'

Aurelio.

'Something like that.'

'Well come on, get ready, we're leaving in a second. It was your idea to go on this trip. You better not leave me hanging.'

'I think I'm going to stay here, Aurelio. I don't think I can do it.'

'Like shit you are. Not after you abandoned me all day yesterday. Come on, get up!'

'Seriously, go ahead. I'm really not feeling it today.'

'You're coming. Even if I have to carry you there myself.'

We were going to visit the nearby town of San Juan Chamula, before heading on to a tête-à-tête with the Zapatistas – a rebel group that lives in an isolated village in the mountains. I felt like steaming-hot shit, but I knew Aurelio wasn't going to leave unless I went with him.

The flamboyant hostel worker made us sign a waiver, before packing us into a minivan full of yellow-haired, red-faced tourist types. 'This is going to be like a unique experience, like the *real* Mexico,' the hostel worker said as he shoved the form into our faces. 'But, of course, everything real can also be dangerous. The Zapatista rebels have guns, you see. It's just in case.'

I looked at the assortment of expensive but chunky cameras clunking around people's necks, the tightly-strapped bum bags, the cheap-looking, expensive outdoor wear and the one knobhead in big, baggy, multi-coloured tent trousers – another tourist staple. 'I reckon we'll be alright,' I shouted as the door slammed shut.

The road out of town was steep and winding. It was pretty nasty in the van, and naturally we had to pull over to let tent trousers out to be sick, all over his shiny new attire. He got back in looking slightly less smug. I, unfortunately, wasn't far behind him.

My stomach felt like it was constantly about to fall over the edge of a cliff, but I just kept quiet and tried to focus on the passing views. Every colour was there, from the jade green of the long-sheathed grass to the red of the cockerel's Mohawk and the lavender of the home-made dresses worn by the voluptuous women tending to their homes and families. Silver donkeys clambered over hills and valleys with piles of firewood strapped to their backs.

I turned my head away from the window to find someone studying me from the other side of the van.

'Hey, sick man, what happened to your hand?'

I could feel the eyes of everyone on me. 'Nothing,' I shot back nervously. The eyes were still looking. 'I was out at this bar …'

'You got that right. You can still smell the alcohol!' my smarmy neighbour squawked.

'Yeah, well, I was out at this bar and then I was helping this drunk guy home and he was stumbling all over the place and basically, I was keeping him upright, helping him back to his house, when he just buckled and fell against this wall. I managed to catch him, but I got a cut hand for my troubles.'

'You were carrying some local drunk guy?'

'Yeah … what, you've never helped anyone before?'

I looked around at the smug faces surrounding me. They clearly didn't believe me.

'Hey guys, give the kid a break, no?' Aurelio said, silencing the rabble.

As the van swung into town, smiling children scrambled across the square to be the first to greet us, tiny snot bubbles popping out of their little noses. A brisk breeze swept through the streets, a constant presence in the mountains. The small children's lips cracked at its biting cold, their faces smeared red from constant exposure to the sun. 'Hey meester, hey meester, cómprame algo,' one said, shoving an arm draped with local merchandise in my face.

'Sorry kid,' I said, shrugging my shoulders.

'Ándale, no he vendido nada hoy.'

'I'm sorry kid, I really am. Maybe try him,' I said, pointing at native trousers. They rushed over to his side and started tugging his shirt.

'OK guys, gather round,' said Cyril, our guide – a tall, slick bloke with shiny, white teeth and black hair. He took us over to the town church and, dusting down a gold crucifix hanging around his neck, began his well-rehearsed speech. 'Here you will see the meeting of two religions, of two beautiful but different belief systems: the native and the Catholic. What you will see here is totally unique. You cannot find this anywhere else in the world. The people here, they have their own ceremonies and rituals, and if, *if* you are lucky, you might see one of them being performed today. Now, I hope no one is feeling at all queasy,' he said, patting me on the back, but directing most of his attention to a couple of pretty girls from Belgium.

'Man, this whole thing feels like a bit of a fake,' Aurelio whispered to me as we edged towards the church. 'It feels like a bit of a museum or a historical production, you know?'

'Yeah, you're probably right,' I said, trying to pay attention, trying to stop thinking about the mirror.

'I feel bad, man. I mean, this is my country, these are my people, but it all feels kind of fake. We're just going to flash a million pictures and leave, you know? Like, it's the opposite of what's got everyone so excited.'

'Sure,' I said as we followed the rest of the tourists in, stooping as we passed through a low-hanging doorway and into a cave filled with thick smoke and the stinging scent of incense.

Candles dotted the floor, providing the only light besides a thin shaft of intense white that crept in through a tiny hole in the roof. Dripping wax threatened to ignite a crunchy carpet of pine needles scattered beneath our feet. I ran my hand along a row of wooden pews that stretched back into the darkness, until I met a small altar sat in the centre. I inhaled a thick helping of dust, candle smoke and the unmistakable stench of alcohol. The smell of wet earth drifted in from outside.

'We're in luck,' Cyril said, hushing us with a finger to his lips.

Towards the back of the church, veiled by the almost-total darkness, a man in striped shorts and a ribbony hat poured pure alcohol on a small patch of the pine-covered floor, blessing its fertility and praying for a good harvest, mumbling his verses in a low hum that rang around the room. He stopped and stood in silence, his head dropped against his chest, his legs looking like they might give way any second. He stayed like that for some time – Cyril looking on in keen anticipation – before he began to move again, slowly lifting his right arm and placing it under his jacket. Then, a flutter, a struggle, a cold-blooded murder. The man plucked out a chicken, wrung its neck, snapped its head off and let the still-warm blood drop to the floor.

'This is to ward off the bad spirits,' Cyril said, trying to restore some colour to our white faces. The girls from Belgium sloped against the church's mud-and-plaster walls, struggling to keep it together. 'Just wait,' he told us, sensing the man was saving the best until last.

I strained my eyes to see through the darkness of the church but couldn't quite make out what was going on. Then we heard a seal pop and more liquid pour onto the ground.

'Is that Coke?' Aurelio shouted

'Shhhh.'

'Sorry, but seriously,' he whispered, 'Fucking Coca Cola?'

'The gods have a sweet tooth I guess,' Cyril said, giving me a laddish wink.

'Seems like our mate too,' Aurelio said, pointing at stripy shorts as he guzzled the rest of the Coke down, before letting out a rip-roaring belch and casting the can to one side. He took one final look at the dead bird, before shuffling past us and out the front door of the church, lighting a Marlboro Red as he surveyed the outside world and made his way down the street.

'Well, that was pretty amazing,' I said as we crawled back out of the church, the overwhelming daylight blurring my vision.

'Do you really think so?' Aurelio blurted out.

'Yeah, I thought it was pretty mind-blowing. Especially the bit at the end. Pretty gruesome, but really interesting,' a salesman from Derby chipped in.

'I wanted to be amazed, I really did. But I wasn't,' Aurelio said. 'Snapping a bird's head off and pouring your favourite drink on the floor seems, to me, no crazier than drinking the blood of some dead guy.'

'What are you talking about?' I said.

'The same things move us all, man. The same things push us into doing what we do and how we do it. We're all scared by the same confusing questions.'

'Don't think it'd ever occur to me to sacrifice a chicken, Aurelio.'

'That's not the point …'

'Right, let's move, everyone!' Cyril shouted, corralling us back into the van. 'It's time to go and see the Zapatistas.'

Cyril gave us a brief on what we could expect from the rebel group, along with a particularly bloody account of their history.

'Are they, you know, like still at war?' a girl from London in an olive-green beret asked Cyril.

'Let me put it this way: the first thing you'll notice is the guns.'

We can only have been an hour out of San Cristóbal, but it felt like we'd been travelling for days. Great waves of hills tumbled over each other either side of the van, the sun bearing down and not a sound in the air, save for the gentle whisper of the breeze through the tall grass that lined the banks of the road. Fields of corn gripped onto the hillsides, determined to win the battle for life, a steep drop falling down below them.

Cyril seemed nervous, or maybe it was just me. Some of the group had opted out of going – already on their way back to San Cristóbal's comforting coffee shops and reggae music. Just a hard-core few remained. No one spoke. We all just looked out the window thinking the same thing: no one would ever find us if we were somehow to disappear out there in the ocean green of Chiapas' endless, undulating valleys.

The van stumbled to a halt outside a metal gate. A sign: *Land of the Zapatistas – here the people govern and the government obeys* put us in our place. Two stern and upright women stood guard, their rifles pointing to the skies. They wore black and red dresses, sporting long, plaited hair, their faces covered by woollen balaclavas. They stood proudly, a steely determination in their eyes and a rigid belief in their cause.

We were made to hand over our passports and register in an old, flaky book. Our documents were taken hurriedly to a central committee in a hut adorned with political murals somewhere off to our right while we waited out in the sun. Cyril had decided not to join us; he sat in the van listening to Bon Jovi tapes instead.

As the minutes passed, my nerves began to fade. Rich, fertile land spread out as far as I could see. Young boys and girls fetched water from a well behind the village shop and in the distance sat the studious silence of the community school, teaching knowledge-hungry children a blend of old and new.

'Looks pretty idyllic, doesn't it, Aurelio?' I said as we stood waiting in the street.

'That it does.'

A couple of armed guards moved slowly over to our group. 'Señores, por aquí.' We had been summoned.

I don't know what I expected – maybe a pack of angry, armed militants, or an intimidating bunch at least, but there sat a frail couple, infinitely older than the walls that surrounded them. I was probably taller than both of them put together.

Bahlam and Xochi began to speak gently and clearly, a cold and suspicious air penetrating their words, the eyes beneath their thickset masks revealing more than the words they spoke. They began by telling us about the legitimacy of their fight, about how the native people had been subjugated in one way or another since the European travellers landed. They told us about how they had taken up arms in 1994, fought the Mexican army and stormed the town hall in San Cristóbal de las Casas. They told us about the hardship of fighting for a life of their own, and how the Mexican government had done its utmost to suppress their nonconformity and bring the community back into touch. We listened intently, submissive to the words of a life and a struggle we would fail to truly understand.

'Do you ever think you're fighting a losing battle?' a fellow tourist in a long, white dress asked them.

'The only thing we've lost is our fear,' Xochi said. 'We're fighting for what we believe in and doing the best by our people. That means everything to us.'

'But do you ever lose hope? Do you never just want to give in?' I asked, shocked that I'd spoken out.

Xochi considered her answer for a second. 'We always knew it would be difficult, but when giving up means losing everything …'

… 'No matter how painful or difficult it gets,' Bahlam stepped in, 'we have to believe it'll be worth it – we have to believe. And look at everything we've made for ourselves,' he said, proudly nodding towards the open door.

I looked at the floor and then at my hands.

'Everyone's fighting their own battles,' Xochi said.

'Ain't that the truth!' Aurelio exclaimed.

'We're proud of what we've done and we're proud you've come to see us. Please, feel free to explore our community, if you wish,' Xochi continued, rising to her feet and guiding us outside.

I spotted a girl peering out from behind a building some twenty metres away. She kept a watchful eye on us, half her face hidden.

As the others ran off to take pictures, Aurelio and I moved over to where she was stood. She looked older than I first thought, a lively decisiveness running through the blood in her cheeks.

'Can I sit here?' I asked her.

'It's your step as much as it is mine,' she answered.

'Thanks. What's your name?'

'Matilda. And you?'

'Simon. Nice to meet you.'

'How about your friend?'

'My name's Aurelio. It's a pleasure to meet you. How old are you?'

'I'm 10.'

'Wow, you look much older than that …'

We sat there in silence for a while, letting the immediate world around us be all that existed in that moment. We looked out at the fields of corn shimmering in the mountain breeze and the bulky, white clouds racing across the sky, over the hills that lay in the distance.

'It's pretty beautiful here,' I said.

'I like it. Where are you from?'

'The United Kingdom. Heard of it?'

'I think so, yes. What's it like?'

'Nothing like this. Lots of people in a hurry. Lots of people looking for answers they're unlikely to find.'

'Do you think I'd like it?' she asked.

'Yeah, maybe. Do you like big cities?'

'I'm not sure … I've never been to one.'

'Oh, right. And do you like living here?'

'Yes, of course. It's safe and I'm free to think whatever I want to think. That's quite important.'

'Yeah, I think it is.'

'If you can't be who you want to be, then you need to escape – you need to find that place,' Matilda declared.

'Would you say you're happy?' I asked her.

'I want nothing more than what I've got. So yes. Are you?'

'Sometimes I think I am.'

'Come on! We're the happiest people in the world!' Aurelio shouted, throwing his arms in the air like he'd just scored the winner in the FA Cup final.

'Good for you,' she said, smiling.

We left Matilda sat on the step, gazing off towards the corn fields. She was incredible, mature – a person older and wiser than her short time on this planet. Next to her I felt ignorant, stupid even. She seemed to get life, to understand it, dominate it and beautify it. She complemented her surroundings, whereas I seemed to be at war with mine.

'Hey, man. So was it you?' Aurelio said quickly as we wandered back to the van.

'Was what me, Aurelio?'

'You know, the mirror.'

My muscles tensed up and the bitter taste returned to my mouth.

'Aurelio … we've had a really nice day, can we just go back to the hostel and forget all about it?'

'See, I think that's your problem.'

'My problem?!'

'Yeah, I think maybe you're problem is that you never face up to anything. You just keep running.'

'Running?'

'Yeah, like I said in Puerto Escondido, running away. I think it would probably help if you were honest about stuff. Just look at the Zapatistas taking everything into their own hands. It's fine to be scared, man. It's fine to be freaked out by stuff. That's just life! But you gotta accept that and face the things you don't like sooner or later. Otherwise it's all just gonna keep getting worse and worse. I mean, shit Simon! Puerto Escondido scared the living crap out of me.'

'What would you know about that?'

'Hey man, I'm just saying … I don't mean to cause offence or nothing, but I do think it would help you just to talk every once in a while.'

'And who are you to be lecturing me on facing up to problems?' I snapped.

'Sorry, man. I'm just saying, it could help.'

'And what about your problems? How did you manage to come away on this trip at a moment's notice? Where's your career? Your girlfriend? Don't you think it would help you to focus a bit more on the wide, open spaces in your own life?'

'I …'

'I told you, mate. I'll talk about it when I'm ready.'

Aurelio just stood there, stunned, before he turned and slowly continued his walk back to the van, shaking his head.

'Hey, Aurelio. Wait up! I'm sorry mate,' I shouted, calling after him. 'I'm sorry!'

'Don't sweat it, man,' Aurelio said, turning to face me. 'I just hope you know I've got your back, that's all. You know that, right?'

'Thanks, it means a lot. It really does.'

'Any time.'

'I really am sorry. I don't know why I reacted like that. I think I'm just having one of those days. I don't really deserve your support.'

'Man, seriously, no worries. I was probably pushing a little too hard. Let's just put it behind us, yeah?'

'Sounds good. So, how about we head on to Mérida?'

'I'm sorry, Simon, but listen, you're going to have to go on to Mérida alone. I'm heading back to the capital for a bit. Got some stuff I need to sort out.'

'What? It's not because of what I said, is it?'

'Course not. I forgot to say, I got a phone call from my folks and my dad's got this project he wants some help with – something about earning my keep. He's got this crazy idea that money doesn't grow on trees. But, hey, I don't think it'll do you any harm to spend some time by yourself.'

'OK, mate. I guess you're right.'

'Course I'm right. You'll have an amazing time. I'll catch you up at some point anyway. You won't be able to keep me away for too long. Now come on, let's go annoy some tourists.'

23

There was no avoiding the fact, the boat was slowly sinking. The captain, oblivious or else indifferent to our plight, perched himself on the back of our narrow, wooden vessel, his gaze fixed on an indistinct point in the horizon as we gently chugged along the muddy river. I fished a bit of moss out of the water and landed it on his head, trying desperately to get his attention. I pointed at the brown, jungle water pouring in through a crack in the side of the boat, remonstrating with him that if we didn't turn back soon, both of us would meet a murky end. He heaved a heavy sigh, having already resigned himself to a miserable marriage with his sinking boat. Giving the rudder a tweak, he threw us around and pushed back up against the current of another failed attempt, his silence shattered by the frantic thrashing of the motor.

Having left Josefina bobbing back at the port, we picked up the pace, buoyed by Sofia's energetic purring, carving our path through the water at a decent speed. The jungle loomed above us forcing our attention forward, straight ahead. We sat and waited, searching for our signal to stop, the tunnel growing darker the further we ventured in. Not a twitch from the captain, his narrowed eyes focused with anticipation.

Suddenly, he sat up straight and Sofia made her way over to a steep bank on one side of the river where a faint, forged path led directly to the lion's mouth of the jungle. I made my way over to the pointed end of the boat, where, shifting my weight from water to land, I started to climb the staircase carved into the wet bank of the river. Each step was harder than the last as I dug my feet into the damp earth, feeling myself battle with hundreds of years of rain and mud that tried to carry me back down to the water. I glanced over my shoulder, my lungs panting – heaving – trying to gulp down as much oxygen as possible. The boat had disappeared. The captain had abandoned me to the jungle.

I continued forward, treading with care, compelled by the untamed roar of the forest before me. Vines swept down like grand theatre curtains, framing nature's dialogue: the bellows, croaks, whistles and crows of life in the jungle. I stepped cautiously past giant trees and ferns, bulbous drops of sweat slipping off my body and draining back down to the earth. Squinting,

I could make out a shape of dark grey just ahead, a floating buoy in a sea of green – a vestige of civilisation.

My foot hit something hard, a stone buried deep into the jungle soil, and then another, restrained by hundreds of years of undergrowth, a barely recognisable wall growing out of the sheets of green, tangled in nature's grasp.

The wall led me to a narrow, stretching tunnel that ushered me into a swirling black hole, the light fast disappearing behind me. All I could do was keep walking on, trying not to think about who – or what – I might be sharing the space with. My hands, tentatively outstretched in front of me, worked their way through the sticky yarn of spiders' webs. My heart fluttered like a hummingbird, yet my feet kept moving with a growing inevitability. Edging my way through the darkness, cold, moist stone either side of me, I reached out and felt a step – a slimy stone slab. A golden coin hung above me, slowly growing bigger and bigger: a stream of light spilling in fresh life. I could hear the sounds of the jungle again as I emerged into a forgotten past. I had made it.

The sun drifted in through the few gaps in the forest rooftop, painting an amber-spotted quilt on the floor. I was alone in Yaxchilán, a small sliver of Maya civilisation frozen in the tropical heat of the southern border territory – a little detour before I headed on to Mérida.

As I stood there, my baggy T-shirt stuck tight to my chest, the jungle seemed like the perfect place to avoid living in: crazy animals, intense heat and danger at every turn. It seemed impossible that anyone could build a city there with little but their bare hands, but the Maya had done just that: churches, houses, schools, all lost to the jungle.

I took a seat on the lemon-green grass and marvelled at the incredible scene of nature vs man. Yaxchilán had once been a bustling city, but with the passing of time, nature had reclaimed its space and swallowed human life – vines, leaves and plants eating into the remains of a pre-Hispanic community, now just a temple to man's fight for the infinite. It was a battle we humans were always destined to lose.

Yaxchilán's main square, its hub, was close to the exit of the tunnel I had just arrived through. Three pyramids enclosed the square, making it feel almost like a football pitch – a field where dreams were shared and lost. I tried to imagine myself living there one thousand years before. My hand pressed up against the ancient stone, I could hear the pulsating heart of the Maya kingdom, the steady beating of a pig-skin drum getting faster and faster, echoing across the natural auditorium, bouncing around the buildings and down into the valley below. I could feel the presence of an ancient people and their panic – the steady, progressive panic at the realisation they would have to leave this place and make a journey into the unknown.

A large stone storybook stuck out of the ground in one corner – a stela immortalising a story that needed to be told, a life changing event like the birth of the son of God, the handover of a dynasty to a young and sprightly king, or a great battle fought to protect the kingdom. Or maybe just a monkey wearing a dress. Yep, as I cast my eyes over the ancient artwork, all I could decipher was a pack of tranny apes prancing about as if dancing at a school disco. Maybe it was the Maya's idea of a joke. Maybe they saw us coming.

The grand palace – the big mother of all the pyramids – sat far above the central square, a trail of crumbling stone steps leading up to its summit. The incessant, jungle heat sweat the life out of me by the time I reached its top, and for the briefest of moments, I doubted it'd be worth it. But as I took my place on Yaxchilán's throne, high above the dense green carpet, scanning the earthy brown of the river and Guatemala beyond, I began to smile. That, over there, was a whole other life. Just over there was something else to explore, people to meet – another country, just the other side of the river. Suddenly, the world seemed too big and time too short. I suddenly became aware of all the billions of possibilities I'd sheltered myself from. I suddenly realised how little I knew.

I've always been a bit cocksure, if I'm honest. I've always thought I'm a bit worldlier than the next person. I've always thought I was travelling the world by turning on the TV. For whatever reason, I've always felt like I was in touch with everything, everywhere. I've always been proud of how much I can reel off about current affairs. What, the DRC conflict? West Bank settlements? Muslims in Myanmar? I love to churn out eloquent monologues on how and why the situation will or won't change and just what measure might be taken to sort the whole thing out. I've always thought I had all the answers.

But there, among the smells and sounds of the forest, the deep history running through the land of a life and a people I had no idea even existed – it all felt so incomprehensible. It was all so alien to me. That jungle was thousands of years old. The view, the tree tops – everything I saw – was the same view the Maya saw as they built these pyramids. The same river still flowed through, sinking boats with drunk captains. The air still moved through the chattering trees, taking life and planting it elsewhere. The birds still woke up each and every day as the sun reached its throne. People had come and gone, but that, the *real*, had remained exactly the same for millennia.

There, in Yaxchilán, the solid foundations on which I had constructed my very definite views of the world, all became so incredibly fragile. From the most trivial to the insanely complex, I'd had a great knack for reducing life to simple pint-size patter, when, in reality, it is too big for any of us to comprehend. The more I explored, the more deeply I foraged, the less I seemed to understand. Me, there, on that pyramid – just a tiny piece.

I closed my eyes and imagined what my life might be like if I gave it over to the road – what it would become if I renounced upward trajectory and focused on the here and now. I thought about what would happen if I never went back home. I imagined where I would work, how I would move and what I would see. I wondered if I'd feel lost without any fixed goal. I wondered if anyone would miss me back home. I wondered if I would ever think about the past, or if I'd just drift towards the core of time itself. Perhaps time itself would become irrelevant.

And, just as I straddled that mental hurdle, just as I knocked on the door of enlightenment, something hit the back of my head.

I put my hand up and ran it through my hair. It came back with a dense and slightly-pongy mass. It looked and smelt like shit. Literally shit. I looked up, and there it was: a monkey, looking unduly proud of itself with its soiled hand pressed joyfully to its bottom. A monkey had thrown its shit at me. Brilliant.

It made me angry, really angry. I wanted to shout something, I just wanted to shout. So I got up and spluttered the first thing that came to me. 'Yeah, well, that's exactly why you're in that tree you cunt!'

Nil points.

You can take the boy out of Swindon, right?

When I got back to the river, the boat had reappeared – the captain was asleep, tropical sun washing over him, life's finest medicine. He'd made it. He'd found what made him happy and stuck with it. I envied him for that.

24

Returning to the port, I tipped the captain and made my way back up to the dirt road that had led me to Yaxchilán. I flagged down an old Toyota pickup, hopped in the back, and headed slowly north along winding, backcountry roads. I'd managed to persuade the driver to give me a ride in exchange for an old Swindon Town football shirt with *Fjørtoft* on the back. I was reluctant to hand it over, but it was that or hard cash. He was also quite interested in my camera, but I took the initiative and imitated Fjørtoft's classic plane celebration and that, together with the shirt, was enough to secure a ride. Swindon had been living off the golden glory of the '94 season for too long anyway.

With the shimmering sun at the very top of the sky, we chugged along a straight, hypnotic road, a playful breeze doing its best to wring all thought out of my hard-packed head. Life had long since felt as light. My decision to abandon home felt vindicated, my journey worth every step. I had somehow made it all, everything that I had seen, if only by rejecting the safe trappings of normal life. I lay back against the rusting exterior of the van and closed my eyes, the sun gladly resting against my face, raining warmth down on me with no cloud to obscure its view.

The changing scene around me was impossible to corroborate with the country I had arrived to. It was still Mexico, of course, but to think that it belonged to the same land that spawned Mexico City, Puebla, or even Oaxaca was incredible. I had read about warring civilisations, the fight for control of land and resources – an image which made complete sense when painted against the arid, harsh landscape of the mountainous Mexican altiplano, but this was another terrain, where Maya astronomers and thinkers battled to tame thick forested expanses. The land had flattened out, the heat ratcheted up, cactus giving way to sugar cane, avocado trees and grazing cattle. The frenetic pace of the Mexico I had lived since arriving was being lulled into a wheezy submission.

We passed through sleepy towns sedated by the seductive callings of the afternoon siesta, where people swung in hammocks next to the open doors to their mud-brick, conical, pizza-oven houses, the bolshie heat refusing to budge, obliging all to take some time out. The life of each town was drawn to the invasive carriageway running through its heart. Man and wife, dog and cat, sat outside simply watching, observing, conversing not with each other but with the rich dialogue of daily life unfolding around them. Turkeys wandered around, chests up and out as if they owned the joint. Wood fires burned away, heating wodges of yellow tortillas and giving off that unforgettable smell of mankind using nature to its own end. Children chased after chickens, captivated by the magical landscape, pulled by fear and intrigue to the dark enclaves of the surrounding jungle, where rumour and legend cast spells over their imaginations, turning the slightest movement into the powerful strides of the mythical, black panther.

We passed a large, three-wheeled cycle cart, pedalled by a slight old man, with a heavy rock of a lady sat in a plastic chair on a platform over the front two wheels, shielding herself from the sun with a faded red-pink umbrella, unaware of the rapid rivers of sweat coursing from the old man behind her.

One town melted into the next and, as we marched on, I abandoned each of their stories in favour of my own journey. At times I tried to focus on an isolated emotion, a feeling rather than coherent thoughts. I tried to let calm and peace embalm me as I contemplated the lively fields of green around me. Yet no matter how hard I tried to shy from solid thought, I inevitably returned to the same defining moments or decisions in my life. I found myself delving deeper and deeper, spiralling down in circular motions, revisiting moments buried deep in my consciousness, each time dwelling on the same emotions with a more profound sense of melancholy and regret. I tortured myself with the things I might have done differently, the words I wish I had spoken, and the actions I longed to have taken. Despite my distance from anything that resembled our lives together, I thought about Carla. I wondered if somehow she might be thinking about me, if she might be thinking about us. I found myself wishing she was by my side, sharing everything I was living. But then I would shake myself down and try to move on, to forget, to forge my own path and write my own story.

'The thing is, I feel like we can be too dependent on the relationships we form with others,' I said to myself, my muffled words flying off behind the truck and into the sky. 'Right?! Yes! We measure our lives through those interactions – we allow them to define who we are and change what we want from life. We almost *need* those relationships in order to feel human, to feel part of everything else that's going on. We pour ourselves into conjugal moulds and create something new, something shared. And once you meet that person, once you make that connection, you will always leave a part of yourself behind. You'll never be the same again afterwards. Because there will always be an afterwards, a postscript, a coda. One of you will always go back to being alone. And you'll never be the same again. You'll never go back to just being that *you* from before. That past – what you shared and fought for – that's *you* for the rest of your days. And that's kind of hard, right? I mean, to think you can just give away portions of your life, helpings of yourself, to some joint cause that can end just like *that*, that's really tough. Because time will eventually catch up with you … well, with one of you anyway. I know, I know, we should just be grateful, but it feels like there should be a happy ending, doesn't there? Wouldn't that be fair? …'

The car gently arrived to a standstill, its tyres scraping over loose gravel. I had no idea where we were.

'Drinks break,' the driver shouted as he peeled himself away from the front seat of the truck and off into the night. He was going to Mérida and there was still a long way to go, but he was doing his best to pass the time by packing his cab with beers.

I sat on the grass for a while and waited, surrounded by the sounds and smells of the damp heat of a tropical world, listening to the high-pitched purring of the cicadas in the background. The light of the day was beginning to fade, the sky moving through its catalogue of reds – from crimson and blood, through burned orange and pinks, then back again through purple. A solitary cat strolled out of the undergrowth, took one look at me, hoicked up a hairball and carried on to the other side of the road, brushing up against a barely legible sign: *Welcome to Kabah.*

An old lady ambled up the road, leaning her weight fully on a knobbly cane, edging towards me like a determined snail whose hungry gaze is fixed on a sprouting vegetable patch. She came right up to me and stood still for a while, unsure what I was, or why I was there. She poked me with her stick; I gave out a nervous laugh. She seemed surprised to see that I was real.

She began to speak to me, her voice deep, concerted, playing with the sounds of Maya – Tzeltal – her native tongue. Her low and guttural tone forced through a steady breeze that made the hairs on her chin wobble from side to side. As she took my hand in her own, I tried to tell her that I had no idea what she was saying, but I was mesmerised, enchanted, my eyes glued to hers, my hand held tightly to her chest.

She put my hand on her heart and began to pray, her head hanging down loosely onto her chest. A slow and gentle tear rolled down the jagged contours in her face and fell to the floor. She held out my palm and looked deeply into it, scrutinising each and every crease, as if it told a different story. She looked deep, deep, *deep* into my eyes and began to speak to me in a rich, expressive tone, her bottom lip trembling as she spoke. Feeling the fast-emerging stars settle down to listen, I followed every word she said, allowing them to pass through my skin and take form once more. It seems strange now. It seems improbable, impossible even, but I understood each and every word she spoke.

'Simon, I can hear you. I can hear your inner voice, your well-covered emotions, everything that you buried not so long ago knowing that someday it would surface again, uglier than when you left it. You knew you would have to face it. And you are. There's no quick solution, no fast track to happiness. Your story will always be yours. But you have to keep taking those steps, you have to keep searching. The answers may or may not come, but that's not what's important. You need to keep asking those questions. You need to keep shedding that skin of yours. The night may grow darker than it has been, but it will draw to a close. You *will* eventually find what you're looking for.'

And, just as I scrambled for my abuela's photo, the old lady disappeared somewhere into the night, a dark shadow against the violet sky. It was just me and the buzzing crickets again.

The driver returned shortly after, a big, brown bottle under one arm and a friendly sort of girl on the other. I hopped into the back of the truck, obeying the old lady's instructions. I was on my way.

25

Carla,

I know this is crazy and that it makes no sense to write a letter to you – you'll never read it. But in some small way it helps me to keep you close. Somehow it helps me thinking these letters and words might reach you – that somehow they'll fall in between the cracks and find you.

Do you remember when my abuela was in hospital and she asked us to go and explore? And we made that promise to find her old house, where she grew up? Well, here I am, travelling through Mexico, just like we always said we wanted to do. It'll be a challenge, but I'll do my best to find it. I thought you'd be happy about that. You always used to say we should come to Mexico and live out our dreams. I should probably do some more of that.

I'm trying to give my life over to chance and let the wind carry me wherever it needs to carry me. I'm trying to plan less and just allow myself to enjoy whatever life sends my way. Sounds a bit cheesy, right? Well, it's all in the name of becoming a better person and finding a new way to be, if that makes any sense.

Sometimes I have these dark thoughts, Carla. Sometimes I wonder if I should seek more help, but then I think that maybe that's the problem: everyone else chipping in with how I can get better or what I need to do to move on. I think I probably just need to forge my own path and take care of this myself. I just don't know when that will all happen. What if I feel like this for the rest of my life?

I know what you'd say, but it's not that easy, Carla, I promise you. When you're the cause but also have to be the solution, what then? How does that work? I guess it's all just a bit overwhelming at the moment. In some ways I feel much better than I have in a long while. In some ways I feel free, refreshed and invigorated. But then it can always come creeping back, sometimes harder and faster than before. That's what scares me. I don't feel like I'm the one in control.

A lot of the time, I feel like I'm kicking against a fast-flowing river that threatens to sweep me away as I try to grab onto whatever I can to keep myself afloat. Sometimes that's you; sometimes the memory of what we had is the one thing that stops me from going under. Then sometimes it's what feeds the water rushing past me; it's what sends me rushing down, flying towards a dark and lonely place.

Like I said, maybe I just need to let myself go with the water for a while. I'll let you know how that goes.

Miss you so much,

Simon

26

Mérida is famous for two things: hats and hammocks. I had neither.

Being in Mérida is like wearing your entire wardrobe of clothes – woollens and delicates included – for a light- to medium-intensity jog across a desert. Hitting a brick wall as the sun starts to fall from its perch, Mérida retires – it gives in. The lead-weight heat slows you down, putting you to sleep. You're there, you know that you're there – your body is there – but your mind has already folded in on itself, incapable of further action, thought impossible. In your weary state you have to keep reminding yourself of the most basic processes. Right foot, left. Right foot, left.

Walking around the old, pastel-painted streets in search of a place to stay, I could hear the city trying desperately to breathe, trying to make it through a cauldron of thick, boiling soup: a gentle cough, barely respiration, just enough to show that there was still some life left. The air was deathly still, human interaction at a premium. Some people were just strewn across the pavement, incapable of moving any further, collapsed in an immovable heap, a signed will in a pool of sweat by their body, a sad tear for all those final goodbyes that were never said. Those that had got home would just sit, all pensive activity beyond them, their faces awash with disbelief, each sat face to face with another fiery afternoon, unsure of how they managed to live through the last and how they might make it through the present. A treasured few were lucky to be comforted by a gently purring fan – chipped wooden blades whirring above fading '70s decors, moving hot air around stale vats of stagnant nothingness. It was just a question of sitting, conserving energy and moving as little as possible. These were dead hours.

I, of course, never an advocate for the old *When in Rome*, thought I should throw caution to the wind and carry on as normal. In the comfort of my air-conditioned hostel room, I chucked on a fresh shirt, slung on my trusty flip flops, and with a map under one arm and a bundle of naivety under the other, I left for the street. It wasn't long before those who hadn't made it home started crossing the street to avoid me, terrified by the drowned rat dragging itself from one corner to the next, its shirt now a completely different colour to when it had left the hostel.

'You might want to take a hat,' the hostel owner had ventured.

'Yeah, I'll be alright.'

Red-raw scalp.

I had probably only walked about two blocks by the time I gave up, if truth be told, but that was enough. I had got as far as any fit human could manage.

Standing in the central square, dense sweat racing down my forehead and stinging my eyes, I took a moment to survey my surroundings.

'Right, what have we got here?' I muttered to myself. 'Yep, government building, check; mural, check; café under archways, check; hordes of tourists dressed entirely in flannel, check; ch … oh wow, yet another bloody church.'

'Don't criticise the word of God, man,' a self-righteous American stood next to me proclaimed.

'Pardon?'

'Ha ha, pardon! I love it when you guys do that! Pardon me, could you pass me a bo-ul of wa-uh. Ha ha, you guys crack me up.'

I left the tourist cackling to himself and went into the church convinced it was bound to be cooler than the hellish heat of the outside world. I looked around, unsure whether I could even be bothered to take in yet another religious building; yes, it was beautiful, yes it was less gaudy than the rest, but essentially, it was still a big room with a cross and a lot of people playing *Who can be the quietest?* Besides, I was still sweating like I'd committed some heinous crime, something really ugly. Just as I made to leave, there was a tap on my shoulder. 'Siiiimon.'

Before I turned around, even before I dared turn my head, I knew it was very unlikely to end favourably for me. It sounds like her, I thought. It sounds like the lovely but slightly intense one from Cholula – the one I thought had probably done a fair amount of Internet research since I last saw her. Why accept the friend request? Why dammit?!

I turned round.

'Iiiissss meeee!' Elena screamed at my face.

'Wow, what a massive surprise. It's great to see you!'

'Yessss issss amaaaazing. I can't believe it,' she said excitedly.

'What are you doing here?' I asked, suspecting I probably already knew the answer.

'I just come on vacation!'

'I thought so. Did you come on your own?'

'Yes. I just come on my own.'

OK, likelihood of her being a bit of a psycho increasing.

'You want a drink?' she asked.

She'd backed me into a corner. I couldn't say no. I was sweating so much that she'd know I was lying if I declined. I was parched, there was no hiding the fact. There was no way I could say no. 'Yeah, absolutely, yes I do. Sign me up!' I said with a slight grimace.

'Sine me what?'

'Don't worry. Let's just get out of this church.'

We moved quickly across the main square, I slightly ahead of her, afraid she was trying to lure me into a well-constructed trap. I considered the chance that this might all be slightly dangerous and the fact that my mum had always warned me about these kinds of situations. 'Watch your drinks and mind the winks,' my mum used to say. But I just had to be the one in control – that was the rule. So we strode from one block to the next, Elena hanging just behind me, slightly perturbed by the fact that I was clearly freaking out.

'Let's just find bar. Any bar,' she said.

'Yes, that's what I'm looking for,' I snapped back at her. You call the shots, Simon. You call the shots!

And that's when Cantina Peking emerged from the shadows. It looked sufficiently dingy for me not to have to put up with her expecting looks for the next few hours, while also being dirty and cheap, and so likely to shake any idea she might harbour that I had more than two pennies to rub together. It also looked even less likely to be anywhere she might try to take advantage of me, sexually speaking. I dragged her inside before she could say no.

Mr Wong's tavern had all the class of a kick to the spuds. An assortment of poster girls with massive tits hung from rusty nails sticking out of its mint-green, stained-brown, flaky walls. Fluorescent lighting gave a surgical hue to a scene that you would never want to put under the spotlight. In one corner were the gent's toilets – a semi-cubicled space, where you could see the feet and shoulders of those relieving themselves, a strung-out cardboard box covering the urinals themselves from view, without stopping the sounds and smells of its patrons escaping. It was like watching a bunch of drunk louts pissing in a lay-by.

Tin tables and plastic chairs were scattered across the room, most looking like they may have never been occupied since the sorry place opened its doors. Wong himself, wearing a pair of McDonald's sunglasses and a loud Hawaiian shirt, was perched behind a flimsy plywood bar, serving beer into dirty plastic glasses. It was truly seedy.

'Wha' you wan'?' Wong shouted across the bar, picking up on my gringo appearance.

'Errrr … beer?'

'Yeah, we got beer.'

'Two?'

'Yeah, we got two.'

'Can we have two, please?'

'Yeah, you can.'

Sarcastic bastard.

Wong took his time, occasionally throwing random abuse across the floor in a high-pitched, Anglo-Hispanic-Chinese accent. I wondered how the hell he'd got there. I wondered how I'd got there.

'So, you like it?' I asked Elena, convinced I had done enough to make her never want to see me ever again.

'Is different,' she said. 'But I like it. I like everything you like.'

Right. God. I thought I was a bit of a gent before this trip. I wanted to believe that I was a nice guy, a decent bloke, but honestly, I'd just spent the night with her. That was it. I hadn't even wanted to do it, I just thought I owed it to the trip. It wasn't something I was really ready to do. It was the booze and the trip, the trip and the booze. I certainly hadn't expected to see her ever again. She seemed like a really nice girl, but the whole thing was awkward! It wasn't even like it'd been any good. *I* hadn't been any good, that's for sure. I'm pretty sure it was one of those two-pump slumps. One of those ones where you apologise afterwards and they say, 'No, don't say that.'

'It makes it worse right?'

'Yeah.'

'I already said it though.'

'I know.'

'Probably forget about this, right?'

'I think that's best.'

It was definitely one of those. I don't know why she liked me so much. There was no reason for her to think I was anything other than a complete waste of space.

'So tell me about you,' I said, doing that sippy-drinky mime thing to Wong, getting the old dog to bring another couple of beers across, my eyes lowering nervously to the floor immediately after. I was resigned to my fate. I knew I was too much of a wimp to back down.

'Well, I born in Izúcar de Matamoros in state of Puebla. I have two sister and one father and one mother. I went to school, then I want to get job but my father say I have to study. That's OK, I say, but what I want to study?' ... 'What I want to study? I'm asking you.'

'Errrr ... biochemistry?'

'Noooo, you crazy! I want to study be a chef.'

'So that's why you're such a great cook?'

'No, I say I *want* to study be a chef, but my father say no, you have to make the money, you have to make it. So I study be a lawyer. Better he say.'

'So you're loaded. Do you have loads of money?'

'No. Well I have some. I buy a beer ... or two.' And at that she exploded with laughter – the high-pitched kind you might expect from an absolute maniac convinced they've cornered their prey. Once she'd calmed down, I ordered her another beer. She wasn't going to stop at two. Not if she was going to put us through what I thought she was going to put us through.

Wong started serving with more panache, getting into his role as filth facilitator, giving me a wink or two. I went to the toilets and let off an absolute floorboard-creaker of a fart, making no attempt to cover my tracks. If I was going to be a lad about this, I owed it to lad-dom to get into the role as much as possible. Besides, I'd already had a few before we got there. I was fairly well toasted.

I walked back to the table and accidently kicked its wonky leg, sending beer flying all over the floor. Wong walked over and threw down a dirt-black towel. He didn't seem too concerned.

'And what about you? Tell me your story,' she begged.

Were we really going to do this?

'No, nah. … it's just … my life's been pretty boring.'

'Come on, I tell you about me.'

'I know, but really, there's nothing interesting. I'm just an ordinary guy.'

'I don't believe you and if you don't tell me, I'm gonna scream and tell everyone how you try rape me.'

'But I didn't …' I stuttered, my jaw dropping. She didn't look like she was bluffing. She had me right where she wanted me. 'Well, I was born at the grand old age of zero in a town called Swindon.' I said, trying to make her laugh. She didn't. 'I had a mum and a dad and I went to school. I kind of liked school, though not at first. Obviously at first, all you want to do is watch TV and sit in your Thundercat pyjamas, but eventually the security of it got to me. I felt safe there. I suppose I always felt ahead of the average. I felt like I was doing alright. I knew my place. I could joke around. Some of the teachers liked me, others really didn't. Some said I wasn't reaching my potential, others said I was ahead of myself. I didn't really listen to either.

'I wasn't the most popular kid at school, but I had my group of friends. I'd play football when the cool kids let me, but it would never be long before I embarrassed myself. Yet there was a kind of grinding acceptance that I would keep trying, a glimmer of hope grasped from the odd defence-splitting pass – the quiet beginnings of pride – before I went and scored the world's most-humorous own goal.

'I suppose my biggest weapon at school was my humour. I could make people laugh. But my crimes weren't always victimless. There was one kid called Bernard Cummings. I think it was in geography class with Mr Bampton, we tied Bernard's shoelaces to the desk and then shouted, "Fire!" The poor lad, who was prone to nervous breakdowns, tried to run out the class, but only managed to fall with his desk to the floor. Mr Bampton gave

Bernard a right bollocking, of course.'

'Poor Bernard.'

'Yes, poor Bernard. He was a nice kid. Harmless. If I ever see him again, I'll apologise.'

'And after school, you go to university?'

'I did, yeah. It was good fun. I did business management but I have no idea how to manage a business. I've not even got close to one. It was just a lot of drinking to be honest.'

'It sounds fun.'

'It was. Lots of jokes, not much studying.'

'And this girl you tell me about?'

'Whi … she … well, she …'

The silence was awkward. I'd waited too long to respond. I was stuttering and stammering, but what could I say? I could have denied it, I could have brushed it off, acknowledging the distance I had gained by coming to Mexico. I could have lied. I *should* have lied. I should have erased years of history just like that. I should have just left it behind. Wasn't that why I was in Mexico after all?

But I didn't. I tried to fight it. I tried every trick I'd learned and honed until that moment, biting my lip and tongue, but my eyes began to fill with water and, I'm kind of ashamed to say, I started crying.

'She died.'

I wanted to run at that point – to get out of there before I was made to confess any more, before I opened up, but the eyes of the bar were fixed on me. I was glued to my chair.

It wasn't a nice feeling, but if you've ever been in a situation like that, you'll know that it's like pulling a plug on the Atlantic Ocean – a giant body of emotion, present for as long as you can remember, flushing out at full speed. The weight behind it was so great that there was no way I could stop. Once it had started, there was no going back – out it flowed.

It was pretty embarrassing. The poor girl had no idea she might unlock this Narnia personality with one simple question. Wong almost looked worried.

I'd have liked to have told her all about how I was feeling, but I couldn't really put it into words anyway. Those feelings were far too complicated for me to describe back then. I would have liked to have been able to describe them – as Aurelio said, maybe it would have helped – but I couldn't.

Some things stay with you for a long time, probably the longest time. They're what require another layer of skin, another you. And underneath it's still there, of course. Eventually the cards will tumble. Eventually all will lay bare. But in the meantime you can do a pretty decent job of hiding it away.

'Are you OK?' she asked.

'Yeah, I ... I ... I'm fine,' I stammered, doing my breathing exercises. 'Shall we get some more drinks?'

I went to the bathroom and washed my face. The incident was forgotten there and then and we got back to the serious business of making the most of our luxurious surroundings. The beers kept flowing and there was tequila and rum. There was one point at which I swear I fell asleep during one of her stories, a small bundle of saliva edging its way down my face. She didn't seem to notice or care. We were there until Wong flicked the lights off.

'Time to go fuckey,' he said in his charming way. It was only about 8 pm.

'Hey, Wang!' I yelled on my way out. 'You know where this photo is?'

'It a joke? It's Mexico. All look the same!'

I was tempted to strike out, but I didn't. 'Is ... it ... Mérida?' I asked. 'Look at the photo, Wang.'

'My name Wong.'

'Whatever, look ... at ... the ... photo.'

'Yeah, I know the place,' Wong said, his voice rising and his eyes igniting.

'What?! Are you kidding me?! You know it?!'

'Sure ...'

'Can you take me there?' I said in a hurry.

'It cost you. One hundred dollar.'

'Of course. Just take me there. Let's go!' I said, slinging back my rum and coke.

We left before Elena had a chance to intervene. Wong walked at some pace, bent forward, his feet barely touching the ground. I grabbed Elena's hand and dragged her through the placid crowds of weary people, racing after Wong as he weaved his way across the city.

'Do you think it safe?' Elena asked.

'What?!'

We had thread ourselves through the entire city before Wong pulled up at the end of a dark, abandoned street.

'Pay. Now!' Wong exclaimed, thrusting his hand towards my pocket.

'Hang on. Is this really the place?' I slurred.

'Oh my Gat. Trust Wong. He know what you look for.'

He was gone as soon as the cash had left my wallet.

I walked slowly forward, my feet clumsily traversing the slippery cobblestones. It was hard to make out one house from the next. A sickly street light coughed weakly in the near distance.

'Simon, we have to go,' Elena begged.

I shrugged my shoulders as I turned to face a white house with potted plants along the windowsills and a stained-glass window above the front door. I held up the photo and brought the house into focus, then looked back at the photo. It was all there: the intricate iron covering the windows, the cracked blue tilework and the concrete step leading down onto the street. It was all there. Yet … somehow, somehow … it just didn't feel right. There was something missing. I turned over the photo and checked the address. It was completely wrong.

'Maybe they changed the street names,' I said, shaking my head.

'You really want find this house, right?' Elena said, clutching my shoulder.

'I have to find this house. It's all I've got left.'

'Don't be angry with yourself. It's not fair. You do your best.'

'It's just … ever since everything happened … I've had no control. For once it'd be nice to get it right. It'd be nice to keep my word.'

'And you will. You will find the house, Simon. I know it.'

'It's the least I can do,' I said, deflated.

'You're a good person, Simon.'

'You have no idea.'

'Well, from what I see you have a heart made from gold. Come on, let us go back to the hostel,' she said, taking my hand and walking me away from the house.

I fell asleep as soon as my head hit the pillow, my shoes still firmly on my feet – the booze and the heat made sure of that. But I awoke with a start in the middle of the night and couldn't remember where I was. I got up and moved to the window, looking out onto a lifeless street. Not even the slightest hint of a breeze. A cat slinked past tightly-packed bin bags and leapt onto the bonnet of a car, settling down and drifting off to sleep. I suddenly felt an urge to pack up my things and leave.

'I'm sorry,' I whispered to the deaf, still air of the room as I pulled the door to.

It was a shame really. For all the sweating, Mérida was a really beautiful city – all creamy shades and dreamy parks. The place really seemed to come to life at night. The city's squares and corners were lined with smitten couples, both young and old, slowing down and taking time to be together, sharing a moment away from the glaring heat. Latin, cha-cha rhythms pulsated beneath the flagstone streets, infecting its residents with endless romance and passion. But it was time for me to catch my bus and keep a little ahead of my mistakes, taking my usual route out. My head tried to empty itself and just let my feet drive me forward. Amendments could wait. I was off to the beach again.

27

Dear Ma,

I'm sorry it's been so long since I last sent you an email. I'm not very good at keeping in touch, am I?

Mexico is keeping me really busy. I'm seeing a lot of the country and meeting loads of interesting people. I've got to a bit now that I suppose you could say is the least like anything back home. The scenery, the people, the food – there's very little of anything we would recognise, Mum. Everything is so completely different. I'm doing my best to communicate with all the local people, but you know my Spanish has never been up to much. I do feel like I'm improving though, and now that I've been here awhile, I feel like I understand pretty much everything. I couldn't say the same for my Maya unfortunately – that's the language a lot of people speak where I am at the moment. It sounds completely foreign, totally alien. I like to think there are other ways of understanding people though. I'm doing my best.

I've seen so much already, Mum. Each place has been eye-opening and every step has been worth it – each move has been challenging in its own way. I've met loads of different people – some interesting, others good fun and there's been some weird ones too. Some have helped distract me and some have helped teach me a thing or two.

Obviously I'm still having my moments, Mum. Sometimes I feel like I'm being a bit of a shit, like I'm just a bit of a horrible person. Sometimes I feel like I don't really deserve the life I've got. Sometimes I look back at my life so far, and above anything else, I feel regret: regret for the things I've done and regret for the person I've allowed myself to become. There's a lot of negative energy there still, but I'm hoping that time will help me get myself back on track. I'm sure I'll figure it all out before too long.

Anyway, I want you to know that I really miss you guys. I've always been a bit stunted in that department – telling you guys how I feel. I'm sorry about that. You only regret it in the end.

I'll send you a proper update soon. I might even take a couple of pictures!

Love,

Simon

28

I'd reached the tropical paradise of Tulum: white sand, mint-green waters, palm trees and furry coconuts, all overlooked by cliff-top Maya pyramids. My speedos were on quicker than you could say, 'Worm in a warehouse.'

I only lasted about 10 minutes in the sun before I had to crawl to the shade of a nearby palm, the sand sticking to my sweat-drenched body. I looked up at the jagged silhouette of the leaves against the beach-blue sky. A bird hopped around unopened coconut shells. I kicked back, closed my eyes and listened to the lulling purr of the ocean, my mind synchronising with the movement of the waves, losing itself to another place and time.

Breathe in … and out.

Breathe in … and out.

I opened my eyes and saw Carla sleeping peacefully next to me beneath the staggered shadow of the palm tree, a weightless smile spread wide across her face. It made my heart stop to see her.

'Do you remember the one and only time we went on holiday together?' I asked her.

She didn't move a muscle, her body at complete rest.

'We spent months trying to pick a destination. You wanted a bit of art, a cheeky museum or two. You were never that swayed by sun or sand, were you?'

…

'Whereas I think if we're calling spades *spades*, we both know that the only thing I really cared about was being able to drink beer with a sun burn. I guess it's testament to how much you loved me that you were prepared to be seen with me even when my skin was falling off. I'd always thought you would tolerate me no matter what, but that was a whole other level. Not that I wouldn't have done the same, of course. You know that, right?'

…

'We were on holiday in Barcelona. It seemed like the perfect mix of art, music, food and dancing, for you, and cheap beer for me. We'd gone to the beach – something I didn't even know Barcelona had – as a trade-off for going to the Sagrada Família. "Why visit something that hasn't been finished?" I reasoned with you. "You're rewarding inefficiency." "It's a work of art," you said. I spent the whole time at that church dreaming of covering myself in sand.

'By the time we got to the beach, it would have been about three in the afternoon and the hottest part of the day. "You don't need sun cream after two o'clock," I said.

"*You* definitely do."

"'Nah, you'll see," I said, cracking open a cool one, digging my feet beneath the surface of the sand, and closing my eyes.

'I could hear your voice in the distance, laughing and having fun. You were probably getting hit on by some bronzed native with jewels that would break the scales. I had foolishly thought that the predominant style in Barcelona would be continental-retro. And yes, there were a number of tanned locals squeezing their bumper packages into tight Lycra lockers, but that didn't mean it was a look that everyone could pull off. I've never felt so white. And then there was my manhood, which barely made a dent on my bright-yellow pants. It was sort of like when you strain to try to see an animal in the distance, and you want to believe so badly that it's there that you almost start to see it, before finally admitting that you can't, you just can't. Chill Simon, I told myself. You're golden mate. No mega dong is going to be distracting Carla from your killer one liners. You just need to do like the locals, settle back and enjoy the sun. So that's what I did.

"'Oh my God, Simon, you look really red."

… "What?"

"'Are you asleep?"

…

"'Oh God, Simon, did you fall asleep?"

… "Where've you been?"

"'I went for a quick swim, though by the look of things, it might not have been that quick."

… "It hurts."

"'You look terrible, Simon. You look like a really angry crab."

"'It hurts."

"'Let's get you back to the hostel."

'Hostels, you'd said, are *more fun* than hotels. Now, that may well be the case, but I had no reason to be fun, much less when I was suffering third-degree burns. My beach-sleep-error was made public knowledge very quickly in the Hostel el Sol. Every raging turn in the night, every scream as I got into the shower, every messy number two – though irrelevant to this story – was known and suffered by all.

"'There is solution," I was told by the chiselled hostel owner.

"'What?"

"'Vinegar. Rub it on you."

126

"'Are you sure?"

"'Yes, it's famous remedy here in Spain. It turns lobster to lion."

'Now I'd suspected that Mr Swish might have had eyes for you – in fact, he'd told me as much. "I want to sex your lady."

"'Thanks."

'So why I'd given credence to his clearly ridiculous suggestion of vinegar beggars belief. Yet there I was, literally dousing my crusty body with the pungent stuff, in the vain hope that the pain would stop. It didn't. And now I was peeling in big, yellow lumps. And now I stank of stale fish and chips.

'There's nothing quite like going abroad to make you feel totally wrank, is there? I mean, the French are all good food, better sex and nonchalance to boot; the Italians are more seductive than Casanova; the Germans are so sure of their own greatness that you end up apologising for absolutely everything, and as for the Spanish, let's just say they're better than us at everything.

. . .

'What's that? Yeah, of course I remember David Seaman's incredible penalty save at Euro '96 and his even-greater moustache, but I think that's the only time in 200 years we've been able to feel an inch of pride when placed in the same arena as the Spanish. It's just, we British, we're a European anomaly. We possess none of the jazz, zero joie de vivre and we're rubbish at organising things. We don't fit in. And there's no better example than the two of us wandering down Las Ramblas.

'Barcelona was a place of seduction and romance. Passionate music permeated the hot air, awakening the night from its slumber and making our blood dance around our bodies as silky, tanned people dedicated their time to falling in love. It was all so sleek. And then there was us. We just didn't fit in. You, perhaps, could have made a pass at being local, at being part of that beautiful city. But I, tomato red and reeking of vinegar, looked like a pus-filled spot on a beauty model. I was barely able to walk, if you remember. And when I did, I did so trying not to move a single muscle in my body, keeping my top half as rigid as possible and moving my legs without bending my knees. Worst of all, I was also covered head to toe in a bright-white, paste-like cream that the chemist had made me buy.

"'You feel no pine," she'd told me.

"'No pine?"

"'Yes, no more pine."

"'Oh, pain?"

"'Yes, no more pine for you."

'And when she said no more pine, she meant it. Although leathery and smelly, my skin now felt icy cool. What did hurt, however, were the sideways glances, the double takes, the spitting out of drink as I went past, and the fright I gave myself at my own ghostly reflection. Do you remember?

…

"'I think we should probably head back," I sulked, my tail well and truly between my legs.

"'Don't be a boring bastard, we'll have a great time," you said. "And if anyone looks at you funny, I'll lamp them."

'We went and had a bit of a dance, well you did. We ended up in some Salsa club and this time I had a genuine excuse to sit it out. Dancing would have just made me more irate, and I think you were probably happy to have some time to disassociate yourself from me.

'The creep from the hostel showed up, quelle surprise, and made a beeline for you. You accepted a dance and did that cute look-over-your-shoulder thing to me as he whisked you off to the dance floor. I knew you wouldn't do anything, but he didn't. Standing there, watching you be swept up by a flailing Lothario, I had to admit to myself, that in your position, I probably would have. It was something about the grease in his hair, about his tanned, weathered exterior, and his immaculately-ironed shirt tucked precisely and neatly into his pressed trousers – a bare ankle resting on his suede loafers. This was not a man who had time for socks.

'You danced and twirled together, and got a little bit closer than two human beings should probably be comfortable with. If you'd been harbouring an unsightly cold, it would have been a one-way ticket to snot-plagued mornings for that young lad. As it happens, he got away with it.

'You were the kind of girl who didn't worry about any of that though. You couldn't have cared less what anyone thought about you. You just wanted to have fun and put smiles on faces. Had he made a move, you would have politely turned him down, I'm sure. That's the kind of gem you w … you are.

'And that was Barcelona – now consigned to the changing seasons of my mind. Even now as I try to look back, there are little details that elude me, moments swept away by time. I do my best to hold on to everything, Carla, but sometimes it slips away. I've *become* afraid of losing, I think – afraid of losing it all. Everything seems so fragile – as thin as paper and as brittle as glass. Sometimes, when I play back my memories, I feel like I'm looking at them through a frosty window, watching them as they freeze and crack with the winter cold. I don't know how to protect them. I don't know if I can.' … 'Wait, where are you going?'

…

Gone.

I looked out to sea and wondered where she might be. I reckoned she might be just the other side of the blue – out there, somewhere, just out of sight, floating in the middle of the ocean, waiting for me to join her. I so desperately wanted to find her again. I wanted to be with her, to feel her and touch her. I wanted to make her laugh.

The sea continued to breathe, in and out, in and out.

I didn't stay long in Tulum. It's a real danger when you're travelling. You get into this habit of scratching your feet before you've worked up a decent itch. It's easier to pack your bags and move on than it is to get to know a place properly. But that's the traveller's prerogative: no duty to anything other than the road. Time for something different, time to leave it behind. I'd go back if I needed to. I was just wasting time at the beach.

29

Hola Simon,

Encantado de ver que tienes un tiempo antiguo derecho de la misma. Ha ha, did you get that? There's this thing on Google that translates everything. It's like I can speak Spanish! I reckon one day we'll probably all be programmed with different languages in our voice boxes anyway. That'd be great, wouldn't it? That way you would be able to download a different language or setting. Like you with that Maya or whatever it is, you'd be able to go straight up and ask someone where the swimming pool is or what the weather will be like at the weekend. Amazing what you can do nowadays.

Speaking about technology, you're all mouth with this camera, my love. Where are my photos? Even if it's just a picture of a sign or something, you have to send us everything, my darling. No good us giving you a camera for your birthday if it's just going to sit rotting at the bottom of your bag now, is it?

Anyway, I just want to say that I understand completely what you were telling me about being able to understand people even though you can't, about there being other ways to understand people. I remember once I was collecting money for Barnardo's down in town and a person who had some kind of speech impediment came up to me and popped 50p in my bucket. And, no word of a lie Simon, he said something bless him, and I turned to Jill, who was collecting with me, and she looked all puzzled and I had to translate for her. 'He said *have a nice day*,' I told her. She couldn't understand how I'd done it, but I tell you, Simon, I've got a way of connecting with people. I've got a way of understanding them and connecting with them on their level. It's a gift I have. And I think I've passed it on to you.

So tell me, how's Mexico? Have you got any closer to finding your abuela's house? Sounds like you're seeing some magical places, my love. I'm really pleased for you – and a little bit jealous if I'm honest. I've been telling your dad that we should go backpacking around South America, but he doesn't sound too keen. 'If I want the shits, I'll have another vindaloo off Ahmed. At least I'd be in the comfort of my own bathroom.'

I think it's all ever so romantic though. Just me and the road, the road and me. And I'd have time to read. I never have time to read, Simon! As for getting tipsy on a school night – Lord help me!

You make it sound like a journey to another world, Si. My own little Louis Armstrong, bravely going where no man has gone before, into the unknown, never to return! Well, definitely to return. You're not thinking of staying there are you?

I tell you what though, I'd love a go on those Caribbean beaches you've told me about. I've always wanted to scramble up a palm tree and fetch down a big hairy coconut, smashing it open on a rock and drinking the delicious milk. I fancy I could make a fist at living on a dessert island somewhere. Yeah, I reckon I could. I'd go fishing at first light and cook on open fires, slowly building my rainforest city. My house would be built in the trees. I'd be largely land-bound at first, but I'd eventually become more at home in the trees. Like those Kombai people – have you seen them, Simon? Absolutely incredible! Truly inspirational people they are. They live in trees! And we complain about having to pop down the corner shop to get some milk. Just imagine it!

Now, listen Simon, about you being a bad person, what on earth has made you think that? I don't want to get too worried about you, love, but I don't like to hear you say things like that. Especially when we both know there's nothing further from the truth. You are one of the most honest, bravest, and good people I've ever had the pleasure of meeting, my love. You've got a heart of gold, my darling, and everyone knows it. I've never seen you do a bad thing in your life, so please, please, please, please don't feel like that. Just promise me the minute, the very minute you start feeling like that again, you pick up the phone and we get you back home. I know you're saying this trip is doing you a lot of good, Simon, but you've got all the love you need here. Just don't be too proud, my son.

I'm going to leave you for now, Si. Please do keep writing to us. You know that we love you very much and nothing is too big or small to support you.

All our love,

Mum

PS Dad says to tell you he's just got back from watching Swindon get thumped by Yeovil. That'll be him in a strop for the next week then.

30

It was about half seven on a balmy morning in a sticky port city that I realised I'd tried to sleep with a prostitute. And that was only because of the raging storm taking hold of my gut.

I'd never thought it was something I would need to do in life – it's not something that had ever really crossed my mind. It would have been near impossible for me to imagine exactly how it would come to pass, but this is me and I'm capable of finding my way into deeply weird situations.

As I sat in the bathroom in all kinds of pain, I could hear her stirring in the bedroom – her feet freeing themselves from the sheets and dropping slowly to the tiled floor, seeking a pair of stiletto heels.

'Is it OK?' she asked in her sexy, Latin lilt.

What? My stomach? The situation in general? The fact that I'm talking to a prostitute through bouts of diarrhoea, sat on the bog with a paper-thin door as my only reprieve?

'No, not really.'

'I go for doctor.'

'Actually, it's good. Está bien. Don't worry.'

Silence.

Had she finally gone? I pinned my ears to the door, straining to detect any movement. Then I heard a noise. She was up to something. Maybe she was reaching into the pocket of the jeans I had thrown to the floor in my rush for the bathroom.

'Are you looking for my wallet?'

'I find but has no money.'

For once I was glad I'd managed to spend absolutely everything the night before. I was actually glad. 'Did we, you know, did we actually do anything?' I shouted from the bathroom.

'No, you too drunk honestly.'

'Are you leaving?'

'Yes, I go.'

'Hang on! I've got this photo. It's in my bag. I was just wondering if you could take a quick look at …'

SLAM!

'Well it was nice to meet you.' Just me and the off-white porcelain then. My head sank into my paper-dry hands. It was going to be a long old day.

'Well, hello, butt boy! You're looking good,' Aurelio said, poking his grinning face into the bathroom. He'd sent me an email when I was at the beach telling me he was bored and ordering me to meet him in Veracruz. The fact that he was late in arriving should have come as no surprise.

'Why did you have to show up now?! Of all the moments in all our lives …'

'Calm down, Grandma. You'll be fine. So, I saw this … how do I say it? … I saw this interesting lady with high heels and a lot of makeup walking out of the room when I came in …'

'Yeah, OK, mate. We'll talk about it later, OK?'

'That's if you survive this bout of Montezuma's revenge.'

'Right.'

'How can I help, man? Beer? Water?'

'Water. Just water, please.'

It was a painful ordeal, only compounded by the fact that Aurelio chose to sit by my side the whole way. He told me he wouldn't be able to forgive himself if something happened to me, but I knew that really he just wanted to nurse me back into action as fast as possible. Still, as strange as it was to have a spectator, it was nice not to have to suffer it alone, even if Aurelio did insist on playing wall-to-wall Trance. Besides, his weird concoction of water, salt, boiled rice and lime did just the job. I was back on my feet before the day was out.

Veracruz is one of those places where you're happy just walking about, watching life do what life does – people shouting, laughing and crying, every expression amplified by the stiff coastal breeze, everyone and everything just that little bit louder.

We plodded along the famous Malecón coastal road, yolk-yellow houses and seaweed-green shops to our left and the choppy Gulf of Mexico to our right. I could taste every grain of salt in the hot, heavy air, my hair slicked back with sweat. American cars rattled along with their hoods down, the sun splashing across them with its lemon stare. A group of men in Hawaiian shirts huddled around an upturned bin, chewing on beefy cigars and staking their pride on a game of dominos. They spoke a Spanish I could barely understand, their tongues making no effort at all, lulling around the language and giving up in retreat of the afternoon heat. Ladies with stiff perms fanned their glistening faces, mopping their brows when no one was looking, being careful to keep their well-rehearsed makeup in place.

We walked on, drawn by the distant sounds of an orchestra playing the unmistakable rhythms of Latin music, our feet tapping and skipping to its addictive pulse. It took us to the city centre where a troupe of dancers were elegantly skating around as if dancing on ice, ambassadors of the reserved courting of an older generation, of a lost respect where subtlety of touch was valued over the simulated humping of our day. No, this was not Reggaeton, but an orchestral bird song that was mirrored by the gentle sliding and stiff backs of the smartly-dressed dancers. In the centre of the square, a Danzón orchestra slowly worked their way through the old classics my abuela used to listen to whenever she wanted to take herself home. The elderly *veracruzanos*, impeccably dressed in suits and dresses, with shoes shinier than a big, brass button, danced with their loved ones, each with a big smile on their face. Everyone looked endlessly happy. Life was present and that was enough.

The orange sun crept through the gaps in the slow-aging colonial buildings that enclosed the square, their bright paint gradually peeling away, an accepted casualty of the coarse sea air. We took a seat at a café under the sturdy arches along one side of the square and ordered two Veracruz-style coffees, unaware of what that entailed. This being a touristy spot, there was an easy route that was not to be taken. Why just bring out a cup of coffee? Why?! No, any opportunity for showmanship and flair was quickly pounced upon. A waiter appeared with a slightly nervous look on his face, clearly at odds with the daring act that he was about to undertake. He placed a cup before me with just a measly espresso shot at the bottom of it, for in Veracruz no one drinks their coffee unless it has been topped up by piping hot milk poured from a great height. The higher the better! And so, as a single bead of sweat edged its way to the shiny tip of his nose, Esteban took aim and began to pour. Hot milk splashed everywhere, but finished mostly in the cup. He looked relieved and even a little proud. I was astonished.

I leant back in my wicker chair, letting the honey glow of the late-afternoon drip over me – the sound of Danzón music warming the coldness of my repentant heart. I felt like I could have been back in Hemingway's Havana. It was all cigars, rum, coffee and insatiable sweating. I started looking around me for potential spies, suspecting most as working either side of the law: a couple of blokes in panama hats and pencil-thin moustaches; and a lady in a scarlet cocktail dress stirring sugar into her coffee with passionate fervour as she flickered her spindly eyelashes at passers-by.

'You know, I think I like this city,' I said, ordering us a couple of beers.

'No shit, you seem to be making the most of your time here!'

'Ha ha. What can I say? It's been very hospitable.'

'So, tell me, Simon, how did someone like you – the pure, innocent Brit – come to spend the night with a prostitute?'

'OK, before we do this, can I just confirm that it is something that people do here?'

… 'What, pay for sex?'

'Yes.'

'Well, I'm not sure I like your tone, brother, but yes, it's been known to happen.'

'That's what I hoped.'

… 'And?'

'And you promise you won't judge me?'

'Man, you know I'm the last person to judge.'

'So, I was lying in bed, enjoying our hotel's beautiful sweetcorn tile floors and turquoise wood decor, when a seething bass line crept into my room. There was no way I was just going to lie there and ignore it. It deserved better than that.'

'Yeah! I knew you loved Salsa music!'

'It shook me right out of bed and into my least-creased shirt. I was lost and massively sober, trying to find the source, when a fat and vaguely threatening man with a kipper tie pinned to his barrel belly ushered me into what I believed to be his bar. It wasn't.'

'What was he? Hit man? Gigolo?'

'Well, he worked there, that much was true, but it wasn't a bar. It was a strip club, as it turned out. But being as it was just shy of 11 pm, the dark room I shuffled into was completely empty.'

'Ha ha. Of course it was, you clown!'

'The stink of cigarettes and rum was giving me a headache. I immediately wanted to leave, but the fat man was standing stubbornly in the way of the exit. So I sat down at a white plastic table, pretending to know exactly what I was doing. "¿Qué va a querer joven?" a waiter asked. "Dame una cuba libre," I said, in my most commanding Spanish.'

'Bullshit you said it in Spanish!'

'Hey, I've been getting the hang of it since you deserted me. I've maybe even got a little cocky, you could say.'

'Brilliant.'

'And so the drinks started coming. Silly old Silk had forgotten to put the prices on their menus, so it was a bit of a roulette. Luckily, I'd also forgotten to take $250 out of my wallet before I'd left the hotel, so I was able to throw down a cheeky rum or two without thinking too much about the consequences. I was sat there all on my own, pretending to enjoy myself, for what must have been about an hour before anyone turned up and even then it was a fully-clothed stripper carrying a small holdall of props and what looked like a miniature gun. She seemed a bit put out that anyone had got there before her, but after a quick chat with the bouncer, she let out a great honking laugh and disappeared backstage.'

'Nice.'

'It was degrading. Silk didn't fill up until about 3 am and by that time I was … well, you've seen me before. The crowd was, at best, middle-aged and if I looked hard into the eyes of my fellow patrons, I detected as many tears as I did aplomb. This was a home for losers and I was at the heart of it.'

'Ha ha! We've all done it, man. We've all done it.'

'From what I remember, a man who might have just about reached my waist bumped into my table, smashing my near-empty drink onto the stone floor. At first I thought he wanted to glass me, but I soon realised he was prepared to make amends. My consolation prize was a dance from the cheapest on offer. It'd be wrong of me to say she was unattractive, but even then, in the darkened, smoke-filled room, I suspected she might have been some way below my lowest standards. It's worth mentioning here that I was once bedded by a girl who looked like Henry the Eighth.'

'Ouch! The one with the massive, bloated body and thin, little legs?'

'That's the one. Yep, it probably wasn't going to be my night.'

'So you took her back and sealed the deal?'

'Not exactly. If I tell you my wallet was empty before we got back to the hotel, you can probably imagine just how much I'd drunk.'

'Ahhhh man, you mean you couldn't even compete? What a waste!'

'Errrr, yeah. You know what, I'm kind of glad if truth be told.'

'Why?!'

'Because it's not me, Aurelio. It's not me … I don't know, I guess I felt like I owed it to the trip – like it was just something that was always going to happen. But it's not me … I don't think it is at least. I just … I'd like to say it was out of character, but I'm not so sure any more …'

'Come on, man. It was just something you did. No need to try and read too much into it. Hey, maybe it'll help you even.'

'Help me?'

'Yeah. You know, maybe you needed to do it. Maybe you needed to get something out of your system.'

'Right. So why did it make me feel so shit?'

'You're real hard on yourself, aren't you? I worry about you sometimes. You'll be OK, man. Why don't we try and take your mind off of it?' Aurelio said, bringing over the waiter. 'Bring us a couple of mojitos!'

The searing air eventually carried us onwards as we zigzagged along bustling avenues back towards our hotel.

'You wanna call it a night?' Aurelio asked me as he opened up the room next to mine.

'Thanks, mate. I think I just need to catch up on some sleep.'

'OK, man. Anything you need, you know where I am,' he said, closing the thin, wooden door behind him.

As I lay on my bed in the stiff sedateness of my room, the sound of nocturne life bouncing off the walls, I looked up at the ceiling fan trying in vain to take some heat out of the place – the sound of its shark fin blades cutting through my middle – and I realised that, for all the travelling I'd done, for all the time I'd been away, I was still completely lost. I wasn't any closer to finding my way. I was just going round in circles: the same thoughts, the same places. I couldn't overcome how alone I felt and how far I was from reaching the other side. And that worried me a bit.

There's only so many times you can tell yourself that everything's going to be OK. At some point you have to start seeing results – you have to stop doing the things that aren't you and start doing the things that the *old* you or the *real* you would do. Honestly, you have to stop trying to sleep with prostitutes, or smashing mirrors in the middle of the night. You have to stop disappointing people. You need to stop disappointing yourself. You need to be able to go for more than a day without searching for the fastest escape route. You need to be able to be happy for longer than a bottle lasts.

The fan continued to whirr above me, each stroke more tired and futile than the last. I looked over at my bag of meagre possessions and then back to the fan. 'You can get through this,' I told myself.

I reached out for a bottle and, wincing, took a swig. 'You need to get through this.'

I took a scratched, brown flask of pills out of my pocket and looked, dazed, at its contents: tiny droplets of numbing joy, a big, red button, an ejector seat. I ran my fingers along the jagged ridges of its lid, imagining just how far it would send me as I watched the lights of passing cars sift through the half-open blinds and walk across the ceiling.

Another swig and I let the bottle drop to the floor.

I looked again at the tablets, before watching them slam against the opposite wall and disappear out of sight.

Something, or someone, would have to give. Only time would tell which.

'Can you hear me?'

31

The temperature was hovering close to zero as we reached Mexico City. There was no sign of daylight. The capital's unique scent of sun-baked concrete, pungent flowers and petrol crept through the near-empty Taxqueña bus station. Walking out into the cracked grey of the capital, we were greeted by tired newspaper sellers and shoeshine men waiting for the day to kick in.

'¿A dónde van güeros?' a taxi driver in a pork pie hat asked us, leaning into the back of the car and flinging a door open before we could respond.

'Llévanos a Tlalpan,' Aurelio said, handing the driver his address.

We sat in total silence on our way to Aurelio's house – he barely able to keep his eyes open after heady days of excess on the coast, and I just tired of talking.

I was happy, in a way, to be back in the abrasive grasp of the city – a place where everything and anything happened and I would find it hard to be alone. Thin buildings, small buildings, fat buildings, tall buildings – crammed living, full to bursting of people with dreams of exceeding, with plans that stretched beyond the immediate, of people who were always on the move.

'Back to the cesspit,' Aurelio sighed as we pulled up to the brown gates of his family home. 'You got any change?'

We walked into his house, which was once again completely vacant. The sofa I had slept on when I first got to Mexico looked untouched. Two plates of food covered by plastic serving domes sat next to the microwave.

'Where are we going then?' Aurelio said, unfurling the crisp, yellowed paper of a well-loved map.

'You want to leave straight away?' I asked in disbelief. 'We only just got here.'

'Yeah, man. It kind of depresses me being back.'

The back door opened and a lady with thick arms and a light expression walked in.

'Juanita this is Simon,' Aurelio said hurriedly. 'Simon, this is our maid Juanita.'

'Hi, Juanita. Nice to meet you.'

'The pleasure is all mine,' she said, smiling sweetly and backing into the kitchen.

'You have a maid?!' I stammered.

'Of course!' Aurelio snapped. 'OK, back to the map. What's next? Oh hey, what about that photo of yours?'

I reached for my bag, but Aurelio swept it from under my nose, fishing out the photo and rushing after Juanita.

'Aurelio, the guy at the bar in San Cristóbal said he thought it might be somewhere in the north – somewhere like Guanajuato,' I called after him. 'Maybe we should just go there.'

I could hear the two of them talking in low voices as Juanita mopped an already-immaculate floor. Aurelio emerged with a smug look on his face. 'Right, she said it's probably this place up north in the jungle, though she's never been there.'

'Really? Where?!'

'Yep. It's this place that has a crazy castle in the middle of the jungle and lots of gang violence. It could be fun,' Aurelio said, plunging a steady finger into the middle of the map.

'Well if she really thinks it's there …'

'That's that settled then.'

With the low-hanging sun stinging our eyes, we once again found ourselves battling through the Mexico City impasse, though this time with my hands on the wheel – my feet marching up and down as I tried to inch Aurelio's Beetle forward through the palpable anger of thousands of people going nowhere. We'd come back in and now we were doing our best to try and get back out. It was no easy task.

Staring ahead, straight down Avenida de los Insurgentes' corridor of steel and glass, captivated by the sun's reflection in the changing faces of tall office buildings, I imagined what my life would be like if I lived there. What if everything I was witnessing, everything I could see, touch and breathe, was mine? What if I just decided to leave the past in the past, cut off completely and launch into a totally new life? I felt pretty far from what I had always called home and going back seemed almost impossible – it would just be one massive lie. After months on the road, I didn't feel I belonged anywhere, really. I was just a floating mass attaching itself to other lives and other bodies, feeding off their stories, doubts and fears. And I saw a bit of that in Aurelio too. Both he and I, while complete strangers in many ways, were united by the unanswerable questions we posed ourselves. In that isolated, frozen space, the bubble in which we moved, neither could help but try to make sense of how we'd got there.

'It's strange you know,' Aurelio said, the first to break the silence.

'What is?'

'Sometimes I feel like maybe I don't belong here.'

'What do you mean?'

'I mean that *my* people don't really understand this land. This place used to be a lake, man. Then the Spanish came and drained all the water away.'

'Yeah.'

'And now we worry about water shortages, but we just keep on building. Concrete as far as the eye can see.'

'Complete rubbish.'

'What?'

'About you not belonging here. I can say that, but you were born here, ergo …'

'You would say that, no one ever took you over.'

'Normans, Vikings and almost the Nazis.'

'Yeah, but it's not the same, man. Your history evolved. Mexico, well that was more like a collision with a big rock from outer space.'

'Maybe you're right.'

'We're all right if we believe ourselves to be. Life is a mirror in which you see reflected the reality you choose to believe my friend.'

'Is that poetry or something?'

'What like Neruda or Paz?'

'I guess.'

'Ha ha, no! Have you even read them?'

'No. I always liked Shaggy as a poet.' It wasn't me.

The road carried us onwards, as it always would, now tired of the wayward philosophising of a couple of chumps still a little wet behind the ear. The sprightly ticking of the Beetle's motor ignited our spirits as we contemplated the vast expanse of dusty-brown nothingness stretching out before us. We felt drunk on a sense of awe, an insignificance that frazzled our brains as we melted into nature's design. Driving mile after mile, we lost ourselves to our surroundings, living the infectious *Mexicanness* of it all: the cactus, the volcano, and the huge, dry landscapes of minimal life – magnitude beyond all comprehension.

We passed several small towns that for all their pretence to housing life, looked to be beyond the world of the living – strange one-street towns where dirt and earth gradually covered shrinking houses, man's grip on his fate steadily overtaken by a destiny greater than his own. To simply survive there was a feat in itself – people battling against the inevitable, steep, downwards slope into death itself.

Then, in a show of defiance, a man in a wide-brimmed hat sat on a donkey appeared by the side of the road, gazing off into the distance, the absolute sum of his surroundings – Mexico personified.

'Hey, pull over,' Aurelio said, eagerly winding down his window.

'Excuse me, sir. Do you know if we're going the right way for la Huasteca Potosina?' The man slowly turned his head and looked down into the car. His moustache drooped as he shrugged his shoulders. 'La Huasteca?' Aurelio tried again, speaking at half speed.

'No Spanish,' the man grumbled, digging his feet into the donkey's sides and trotting off down the road.

'I told you, man,' Aurelio said. 'Even I don't get this place sometimes.'

I eased the car into first and crept back onto the road as the sun set over the horizon, blanketing the world in a dark indigo fabric, a few pinprick holes shedding light from a secret world.

We began to climb, winding our way upwards through clouds of dense fog that drifted past us, hiding all life from view. We spent hours curving our way along a pitch-black road, once again eaten up by the silence brought on by our exhaustion.

It was late when we arrived in El Olvido, the town clock omitting a solitary *gong* to signal that lost time between night and day. A drunk stumbled across our path, his indiscretions momentarily spotlighted, until the curtain fell and he dropped back into the shadows of the night, a phantom spirit looking for somewhere to rest.

'So where's the hotel?' I asked.

'What hotel?'

Most places were closed or abandoned, but we eventually found a place with a light on in the doorway: the Hotel Pasatiempos – a lonely looking joint that might just have a bed or two hidden away somewhere. We grabbed our things, locked the car and tried our luck.

The reception area was totally empty, save for a wiry, one-eyed cat guarding the front desk. An exposed bulb gave out a greenish light, painting an eerie expression across the tired hotel walls, which looked like they had long since given up waiting for something to happen. An old, wind-up clock kept its own track of time, accentuating some beats and missing others, the pendulum swinging but the hands frozen.

'Friendly place then,' I said, looking over to Aurelio who was trying to fend off the cat.

'I've felt more comfortable at funerals.'

'Perfect.'

It was now gone one in the morning and we assumed the owner must have been asleep somewhere, possibly a morgue, so we helped ourselves to a key and found a room.

'Right, what now?' Aurelio asked.

'What do you mean *what now*?'

'Well, we can't just go to bed before checking out the rest of the hotel.'

'Obviously not.'

Our suspicions were soon proved well-founded – we were the only ones staying in what was probably the world's weirdest hotel. We crept around from room to room through elongated, haunting silences that were only perforated by our hard, heavy breathing, both of us half expecting a maniac to jump out on us at any minute. One room had a bed with no mattress but a half-full ashtray, another what were quite clearly blood stains on the sheets. But typically the Pasatiempos saved the best until last.

'Fuck me.'

We kicked open the door to the room neighbouring ours, our eyes taking their time to adjust to the deep darkness of the room. We had stumbled on what looked like the scene of a Satanist ritual. Burned-down candles lay positioned across the floor – five of them – the smell of melted wax still clogging the air. The numbers 666 had been burned into the ceiling. A charred doll hung from an improvised noose nailed to the wall above the bed. Sheets had been violently strewn across the room, clearly the result of a struggle.

As I broke out in nervous laughter, Aurelio quickly drained of blood, his mouth open and his eyes wide.

'What, you don't believe in that shit, do you?' I said. He looked like he was about to be sick. 'Sleep well, Aurelio.'

And out went the lights. We were plunged into complete darkness and a bottomless, static silence, save for the territorial clock and the pained sighing of a one-eyed cat.

As the minutes passed and I willed my body into deep sleep, my thoughts bounced from one rock to another. I found Carla floating in the middle of an ocean, stranded on what looked like a deserted raft that had been battered by years at sea, its edges gnawed by the incessant pounding of boisterous waves. She was sat with her knees raised and her bare feet flat on the surface of the raft. Her long hair fell down her naked back and over her face, her head held tight against her body.

I, floating as if nailed to a hot-air balloon above her, shouted her name, failing to hear my strained voice over the fierce wind of the open ocean. Carla just continued to float, unaware that I was just above her. Panicked, I looked around me to try to gain some idea of where we might be. I looked at the colour of the water; I looked for fish below me and birds in the sky. I sought desperately for any point on the horizon, but there was nothing – just me, Carla and the raft.

I closed my eyes, trying to hatch a plan for how I might reach her, and when I opened them again, she was gone and I was back in my bed in Swindon. I was chained to the four corners of the bed frame and I couldn't move a muscle. My mouth felt like it was full of sand and my legs ached – a blunt, creaking pain. I could only see the ceiling and the projected, changing light of people moving on the landing outside my bedroom. I strained to try and hear what they might be talking about, but all I could occasionally detect was the sympathetic calling of my name. They must have been talking about me, but I couldn't decipher what it was they were saying. They sounded sad, concerned, possibly angry. I closed my eyes again.

And so it continued, my mind tormented by memories mixed with dreams. I wanted to fill my head with different thoughts – happier thoughts – and allow my dreams to take me to new places, but it was impossible. All I could do was try to keep my course as sleep dragged me further into the eye of the storm, a long, drawn-out war of attrition.

I awoke to find the one-eyed cat in my face and Aurelio in hysterics at my screaming. I've never liked cats and for what it's worth, I think the feeling is mutual.

Aurelio and I wandered into town along damp, fog-filled streets, looking for somewhere to have breakfast. Straggly stray dogs drifted alongside us, looking for guidance and a hand that would feed. A duvet of cold covered the town, keeping most people locked safely up at home. Even the shops were closed, their shutters drawn. Eventually we saw a red tea towel emerge from the mist, ushering us through a patio door into Doña Sara's restaurant with a, 'Pásenle jóvenes.'

'Morning, Doña Sara,' Aurelio said, sitting himself next to the hot coals of the restaurant's comal stove.

'We don't get too many tourists this time of year,' she said. 'It's nice to have some company! Now, what can I get you gentlemen?'

'I'm so hungry I could eat a horse,' I told her.

'Don't sell that güero. We have cow-brain tacos, cow-stomach tacos, cow-liver tacos, pig-hoof tacos or plain-cheese quesadillas.'

'Quesadilla?'

32

Before this trip, I'd never really strayed that far from home. For me, like many of my mates, holidays used to mean going to EU-Camp every summer for what would be a well-drilled, but ultimately stressful vacation. Trips abroad were underscored by a drudging inevitability as, turning up at a campsite that was even worse than it looked in the brochure – a place where we could apparently get away from it all, but where in reality the imperfections running through every tired relationship in our family were brought to the fore – my parents would finally crack, the budget went to the wall and we all went and got sunburned at the water park. It was the same for every British family at every campsite across Europe. Arguments were routine – an accepted penalty for daring to try and relax. I don't know why people act as if a tent lining is any thicker than a Parisian waistline, but every terse remark, bodily function and childhood strop sounds as if it's just inches from your face. And that was my experience of travel: going to the hypermarket and stocking up on sweets.

Mexico, then, where chips don't appear on every menu and you can't survive by just shouting slowly in English, was a bit of a shock to the system. It was completely different, to the point at which the weird became routine. I was no longer surprised to see someone playing a miniature guitar with a pair of spoons, or shocked to see someone hiding a chicken under their hat. But even after a few months travelling its roads, Mexico could still take my breath away.

'Xilitla is a like a complete detachment from reality – it's a fairy tale,' Aurelio told me. 'It's this surreal, concrete fortress built right here in the middle of the rainforest by a crazy Englishman called Sir Edward James.'

'Never heard of him.'

'You'll never forget him after today, I promise,' Aurelio said, pulling out a thermos flask and pouring a suspicious-looking liquid into the cap. 'A little helping hand.' He gave me a wink and drank up. 'Whatever you do, just keep walking, man.'

I wandered downhill into the untamed forest, unsure of where I could be heading. In front of me sat a bizarre, ornate maze of walls, monuments and stairs choking in the green of the forest. Clumps of white fog began to descend, filling the empty spaces. It didn't take long for me to lose Aurelio as my eyes grew hazy, falling back into my head, wishing my body to rest. Slowly … steadily … I was leaving … time was slowing … and I slipped into euphoric numbness, all colour and shape blending into one glorious harmony of shared consciousness.

Fading staircases appeared out of nowhere, jutting out into the verdant jungle, creating a vivid escape from the human world. I floated from one stair to the next, unable to see anything below me but the dense clouds shifting around my feet. Trees and plants tangled around the concrete, peacefully but assuredly reclaiming the time and space around them, consuming this crumbling, grey testament to one man's desire for legacy.

I kept climbing, just for the thrill of putting one foot in front of the other, sinking deeper and deeper into a living artwork, mesmerised by the profound respiration of the forest around me that ushered me further in, stealing a small portion of my soul with every step.

I started to follow a dark figure, a lady, from one staircase to the next, through passageways, across rivers and along jumbled pathways. I could only see the back of her, but I was convinced she was someone I knew. I tried to move my feet faster to catch up, but kept floating just behind her, a gentle breeze blowing her grey-blonde hair to one side and obscuring the outline of her face. She remained out of reach.

We continued for some time, green passing through grey to brown, red and black. I was drawn on without knowing how or why, a thin thread gently pulling me forward. I was powerless to do anything but follow the path in front of me.

The earth, some way beneath me, began to creak and moan, sending vibrations ringing through the trunks of the trees and shaking the last vestiges of self out of my empty body – small, yellow butterflies escaped my mouth and fluttered into the forest, careless as a freed balloon. The concrete castle around me threatened to collapse, but the vines weaving through its cracked walls just about held it together. I continued on.

We reached an opening – a sweet blue oasis of nourishing water, a slow breeze skimming across its surface. We stopped, she at the water's edge looking down, trying to make sense of her reflection, I just behind her watching the trees around us sway. We remained motionless for what could have been five minutes, five hours, or five days – time insignificant, immeasurable.

A solitary drop of water gathered in the heavens above, growing slowly bigger and bigger until it couldn't contain itself any longer and it fell, rushing like a stampeding herd of frightened gazelle towards the ground, carrying with it the remnants of my soul that had floated away some moments before. We both watched as it sped towards us, each second looking impossibly bigger and stronger. And then it reached the earth with a thunderous roar, unleashing a great ocean upon us, sending giant tidal waves smashing up against the surrounding forest. Suddenly it was all I could do to stay afloat. I tried not to lose sight of my friend, but she made no effort to swim and sank slowly beneath the tempestuous surface of the water. Mustering the little strength I had, I swam over and tried to grab her, but she slipped away and slowly out of reach. I dived down to try and save her from vanishing forever, but my feet, like giant buoys, glued me to the waves above us. I waited, half to see if she might return and half to try and let my oxygen run out, but I just bobbed in despair, helplessly watching despondent bubbles swim past me. I lifted my head above the surface, now unable to recognise anything around me. The water seeped slowly back into the jungle and I was left alone, sat looking aimlessly into the night-grey sky above me.

The sounds of life gradually returned, birds and rivers, as I emerged from the story. I picked up a stick and wrote a message to the gods in the still-wet earth beneath me.

'I couldn't save her.'

33

Simon, my love. You asked me to put together some words about you and our dear Carla. I'm not sure if this is the kind of thing you were looking for, but I have to say, I found the whole exercise sort of therapeutic. I can always do a second version if you like. I've always fancied myself as a bit of an author. It's not that J. K. Rowling's got it easy, but I just find that if I sit down and put on a bit of Bublé, there's no stopping me – the words just pour out. Anyway, I hope I've captured it the way you wanted me to. Just let me know if you want me to make any changes – if you ever end up reading it that is.

I burst into tears when Simon disappeared and we realised he wasn't coming back. He'd been struggling a lot bless him, we all had. He wouldn't admit that, mind. Like his dad he is, tough as old boots.

He refused to talk about it for a long while. He slammed the brakes on and tried to swerve around it. He always used to say he didn't want to let something he couldn't control ruin the stuff he could.

Even though he's not an emotional lad really, he would tell you that Carla is the best thing that ever happened to him. One of those silent types is our Simon though. He seems to keep things bottled up. Valentine's Day was always a bit of a trial for Carla because of that, bless her. Me and she used to sit around the kitchen table, slowly sipping our teas, always on our last biscuit, chatting about our respective men, laughing at just how bloody useless they can be. I mean, it's just three little words – they've done it before and they can do it again, but you practically need to pull a Heimlich manoeuvre to get it out of them. Silly, isn't it? It's just three little words. They don't even have to mean it. Lord, I don't mean it every time I say it. Not like the first time anyway. But what are we doing in this world if it's not to love and to tell people we love them?

But Si, he wouldn't go in for Valentine's Day. He used to say it was about as far from true love as you could get. He used to turn his nose up at all the cards and flowers. And much as I give him stick, you only had to be there after it all happened – after she, you know, left us – to see how much she meant to him, how much he really loved her. He wouldn't speak to anyone for weeks on end, just keeping himself locked up. It was like he'd had his soul ripped right out of him. He'd come back from work and just sit in front of the TV without saying a word. You could see that empty look in his eyes. You could see how much he was hurting, and how hard he tried not to let anyone know. He can be a bit stubborn like that.

The thing is, Simon is, without the slightest shadow of a doubt, one of the most loyal people you'll ever meet. Frighteningly so. It's like he's blind to his own interests sometimes. He gets something in his head and that's the way it is. He sees no reason to think things will change. If he's doing something, he's doing it, and that's how he does relationships.

He was 100% committed to Carla. I remember carrying out a bin bag of all his old FHMs soon after they started going out. I think he might have kept one or two, but he wanted to send a clear signal that he was moving on and that he was a one-woman man. She wouldn't have minded about the mags, I'm sure, but he was so determined to prove his commitment.

I remember the day he told me about her.

'I think I've met a girl, Mum.'

'Wow, Simon, I mean, wow. I'm speechless. Shakespeare's cacking himself up in heaven. Have you really? Me too. Quite a few in fact.'

'I knew you'd be like that. Stop being so bloody pedantic,' he said, rolling his eyes at me.

'Sorry love, come on, it was only a joke. So, what's her name?'

'It's alright, Mum, we don't need to talk about it. I just thought you should know.'

I told him I was glad he'd confided in me and that she was welcome to come to the house whenever she wanted. Obviously I wanted to meet her and suss her out as fast as possible, but you can't just come out and say that, can you?

When she first came round for tea, I thought I'd make a special effort – a peace offering if you will (you know how us women have the ability to instantly be at war with someone we've never even met). I'd made one of my specialities: a zingy gazpacho for the starter, a succulent coq au vin as the main and a big fat jam roly-poly for pudding. Can't beat it. Well, let's just say the dinner was something of a hit. I reckon she was probably one of those kids raised on smiley faces and extra-value pork gut sausages, so you can imagine her face when we went all continental. A right parade of food it was! My husband, of course, in his usual way, tried to mock my efforts. 'Queen popping in for tea is she? You do realise she never normally cooks like this,' he said to the girl. Carla, bless her, just ignored him, and calm and composed like the little angel she is, remarked on what an ever-so-lovely evening it had been. 'Well, you're more than welcome whenever you like,' I said. 'Even if Simon's not here. Lord knows I get a little lonely in the palace sometimes.

And I do.

But anyway, I think Simon feels like he still needs to be loyal. And of course, there's nothing wrong with that, but I'm not sure it's helping him. He doesn't want to – and I hate using these words – but it seems like he doesn't want to move on. It's like he's stuck in a hole that keeps getting deeper and deeper. Maybe, in some ways, somehow, he just needs to put her to one side. He needs to climb out.

The thing is, it must be so hard to do that when the person you have to leave behind is as much of a gem as Carla. She was – is – just one of those people who you like more and more as you get to know her. Some people, I find, light up your world the minute you meet them, only to become more and more boring and drop off the radar. Then there are some you think are dull as old haddock – the growers – who later it turns out are the most interesting people you've ever met: cue BFF. Carla was neither. She was one of those people you hit it off with straight away but who only gets more interesting. She was golden, an absolute winner. Sort of quiet, humble, modest, ready with a joke and a really wonderful listener. I'm not sure I know anyone else who could sit through two hours of me complaining about my husband's dying libido. 'I just want a lovely Greek man,' I would say. And she'd cut in with something like, 'I'd have an Italian.' We had similar tastes, you see. Tall, tanned, romantic and muscles as big as tractor engines. Funny how we both ended up with scrawny, pasty robots, isn't it?

Maybe that's why we got on so well. We were both suffering the same sentence! But she and Simon were perfect for each other in so many other ways. It felt like a summer romance – like one of those perfect loves you see in the movies. I never saw them argue. They just seemed to be very peaceful with each other, like they'd realised that their love might be the best thing that life had to offer. They truly cared for each other. As long as they were together, they could tackle life's challenges head on. Carla would plan everything very carefully so that Simon couldn't mess it all up and Simon would always be there for her when he did. I used to say to Jeff, my husband, 'Look into his eyes. Look into the eyes of your only son. What do you see? Well I'll tell you. Love – pure, pure love. That is someone who would give up anything for that girl. He would go round the world and back for her.

It's such a shame he never got the chance to. It all ended too soon. Life can be so hard sometimes, but we all have to give it our best shot. We all have to pick ourselves up and carry on. I don't really know how that's done, but I think we all find our own way.

And you will, Simon, my love.

We love you ever so much. Everyone does. Never lose sight of that.

Mum

34

As we wound our way back down and round the deep valley and flowing rivers, I tried to put the forest behind me. My breathing, slow and concerted, kept a steady beat echoing around my body, now empty of thoughts. Rich oxygen swamped my blood, nourishing every nucleus of every cell.

I don't feel like we ever really pay attention to the noise of our thoughts – those thoughts that try to keep us awake at night – or the great effort we make to silence them. I'm not sure we ever really know what state we're in until the ticking time bomb explodes and the walls come tumbling down. There, in the emotive jungle landscape of Xilitla, the plug had been pulled once more and I had caught a glimpse of what lay hidden beneath.

But I was leaving that space now.

Sat in the back of a pickup, bouncing up and down as we worked our way across broken terrain, the sun a small, white button trying to break through a tarpaulin of overbearing grey, I looked across at Aurelio and smiled. He smiled back. He didn't have to. I started to feel that the worst might yet be to come, that the further I ran, the more I'd have to confront. But I knew that what was waiting for me the other side was serene. It had to be.

Back in El Olvido, I decided to avoid the Pasatiempos. I wasn't ready to deal with it just yet. I wandered around El Olvido's strange, stunted streets following a bedraggled dog, whose thick teats swung beneath her like a cow's udder. She had a determined smile on her face; she was going somewhere. She stopped by a bag of rubbish and found her reward. I took a seat next to her and watched her feast on someone's meagre scraps, happy to have reached it before anyone else.

'Life's tough, right dog?' I said, watching a couple of barefoot children run along the street opposite us. 'Still, you're doing what you can, right?'

'Maybe we're the ones that make it tough,' she seemed to say, licking her lips and looking at me with big, shiny eyes, before trotting off in search of more undiscovered riches.

I stopped at a corner shop on the way back and picked up a six-pack and a dust-covered bottle of tequila. For his part, Aurelio had brought back a couple of local girls.

'Simon, meet Elsa and …'

… 'Suzi.'

'Meet Elsa and Suzi, the two most beautiful girls in all of El Olvido. We're going to show them the very best Mexi-British evening money can't buy.'

'Well, we have to be back home before 11,' Suzi said, blushing.

'Of course, of course,' Aurelio muttered, pouring her a sturdy drink.

'Hey, Aurelio. Can I talk to you for a second?' I said, ushering him out the door. 'Mate, this seems like a bad idea.'

'It's a great idea, Simon. And I'm not going to have you trying to ruin it for me.'

'I'm not trying to ruin anything, it's just …'

'Look, just come back inside, sit down, have a drink and relax,' Aurelio said. 'If it gets too stressful, we'll just take them home and that'll be that.'

'OK,' I said reluctantly.

'We cool?'

'Yeah, we're cool.'

We walked back into the room all smiles. I did what I had to do. 'So, are you from here?' I asked Suzi.

'Yes,' she said timidly.

'Do you work? Study?'

'Yes, I want to study next year.'

'Cool. What do you want to study?'

'I want to study business.'

'Great! I studied business.'

'You must be very successful.'

'Not exactly …' I said, tapping my finger against an empty glass and looking over at Aurelio, who had Elsa in hysterics.

I reached for the bottle of tequila, by now nearly empty.

'Hey, Aurelio, you want to head out?'

Unsurprisingly, nightlife in El Olvido was a little thin on the ground. For a start, there were more crickets than people, the insect's infectious buzz the town's only soundtrack. Yet while the sensible option would have been to knock it on the head and call it a night, we decided to keep going.

'There must be something going on,' Aurelio muttered as a small figure came into view, zigzagging towards us with all the purpose of a daddy-long-legs in flight. It wasn't until he got closer to us that we saw his boots: tanned leather running from his shins, down his ankles, across his feet and flowing into a pointed tip that curled up about half a metre into the air. He looked like a Mexican elf.

'Nice shoes,' I said. 'Know where we can find some fun at this late hour?'

'You guys not from around here, huh?' Francisco scoffed, taking one look at my battered Converse pumps and letting out a sympathetic laugh.

'What gave us away?'

'Police been shutting down all the parties recently ever since *el Moco* got shot.'

'*El Moco*?' Aurelio asked.

'You don't need to worry about him,' Francisco said furtively. 'But I know where we can buy a bottle, if you let me join in.'

'The more the merrier,' Aurelio said.

So we stumbled back once more to the Pasatiempos, another bottle of tequila in hand, to add a further dimension of weird to an already-strange evening.

Francisco, it turns out, was a raging narco-homophobe. Yep, that's right, in the space of about an hour, we'd managed to draw Francisco on his opinion on civil liberties and same-sex partnerships, his occupation and his apparent inability to drink. You see, Francisco must only have been about 17, judging by his bumfluff moustache and the alarming pace at which he fell to our level and beyond. Seeing his opportunity to antagonise, Aurelio told Francisco all about his lurid man-on-man sexual fantasies and his formidable track record in turning the heads of straight men. It was immediately clear Aurelio had made a big mistake, the room falling silent as Francisco rose to his feet, hoicked up the contents of his gullet and spat on the floor, swearing he would cut Aurelio's balls off there and then. When Aurelio reasoned that Francisco must also therefore enjoy a bit of man love, Francisco spat harder, announcing that he worked for one of the most powerful and bloodiest drug cartels in the region: *Las Hachas*. And that's when he pulled out the gun.

'I'm fucking crazy!' he shouted as he waved a pistol from one side of the room to the other, training its sight on each of us, one by one. Sweat began to wash over his trembling face as he clicked the hammer back and spat again, this time at Aurelio. 'Now, which of you shit fuckers am I going to waste first?'

I looked quickly over at Aurelio, who was rising slowly to his feet.

'Look, Francisco, don't take it to heart. It was just my stupid idea of a joke,' Aurelio reasoned.

'Yeah, fucking right it was fucking stupid.'

'Yeah, but it was a joke. Look, I'll prove it,' Aurelio said as he walked over to Suzi and kissed her. Suzi stood dumbfounded, a little scared. 'Come on Francisco, please drop the gun. We're all friends here,' Aurelio added, trying to mask the panic in his eyes.

The ensuing silence pressed hard up against us, no one daring to breathe or think. All eyes were on Francisco, his face beginning to shake, before he finally broke down, started weeping uncontrollably, and turned the gun on himself.

'You don't fucking know … you don't fucking know!' he cried out.

'Hey, listen, Francisco,' Aurelio said. 'Whatever shit you've got, you leave it behind, OK? You're a good guy.'

'I'm a shit guy – a son of a whore,' Francisco sobbed. 'I deserve to die!'

'We all deserve to die my friend, but first we have to live a little,' Aurelio said, edging slowly closer to the gunman, his arms outstretched, ready to catch him if he fell.

Francisco slumped heavily back into a chair, tears streaming down his face. He told us that he'd not had an easy childhood and with the absence of a father figure in his life, had turned to the local cartel, despite his mother's pleadings. He felt caught up in a web of chauvinism as each gang member tried to outdo the other, upping the stakes in how macho they could be. He'd seen some horrible things. He'd done some worse things. He'd done it all in a quest for his place in the world, somewhere he could feel secure. He'd lost his childhood as a result, the thick smell of blood coursing through the best and worst of those years. And now he wanted out, but there was only one route – be it he or someone else who pulled the trigger.

Sensing the moment was right, Aurelio made his move, grabbing the gun and sliding it in my direction across the floor, well away from Francisco.

And as we all began to breathe again, relief filling the void left by our retreating fear, for some reason I started thinking about how it was probably the closest I had ever been to a gun. There it was, just sat there, a weapon that with just the curl of a finger could strike a person down dead. I could see Aurelio out of the corner of my eye, keeping a hold of Francisco's hand, with one eye on the gun, which I was slowly dragging to the base of my feet.

I could feel the eyes of the room glued to me as I began to breathe more rapidly, taking in huge gulps of air. I could see them watch my body bend and clasp its fingers around the handle of the gun, picking it up, lifting it and moving its barrel closer to my head. The hand clutching the pistol began to tremble, its finger inching its way to the trigger. I could see the room move from relief back to terror again. I could feel my mouth open and my tongue begin to move. 'If anyone here deserves to die, it's me,' it said in such a matter of fact way that one of the girls began to vomit all over the floor.

'Simon!' Aurelio screamed. 'Simon, put the fucking gun down! What the hell are you doing?'

The hand stopped shaking, my eyes refusing to blink.

'Simon! What the fuck, man? Put the fucking gun down. This isn't funny!'

'What's the point? I can't even find this stupid house.'

'No, no, no! We'll find it man, we'll find it! Look, I'll show you,' Aurelio blurted, before scrambling through my bag for the photo.

He kept talking, his eyes never losing mine as he passed the photo around the room. I could see sheer, utter desperation swimming across his face. One of the girls started to say something about British immigrants in Guanajuato. And that's when the ringing started – a high-pitched, piercing screech, the room spinning faster than the speed of sound. I closed my eyes, took a deep breath and dropped the gun back down to the floor.

'Simon … seriously …'

I was panting heavily. 'Ha ha. Chill guys, I was only joking,' I said, feigning a laugh to my friends. 'It was just a joke.'

'Fuck man, what the fuck? I think we've all had enough to drink,' Aurelio said.

'Like shit we have,' Francisco shouted, throwing the door open and fleeing in search of more alcohol.

We stood there for a while, just looking at each other, our hearts pounding and our hands sweating.

'Things got a little crazy there for a second,' I stammered. 'We probably shouldn't have invited Francisco along. Still, he's gone now.'

'Holy shit, you scared the crap out of me for a second there, Simon. You Brits have a real strange sense of humour. Sorry about that, girls,' Aurelio said.

The girls stood there, wondering how, when, if they would escape. Then, just as they tried to make their excuses, there was a knock at the door. It was our narco friend.

We quickly turned off all the lights and hid under the beds as Francisco turned violent again, furiously banging on the door, screaming that he killed traitors.

We found him asleep on the floor the following morning next to his pristinely-polished boots as Aurelio and I made a dash for it, leaving the girls to rue their folly, trapped by the Pasatiempo's increasingly-depressed and tired walls – oh, and the slow, steady scratching of a one-eyed cat.

35

Carla,

I don't know why I'm writing to you again. I know it's crazy. I mean, what sane person writes to someone who's d … e … a … d? Yet here's the pen in my hand, on the page. What else can I do? No one else would understand.

I keep having dreams about you Carla – horrible dreams that you're stuck somewhere and I want to try to rescue you, but can't. These dreams, they're starting to take over a little bit. I try and direct my thoughts to nicer places, but I don't feel like I can.

I'm starting to worry something quite serious might be wrong with me. It's a scary thought, Carla. It's really fucking scary. But maybe if I'm worried there might be something wrong with me that must mean there isn't, right? I mean, crazy people don't think they're crazy. Maybe I just do some weird things sometimes, that's all.

I so badly want to be OK, Carla. I want to be normal again, but there are these feelings of guilt – feelings of such intense guilt – that I can't seem to escape from. I don't know how to get over everything that happened. I don't know what I need to do to get better. Maybe I need to start talking to someone professional again, a doctor. Maybe they would know what to do.

You'd know what to do.

I really hope I'll be OK, Carla. I think I just need to realise how good I've got it. I need to be grateful for everything I'm doing and everything I've got. There's so much to be thankful for. Life's amazing – I've just got to open my eyes a bit wider. Then hopefully we can meet again someday. That would make me so happy. It would make everything, all of this, worth the fight.

I can't wait until then.

All my love,

Simon

36

'He must be round here somewhere,' Sandra muttered to herself, the signs of doubt starting to creep into her once-assured expression. 'And I was sure that today would be the day. It's been almost six years now.'

We found Sandra in the unique position of looking more lost than we did. She had a glazed look in her eyes, as if she had taken the world's sadness on her shoulders and was trying to find its resting place.

'Man, she's probably crazy. Let's leave her alone,' Aurelio barked at me.

'We can't just leave her stumbling around. What if she's properly lost?' Despite the pull of intuition, there was no way I was going to leave her on her own.

'Where are we, dears?' she asked, looking us straight in the eyes.

'Lost, somewhere in Guanajuato,' Aurelio replied.

'Some things never change, dears. My, I love the steep and narrow streets of this ol' minin' city. Isn't the air impossibly fresh? Doesn't every breath promise a million different stories of romance, my dears? Here in Guanajuato, there's just so much darn colour: red, yellow, green, blue, indigo, terracotta 'n' rose. There's so much life. Why, there's even a spider's web of tunnels runnin' underneath these here cobbled streets, right beneath your very feet. Did you know that? Oftentimes Guanajuato seems more fairy tale than reality, my dears. This here is a place to get lost in …'

'OK, so what exactly is it you're looking for?' Aurelio said, cutting her off.

… 'Looking for?' Sandra's face turned blank for a few seconds as she searched the back of her mind. 'His name's Proposito,' she told us. 'An unusually tall man for these parts, with a fresh face and a childish look in his eyes. I met him way back in a youth now consigned to the fadin' corners of my memory. He was, you know, a mighty handsome man, if I do say so myself. We shared a kiss in one of these here alleyways once upon a time. I was young, yet to feel the weight of time on my shoulders. He was vulnerable, all too aware of the fragility of us humans.'

'Right,' I replied. 'I thought you were new to the city …'

'No, not at all my dear. South Carolina born 'n' raised, but been down here searchin' for a love I never truly knew for longer than I care to remember. "Just look for me among these wistful streets," he told me. Each corner looks as hopeful as the last – though the sun don't quite fall as I remember it would.'

'Right, well we should probably be …'

'Won't you come with me for a coffee, dears? My treat.'

I looked at Aurelio and got a big fat *no*, but I didn't have the heart to turn her down.

We found a café with a couple of seats looking out onto the street and sat in a row of three, each with a view of the city beyond. Ranchera music fled the warm confines of the café behind us, sending yearning voices ringing around the surrounding buildings.

Looking down into my cup, I watched as thousands of tiny bubbles knocked the sense out of each other, part of a great-black ocean whose stormy waters threatened to crack the icy-white porcelain containing it and seep back down to mother earth.

'Did you ever go to Pleasant Street, my dears? My, it was quite some sight. Those ol' clapboard houses painted up real nice, a coolin' tonic for the warm glow of the afternoon sun. Those ol' bits of wood with all their stories. None more welcome than on Pleasant Street. The town had jus' 'bout grown 'round it,' Sandra said, her big, furrowed face staring beyond me and off into a distant past. 'Families used to walk hand in hand, contented just to be sharin' the same air as those they loved the most, their shadows recordin' each moment and phrase onto nature's blank sheet below them.

'Sundays were those days that stretched out more than most, my dears, time slowin' down to a near standstill, the gentle breeze just about the only thing keepin' that ol' clock tickin'. We would start with my momma's pancakes, and mighty fine they were too, thicker than a mare's hind and with all that syrup and cream – a real treat of a Sunday mornin'. Poppa would be dressed up real nice. He had this bright-red bow tie with these li'l white dots on. He always said he was dressin' up for God, but my momma was happy he was just out of those oily coveralls. He'd near always get syrup down his shirt as he read the mornin' news, tuttin' 'n' sighin' at the state of the world, the radio playin' Mr. George Gershwin in the background, just 'nother adornment in a house that meant to look untouched. I always begged to put on that man Presley. Boy, could he shake those hips! A white man singin' the black man's music, now there was somethin' to behold. But my poppa never would allow that music in the house. "It'll send you straight to hell!" he used to say. I sure hope he got that wrong.

'Mr Allerton's Trinkets was right next to the ol' school house – the beatin' heart of the local community it was, keepin' that there 'magination afloat before it sank to the bott'm of a deep, dark pit somewhen on those hot afternoons. We used to go every Sunday on our way back from church as a treat for good behaviour. My brother would always complain that it smelt of old people. For me, it was just plain fine – even though it made me kinda nervous sometimes. I used to move ever so slowly through Mr Allerton's labyrinth, entranced as I was by the voices tellin' their stories across the ages. I felt the pain and the joy of hundreds of accumulated souls, all heaped up together in that graveyard of memories. But there was one piece in particular that caught my 'magination – a beautiful postcard by now almost faded outta view: '*Ven a Guanajuato*,' it said. I don't know if I could put my finger on what it was exactly – on why it so captivated li'l ol' me. Perhaps it was the simplicity of the darn thing. I mean, there might have been some mighty fine pieces in that shop, worth quite a lot of money to the right eye, but that postcard was, it was somehow pure – not created for money nor nothin', but more valuable as the time passed, a message what might have changed through the ages, but still remained in one way or 'nother. That make sense to you?'

'Errrr, I … I guess so, yeah,' I said as Aurelio rolled his eyes.

'A fat man in a wide-brimmed hat with a big ol' moustache stood on the front of the postcard, singin' the words, '*Come to Guanajuato*,' with all those colourful houses just over yonder. '*Dear Betty, I think I might have found my own little slice of heaven. It's so romantic here. Seems like everyone just gets along, everyone leaving a little piece of themselves behind. So many stories. When can I expect you? Forever yours, John.*' It made me laugh the whole darn thing – it was kinda cute I s'pose. Somethin' about that card, it just hit me deep. I wondered, if I would have been Betty, if I'd have gone. I wondered what John looked like, what he was doin' in Guanajuato in the firs' place. I wondered if they ever found each other 'gain.

'It's hard to say exactly when my urge to come 'n' see Guanajuato for myself grew too damn present to ignore. I studied art at college and got really interested in the Mexican frescos – Rivera, Siqueiros, Orozco, the three great muralists. I guess I always saw them through that damn postcard, part of that picture of Mexico I had built over all those years. Then I fell in love with Frida Kahlo, a woman I saw in complete control, securely insecure and tenacious to the bitter ol' end. She was so much of what I wanted for li'l ol' me.

'So in the summer of '86 I thought *to hell with it* and booked my flight.

'Guanajuato was just like that city I had walked in my dreams, my dears: the infectious charm, those big ol' hats, they were all there.

'I 'magined myself takin' the steps that Betty had shied from all those years before. I was mighty nervous, of course, but it just felt so right. I was happy, I realise that now.

'I answered an ad posted outside the city's only language school. I hadn't ever thought that I would wind up teachin' English, but it was a means to an end and allowed me to feel like I belonged to this beautiful ol' place.

'I spent my days revisitin' the same narrow streets, sure I was witnessin' each detail for the first time. Everythin' was new and hopelessly romantic, let me tell you …' Sandra said looking into my eyes, searching for my name.

… 'Simon.'

'Yes, Simon. My Mexican friends were ever so excitin' and full of life. I met my fair share of men, each of whom made me feel like the most beautiful girl in this big ol' world, until they left the followin' mornin', when I would never see them ever again. But it was my li'l Mexican adventure. I felt rejuvenated and inspired. This was life as it was supposed to be lived – a constant exploration.

'I was perfectly content with every li'l thing – the afternoon coffee as an excuse to abandon the comfort of my ceilin' fan and take on the suffocatin' heat outside, befriendin' every café in town, before retirin' to the agin' decor of my apartment, throwin' open the balcony doors, invitin' in the sounds of buses stumblin' down cobbled streets, and the matin' calls of street vendors hopin' to trap a hungry belly or two.

'But, no matter how happy I was, time was always goin' to catch up with me somehow, my dears.

'I had phoned home out of duty more than anythin' else. "Nana's real sick, Sandra," came my li'l sister's voice, nearly chokin' on those words.

'I had to go, Simon. I had to go …'

I looked at Sandra, downcast and defeated, and then out over the city. Young, made-up girls pranced around with the self-assuredness of someone who knows they've got it. Young, impressionable guys followed their every step. Musicians moved from one table to the next, offering their well-rehearsed routines to all, each trying to outdo the next as their music fused together into a single, discordant voice. Shoeshine boys scurried about, clutching at blackened cloths and trays full of pots and brushes. Happy palms fluttered in a sporadic, soothing breeze. Sandra stood up and went and fetched us three more coffees.

'Maybe her getting lost here isn't such a bad thing,' Aurelio whispered.

'Mate, she's harmless enough,' I shot back.

'She's a bona fide psycho!' Aurelio said as Sandra reappeared.

'So … where was I, dears? Oh yes, the night before my flight I went to go and meet my friends to see them one last time. We were drinkin' an awful lot of tequila, let me tell you. Maybe I was tryin' to forget it all.

'We hit the streets and joined one of Guanajuato's famous

Estudiantina bands for one last tour of the city. Proposito was playin' the mandolin. We were led round, seduced by the history of each corner and the freshness of that cool evenin' air.

'The tour ended in the Callejón del Beso, where legend has it that an enamoured man bought up the house opposite his chastised lover. The forbidd'n relationship was consecrated as she carefully crept to his house each night 'cross an alleyway so narrow that you'd struggle not to find someone's lips. And whaddya know, somehow mine met Proposito's right there 'n' then. Everyone started to cheer, but I was lost to the moment, dears, sure that I had finally found my prince. "My name is Proposito," he whispered. "I just fell in love."

'"I ... I have to go," I said, feelin' the tears finally fall.

'"Well, you know where to find me. I belong to these streets."

'The years passed by, the numbers tickin' round like a speedin' stop clock. I made some success of bein' back home. Nana left me her house, which I renovated and sold for a handsome ol' price, but not without a bit of a fight, I'm obliged to say. I used the money to start a small antiques business, but I was never much of an entrepreneur, dears. No, not me. It jus' didn't come that easily to me.

'And then there was Pleasant Street – my, how it'd changed over the years. The houses were still there, the colours still as strong as they had ever been, but now life passed it by as if it were in a real hurry the whole time, no time for nothin' no more. I couldn't bring myself to go past Mr Allerton's trinket store, sure as I was it must have been lost some time ago, my magical postcard either buried somewhere in silence, or else lyin' forgott'n among other meanin'less things.

'And then, one crisp fall evenin', walkin' round the park in that forgivin' orange light, I made up my mind. What was I to lose? I knew I'd never be truly happy up there, my dears.

'So once again, I found myself boardin' a flight back to that magical land that I had darn well made my own.

'I arrived back to this enchantin' place, somehow hopin' to pick up where I had left, reignitin' a dream that I'd pretty well hidden all those years.

'I hadn't thought much about Proposito since the day I'd left. Every now 'n' then I would have myself a little laugh at the naivety of it all, rememberin' his dark hair 'n' the sweet melody of his mandolin. But now that I was back, my dears, now it all seemed to be so real. Proposito's beautiful music came rushin' back to me, echoin' round the alleyways, paintin' his face across the city walls once more, takin' me so far back that I thought I might never return to the world of the livin', my dears. "Sin tus besos no puedo vivir," he sang that night. Who was I to deny anyone of a single kiss of mine?

'The harder I looked, the closer it seemed, but the more tired I grew. I wish I could tell you why I was lookin', my dears, but my, I don't think I even know myself anymore. I can see his innocence in most faces that pass me by – the frozen emotions of that balmy evenin' – but I think, deep on down, I know he's not here. I'm probably just chasin' shadows, if truth be told. I'm not even sure I'm here myself any more, dears. Fancy walkin' round some Mexican town lookin' for a man who might never have existed! Not sure what else I might be doin' any rate, but now I can't seem to find my way back. Every turn I take just leads me back to the place I started. It's all I can do to convince myself I'm not just walkin' round in circles. But if I give up hope, what next?'

Sandra wiped a tear away from her mascara-stained eyes.

'So, that's my story, boys. Whaddy'all think?'

… 'Honestly?' Aurelio shouted.

… 'Honestly, we think you're doing just fine,' I said, before Aurelio could finish his sentence.

'It's awful nice of y'all to say so. Sometimes I think I'm goin' crazy. Then there's times I think the whole darn world is goin' down with me!' Sandra said, looking at the remaining drops at the bottom of her cup. 'So, enough 'bout me. What brings a couple of charmin' young men such as yourselves to pretty ol' Guanajuato?'

'Living life, Sandra!' Aurelio beamed. 'We're on a journey! This guy is going to go and find his abuela's old house.'

'Really?!' Sandra said, smiling.

'Well, I'm going to try.'

'Was she from Guanajuato, Simon?'

'I don't know.'

'Well, what do you know?'

'He's got this photo, haven't you, Simon?' Aurelio said, nudging me.

'Do you mind having a look at it, Sandra? It's a picture of my grandma outside her old childhood home. You never know, you might recognise it.'

'Well I'd just love to, Simon. Now, let me have a look at this …' Sandra said, sitting a pair of reading glasses on the bridge of her nose. 'Gosh darn it, is she still with us, Simon?'

'My abuela?'

Sandra nodded.

'No … she died a few years ago.'

'Well then I think I know where she is in this photo. There's a ghost town north of here called Real de Catorce …'

'Real de Catorce … RDC … RDC … the address!' I exclaimed. 'Real de Catorce!'

'Oh my, what an adventure. Most livin' people up there left a long time ago, givin' those darn spirits a bit of peace and quiet. They're all mighty friendly in Real de Catorce. I'm sure as any ol' thing you'll find her there.'

'Amazing! Thanks so much, Sandra.'

'Looks like we're all on the lookout for somethin', right boys?' Sandra said, slapping her thigh. 'Now listen, I'm sorry to leave, but I got a sneaky feelin' tonight might just be the night. It sure was nice meetin' y'all. Coffees are on me, dears,' she added, casting off into the city.

'Thanks, Sandra,' I called after her. 'And good luck with everything. I'm sure you'll find him before too long.'

'Dude, don't give her false hope,' Aurelio said, kicking my shins.

'False hope?! Does that even exist?'

'Don't you start, Simon. You're starting to sound as crazy as her!'

'Look, Aurelio, Sandra is – and there is no escaping this fact – clearly a bit of a nutter.'

'Ain't that the truth!'

'But she's harmless, mate. And what she's looking for is honest enough. Whether or not she finds what she's looking for is almost irrelevant, don't you think? I mean, she's happy because she knows what she's looking for.'

'Man, she don't look happy to me. Like she said, she's just walking round in circles. That's torture for most people. She's got a purpose, sure, but she also knows she ain't ever going to find what she's looking for. And that, my friend, is what makes it all the more crushing. Besides, what was all that shit about ghosts?!'

'Well, who's to say they don't exist?'

'You're really starting to worry me, bro. A town full of ghosts?!'

'I know it sounds kind of unlikely, but what if we're wrong? What if they do exist? What if my grandma really went back to Real de Catorce?'

'She ain't there, Simon. The sooner you get it out of your head, the better.'

'Forget it.'

Sandra's story haunted me for the rest of the day. As we meandered through Guanajuato's evocative streets, I started to realise that I could see in her something of myself. I'd been wrong. Aurelio was right, Sandra was looking for something that she was unlikely to ever find – carrying with her the very demons that she sought to escape. She was a monument to the lost. She was, in many ways, everything I hoped not to become. Yet I felt our destiny was shared. She would never escape the memories that defined her existence. She was stuck in Guanajuato forever.

That evening we joined an Estudiantina musical group as they took excited tourists around Guanajuato's famous haunts. All were captivated by the romance of the moment: the frilly costumes; the close-harmony music paying homage to love in all its guises; the cheap humour sold to all at the lowest price; the tequila which eased us all into a state of amorous healing; and the nonsense of it all, the randomness, the chance that each hidden alleyway might be guarding the perfect love story. I was trying my hardest to give myself over to Guanajuato's infectious charm, but I couldn't get Sandra out of my head. I couldn't figure out how she was going to get happy.

Once the band had played their final note and the tourists had ambled back to their hotels, Aurelio and I settled down for a couple of drinks, keen to enjoy the last heat of the day. I could feel the drip drop of nerves and resignation growing into a steady stream inside me.

'What's up with you, mate? Everything OK?' Aurelio asked.

'I don't know, really. I think I just feel a bit lonely,' I said nervously.

'Lonely? You got me shit stain. What more could a guy want?!'

'Ha, thanks, Aurelio. I'm grateful, really I am. It means a lot not to have had to do all this alone.' … 'Hey, can I ask you something?'

'Sure, man.'

'What do you think happens when we die?'

'Shit, dude. That's quite a question.'

'Sorry.'

'Well, I guess I think we slowly, sort of, disappear. You know? As time moves on, we sort of just slip away.'

'Slip away?'

'Yeah, you know, like we just fade, until it's the right time for us to disappear completely.' … 'Are you thinking about your grandma?'

… 'Yeah … sort of.'

'Hey man, that's just my point of view. It's important you remember that. What's to say I'm even close to the truth, right? I mean, what do you think?'

'I really don't know. I guess I'd like to think there was, you know, like some kind of a hiding place – a retreat. I don't mean *Heaven*, it wouldn't be a place that depended on anything else, just somewhere people could find each other.'

'Who knows, man? Maybe that's exactly what happens. But I think the only thing we got to be sure of is to enjoy the time we got here, right?'

'Sure … I just, sometimes I think about …'

'Sometimes thinking's great, Simon. But, man, sometimes you just got to go with the flow. Sometimes you just gotta let go and let life happen. Sometimes that's all there's left to do.'

'Right, go with the flow … so, are you coming with me to Real de Catorce?'

'What? Are you really going to go?'

'Of course! That's going with the flow, right?'

'Simon, please, don't take offence at this, but Sandra was the craziest person I ever met. There is no reason …'

'No reason?!'

'No reason to take any notice of what she said. Listen man, I think this project you've got, finding your grandma's house, I think it's great, but it's a little unlikely …'

'What's unlikely?!'

'It's kind of unlikely … you know … it's quite unlikely you're going to find her house. Especially when you follow advice from crackpots like Sandra.'

'Well crackpots like Sandra are all I've got. So just go the fuck back to your comfortable life in Mexico City and leave me to do the stuff that matters, OK?'

'Simon … I didn't mean to …'

'We never mean to, Aurelio. We never mean to. But like you said back in Oaxaca, it's what we do to make amends that really matters.'

37

Mum,

Thanks again for the camera. I'll send some pictures as soon as I get a decent connection. I'm currently in beautiful Guanajuato, about to head north to Real de Catorce in San Luis Potosí. I think I might have finally found where Abuela lived. I'm really hopeful I'll find her house or maybe someone who knew her or our family. I might not have much luck, but I promised I would try and I'm a man of my word.

I'm a bit confused at the moment, Mum. I don't want you to worry about me, but it all gets a bit too much at times. I think it's just been a long time on the road. I know my journey isn't done yet. I know I just need to stick at it, try to block out the negative thoughts and just enjoy it for what it is. But it isn't easy.

I think my mind is still too focused on the past. I guess that's the same for most of us really. A lot of us spend our lives looking back the whole time, rather than forward. We spend our entire time remembering, reminiscing about the bad as well as the good, feeding off memories of what brought us to where we are today, how we got there and who helped us along the way. And obviously that's incredibly important, to keep us grounded and make us grateful – to be able to put everything in perspective. That, of course, is true. But when your past is marked by something that you want to change, that you would do anything, absolutely anything, to alter, to take back, to affect in some way, it doesn't help. You become obsessed with the tiniest details and how one simple snap decision, so meaningless at the time, might have caused a tsunami – a tidal wave – of change in the world around you.

I have these dreams that I'm drowning, Mum, or someone else is drowning, but ultimately we're both fully submissive to a giant body of water that tosses us around and pulls us under.

It's just the helplessness of it all. There's literally nothing we can do. We're so powerless, defenceless, defeated.

But I want to believe that isn't the whole story, Mum. I want to believe that we have control, that if we want to be happy, if we want to make changes, we can. I want to find that space, Mum, and I think I will find it. I hope I'll find it. Even if I'm not sure what it looks like just yet.

Maybe it's here in Guanajuato. It's a pretty special place – a treasure of a city hidden away in the mountains of central Mexico. It's almost like it wants to remain undiscovered, like it doesn't want to be found. People wander the city's charming streets like they're stuck in a maze, but happy to be lost, like it's all part of the adventure, not knowing where you are or where you're going next. Maybe that lack of control is what I need.

I'm really sorry to put all that in an email, Mum. It's not really what you need to hear, I'm sure, but sometimes I just need to try to express myself. I think it helps.

So tell me more about home, what's the weather like? Tell me it's raining! It's so beautiful here. The sky is this incredible, bright blue the whole time. Is Dad behaving himself? Tell him I'm thankful for the Swindon updates. Will they ever win? I'll write again soon, Mum, and I'm sure I'll be a bit more chipper. I'll let you know how I get on in Real de Catorce.

Much love,

Simon

38

Departure announcements rattled off the ceiling of Guanajuato's ailing bus terminal. A flirtatious ticket vendor tucked into a slice of cold pizza. Aurelio and I were stood opposite each other holding our tickets. We knew what had to happen, but neither of us wanted to have the conversation.

'Simon, it's been a real pleasure …'

'It really has.'

'It's been one hell of a trip, but I've probably been running away for too long. It hurts me to say it, but I think my parents are probably right. I think it's about time I got a job.'

'What about all that stuff about you being made for the road?'

'Ha ha. That's all still true, obviously. But hey, every road reaches its end, right?'

'Or it just turns into a different one.'

'Exactly!'

'So, what are you going to do?'

'Probably just hate my life for a while! Nah, I'll get some bar work or something; I like talking to people, as you know.'

…

'So … you gonna miss me?' Aurelio stuttered, putting an arm across my shoulders.

'Despite everything, you know …'

'I know, man. Hey, I was thinking, maybe you were right about that lady.'

'Sandra?'

'Yeah, the crackpot. Listen, maybe you were right. Maybe the most important thing is just to keep on looking, no matter what.'

'You reckon?'

'Yeah, why not? Plenty of people doing just that. Plenty of *happy* people doing just that. Now, I don't want to see any more sad faces from you, my friend. You've got everything to be happy about.'

'I guess so, yeah.'

'You just call me if you ever feel like, you know, everything's getting a bit too crazy. You'll be OK on your own, right?'

'I hope so, yeah …' I said, drawing my eyes across the room. 'What am I on about? Course I will. I'll let you know where I end up, wherever that turns out to be.'

'Until then.'

'Until then.'

39

I always felt guilty about not doing more to find out about my abuela's roots. I'm British, I know that; you only need to take one look at me to understand that. I'm tall, white, a touch arrogant and I think it's acceptable to vomit in public. I often have vomit on me in public. But there *is* another side to me. Most people at my school would have thought it was strange to have a grandparent born outside of Wiltshire, let alone in another country. I'd always accepted the fact that my grandma was different, that she was from somewhere else, but I never really took the time to imagine where that somewhere else might be and what it might be like. Sure, we talked about it every now and then, but I never did anything to try to understand it – to understand what being Mexican meant to her.

Yet as I grew older, that started to change. It was something innate, a small sapling of intrigue that grew with the years as I steadily lost a sense of who I was and what I was doing in the world. Then my grandmother died and I was consumed by the shame of my indifference. Suddenly all the questions I could never ask surfaced. I begged to hear all her stories once more, to absorb every inch of detail of that land that I had never seen. I started to moan at my mum for never having encouraged more interest in me, but in reality, neither of us were to blame.

My abuela had come to the UK after the Mexican Revolution looking for a fresh chance and new opportunities. It was only natural that she should try and protect us, and to a larger extent herself, from the history that had chased her out of the country in the first place. She had always talked of Mexico in the way that you might talk about a marriage that ends on good terms. It was part of a tough lesson she'd learned and she was thankful for the experience, but she was also ready to leave it in the past. She would always say that her trip to the UK was what really shaped her, and that's why we spoke so little of that *before*.

So I'd decided it was my job to try to recover my grandma's past. It was something I was supposed to do with Carla, but I was determined to go through with it, even if I had to do it alone.

Could it be that my abuela was really from Real de Catorce? She'd told us so many stories, but she'd never specifically said where she was from, or else none of us had paid enough attention. It was a long shot, but I had a good feeling I'd finally found her home. Something about the place just seemed to click.

A hostile wind whistled through the surreal, narrow streets – the wooden frames of the town's decaying buildings creaking and swaying, waiting for the right time to collapse. A scabby-looking lizard shot out of an empty saloon, angry that an intruder had disturbed its peace. Fading street signs told their own version of the untimely death of the place. Nothing could be done to revive it now. I just had to do my best not to stir the ghosts.

I found one of the few hotels still running and quickly dumped my stuff, before hitting the streets, photograph firmly in hand. The stiff mountain wind continued to beat down on the town, trying to sweep it away for good, silencing all in the wake of its explosive roar. The streets, near-empty when I'd arrived, had somehow filled. Crowds of people had slipped out of the shadows to join a religious procession filing through the town.

Hundreds of pale, crumbling bodies shrouded in black veils and gowns inched along the town's main avenue, carrying giant images and statues of saints and virgins, their sheet-grey, featureless faces locked to the ground. They didn't talk, but hunched over, pained by the sins of their fellow man. Some muttered prayers to a Higher Cause, while others kept complete silence. Solemn drums beat slowly in the distance, accompanied by the slow, sad ringing of church bells, carried on the back of the persistent wind. A mesmerised crowd had gathered to witness the event.

I waited ten minutes or so, trying to avoid eye contact with the haunting pilgrims, hoping they would reach their end, but the waves of bodies were relentless.

I tried to make myself heard over the banging drums and moribund bells, asking some local people stood on the sidelines about the address on the back of the photograph, confident that someone would know where it was. But most were too preoccupied with the procession to care. An old man in a trilby hat with a secretive gaze and a scuffed pair of cowboy boots nodded at first, without letting his knowledge slip. His blank expression remained as he took his time to remember that he wasn't sure if those streets existed and that most people there just used events engraved in the town's history to locate themselves. He told me that he lived three streets up from the giant clock, a few houses on from the green and white post office, where the great fire of 1872 started.

'But what street is that on?' I probed.

'I've never needed to know.'

'Do you know anyone who might be able to help?' I asked him.

'Anyone with a map?'

'Aiiii joven, I don't know. I've never seen a map, but that doesn't mean such a thing doesn't exist. Try Doña Martha – her family helped build this city. She lives on the other side of town, just along from the old butcher's shop that can't be named, for obvious reasons. Though you might have to wait until tomorrow; it's procession, you see. They close off this main avenue, so it's impossible to get from one side to the other.'

'Impossible?'

I looked up and saw the same faceless bodies wading through the town's great oceans of debris, their resolve never diminished, using the little strength they could muster to clutch at their religious icons – a low, coarse hum reverberating through the dead or dying buildings. I wanted to see the beauty in their piety, or have sympathy with their sorrow, but it was just eating away at what little patience I had left. No matter where I turned, there was little to remind me of the living. I kept looking at the parade and could only see a dirty, brown river, washing a clump of numb bodies downstream and into a deep ditch of lost hope. I tried to find a way of crossing over to the other side, but there was no bridge or tunnel. It was hopeless, I wasn't getting any further. So I began to follow the pilgrims to find out where they were heading. We moved painfully slowly, a smell of what I thought was rotting flesh permeating the town's stayed air. We arrived at a square where the great masses poured into the town's old cathedral. I edged my way out of the traffic and ran over to the church's entrance, already blocked off by the current of people heading into its core. I tried to jump up and see over the mass of bodies, but I couldn't. There were just too many of them. I had to give up. I, it, we, were a lost cause.

Despondent, I made my way back to the hotel, locked myself in my room and waited. I considered just packing up my things and getting the first bus out of town, but looking down at the photograph in my hand, I knew that I had to try to find her, that I had to try to do the best by my abuela. I switched off the light and let the ghoulish sounds of the outside world guide me through the night.

I was up early, fresh-faced and shaved. Outside, there were no remnants of the previous day's procession. The rumbling faith had completely disappeared, leaving once more a crumbling shell of a town in sepia to fend for itself. The deafening mountain wind continued to blow whispering voices around every corner – people of a time gone by telling their stories of death and abandon.

I walked down into the centre of town, arriving at the church I had been carried to by the procession. Tall and imposing, it must have once dominated the skyline, its caring eyes watching over its parishioners. But now its pockmarked exterior, home to gangs of wiry pigeons, just looked depressing. It was no longer the heart of the town but the sad reminder of everything its residents had left behind. Here the love story had ended and all that remained, like the morning after a party, were the remnants of a dream that couldn't last.

I entered the church, by now completely drained of its disciples, just a big empty space showcasing the nakedness of religion, the imagery and grandeur left without an audience – no priests, no bowing heads, just a vacuous monument to a faith that had since moved on.

The mob of pigeons had managed to get inside – the fluttering of their wings booming around the church's decrepit domes, the only sound to infiltrate the space. I saw one perched on top of the pulpit. It looked confused as to how and where all the people had gone. Its oily, green back shone bright, caught in the little light creeping into the church through a cracked window above us. It bobbed along the lectern before flying up and landing on la Virgen de Guadalupe.

I sat on a pew, watching the pigeon carefully as it sat and stared out across the church. It turned around, cocked its tail feathers and shit on la Virgen's head, before it flew off into the anonymity of the church.

La Virgen seemed upset. She didn't deserve that. 'It's alright,' I said. 'Most people prefer to play the villain anyway.'

She just stared back at me bluntly.

'I'm still not ready, you know?'

Silence.

'I keep thinking of home,' I told her. 'No matter how long I spend travelling, I keep thinking about home and everything I've left there – about the past I left there. There are so many things I regret, so many things for which I could be sorry, so many people I have let down. I can feel this strong force pressing me down, right on the very tip of my head, spreading to my shoulders and through my body. I feel like I'm at sea, being battered by waves that try to drag me down.'

Nothing.

'But I know I can't change anything, no matter how sorry I am, no matter what punishment I'm prepared to suffer.'

I looked up at la Virgen, hoping for some kind of a sign. She stared down bleakly, avoiding eye contact, a weak smile on her face. She knew she couldn't help. Mine was a life sentence.

'Do you at least think I'll get through this?' I asked meekly. 'I can't seem to talk to anyone about it anymore. Maybe I've done enough talking. I just really wish I could make it out the other side. I want to escape this sadness. I want to stop it from scratching away at my soul. I just … there are times when I think the easiest thing to do … I don't want to think that, I really, *really* don't, but what if *I'm* the problem?'

A single tear fell to the floor and seeped across the floor of the once-hallowed space. I was trying to save myself from falling into the never-ending darkness, from ending it all there and then.

But I was too weak even to do that.

I don't know how long I lasted in the church. For the first time in a long while, I was completely alone – alone in an abandoned building in a time-forgotten town. Just me and my life. Just me.

Outside deep shadows spread like wildfire across half the town. Bitter air continued to blow through unabated, carrying with it year upon year of loss and shame. Soil battered my face like the rain of an ocean storm, my mouth and lungs filling with dirt – my legs, weak against the force of the wind, preparing to buckle.

The streets were now almost completely empty. Ghostly stories and spirits raced past me, bringing life to an abrupt end, rattling the roofs of the few homes that remained and threatening to carry off anyone who dared to stand in their way. This was a space for the dying. You either got out as quickly as you could or settled down to face your fate.

But I had to battle on. There was something that needed to be done, a story that needed to be finished – a tale with an ending I could affect.

I wandered for what must have been hours, hoping for some kind of a sign, some kind of a lucky deal, my shoes now full of grit, like giant lead weights at the end of my legs. I walked as best I could, holding my hands stretched out in front of me to feel my way forwards. I wanted to shout, but all sound was eaten up by the ferocious wind. I kept my face and eyes low, hoping I wouldn't be hit by the swirling rubble racing through the air around me.

I sat down in the road for a while, trying to regain some strength, when I thought I saw something moving in the distance – a slender, creased man coming towards me. I grabbed at him with all the joy of a shipwreck spotting a passing vessel and asked him if he knew about the old butcher's shop.

'Yes, I know it,' he said reticently, blowing off a thick pile of earth that had settled on his upper lip.

'Could you tell me how to get there?'

'Yes, I could.'

'Great ...'

'Yes.'

'Is it close?

'Yes.'

'How do I get there?'

... 'It's opposite what used to be the cinema.'

'Perfect, and where's that?' I could tell I was losing him.

'Take this hill.'

'Yes.'

'Walk up it.'

'Yes.'

'Cross over to the other side.'

'Yes.'

'Take your third right.' ... 'By the old well.'

'Yes.'

'Continue down that road and you'll find it.'

And with that he was gone, fading once more into the grey-brown.

I was feeling a little shaky, but I dragged myself up that goddamn hill.

'You know, Carla, I'm really starting to doubt I'll make it.'

'*Come on, Simon, you can do it!*'

'I know, I know. I've just got to keep moving. I've got to keep believing.'

'*Do you remember that time we queued for hours to get tickets for that band ... what was their name? ...*'

'I.O.D?'

'*Yes, that's right. Ha! Blimey, they were crap.*'

'Yeah ... they were pretty rubbish. But we had a great time, didn't we? You made me lift you up on my shoulders and then you just disappeared in a shot, surfing across the crowd.'

'*I did! And do you remember when you were convinced that you wouldn't get your grades to get into uni?*'

'I couldn't study. It was during the World Cup.'

'*But you got them didn't you?!*'

'Yes.'

'*You see, you always doubt, don't you? But I believe in you – I'll always believe in you.*'

'You always did. Carla, I miss ...'

'*Don't start, Simon. You know we can't go down that road. Now, what's that you can see in front of you?*'

'A well.'

'*And what's that just up ahead?*'

'An old bu ...'

... '*tcher's shop. You see? Don't ever doubt yourself, Si. Don't ever ...*'

... 'Hang on, don't leave me just yet! Can you stay a little longer?'

'*Well, are you going to walk in or not?*'

Behind the counter, a plain-faced young girl sat with the expectant look of someone awaiting an arrival. An old gramophone, propped up against the rotting corpse of a calf, played out a beautiful, moving song:

Tendré que volar,
Para poderte encontrar,
Buscarte entre las nubes,
Y el inmenso azul del mar.

'Do you know Doña Martha?' I hurriedly asked the girl.

She raised her hand and pointed to the house next door, almost managing a smile.

I thanked her, racing out the shop and knocking on the freshly-painted green door.

'¿Quién?'

'It's Simon.' What a pointless thing to say. 'I'm looking for an address. They tell me that you know them all.'

A clunk and the door was open. A short, round lady stood staring at me.

'I'm sorry to bother you, it's just – I'm looking for my grandmother's house. She was from here, I think, but she left a long time ago.'

'Sí.'

'The address is: Guadalupe #42, esquina Tonalá.'

'It doesn't exist,' she declared, slamming the door in my face.

I turned to walk away.

What did I tell you, Simon? Don't give up! She isn't fobbing us off that easily!

'Did it ever exist?' I shouted at Doña Martha through the thick barrier between us.

The door opened again.

'Look kid, it might have existed, it might still exist. What I mean is, that's not how we do things here.'

'OK, you mean the whole *by the juggling one-legged man wearing red on a Thursday* thing?'

'¿¡Qué?!'

'Sorry, how do you do things here? Please tell me!'

'Look, it's like this,' she said. 'Nothing here, is quite as they intended it. Time eroded logic. We each have our own way of living now, but most people govern themselves by those who are still standing, by those who never escaped.'

'Fine. So do you know, or have you ever known an Alma Eterna?'

'She never lived here in Real de Catorce.'

'No she did! I have the photo to prove it!' I exclaimed.

And as I pulled the picture from my bag in a desperate race to prove her wrong, it fell painfully, slowly to the floor and out of sight. I scrambled around in the violent, grey sea below, desperate that this, of all battles, was one I wouldn't lose. The old lady's door slammed shut again as I sank to my hands and knees.

'Wait, wait! Please wait! I can find her! I can find her!'

Silence.

I'd failed. The book had closed and that was that. There was nothing I could do.

Dark clouds clustered overhead.

40

It's snowing again and your dad bloody hates it. He says, and I quote, 'If I wanted snow, I would move to Canada. I want rain. Cold, hard rain that gets up your nose and makes you hate life.'

I've always loved it though, Si. Maybe it reminds me of when you were small and how magical it was for you to see the snow. I remember once you and your best friend, Tom, rushed for your hats and scarfs because you heard your dad shout, 'It's snowing again.' He was talking about the crappy TV reception, of course – such a problem in the Thames Valley region, or so they said. They used to blame everything on the Thames Valley, as I remember. Asthma, rubbish TV, bad weather, petty crime – everything was the bloody Thames Valley. I'm not sure Swindon's even in the Thames Valley! Anyway, when your dad shouted about the snow, your eyes grew huge with excitement – so big and wide – and well, I'll never forget it, all of a sudden you were all dressed up in your little bobble hat and scarf, rushing for the back door. It was very cute. There are many things in life that cause us to forget, Si, but that memory will stay with me forever.

Simon, me and your dad, we're a bit worried about you. We really are. He told me not to say anything, but I can't sit on the sidelines any longer. I know you say it's just a bit of a bad patch, but listen, you have to be brutally honest with us, Simon, my love. Let's call a spade a spade. If you need to come home, that's what will happen. We'll pay for your flight or whatever you need, Si. We just want to know that you're well and in a safe place.

Are you still taking your medication?

Janice came round the other day, Si, to drop some of your things off. They were cleaning Carla's room out. They told me to tell you that they send you their love. No one blames you, you know love? Sometimes we're all just so upset that we forget to reach out to those most in need. It all gets a bit selfish, but we don't mean anything by it.

I know it's nearly the 15th, my love. Please, please, please, if you need someone to talk to, for God's sake pick up the phone, Si. Don't be too proud. We're here to help you, my love. We're just worried about you, that's all.

We all love you very much, Si, and we'll be waiting for you when you decide to come home.

Write soon please.

All my love,

Mum

41

Hi Mum,

Just writing to say that I might not be in touch for a while. I ended up buying this old banger off some lady who lives in Real de Catorce. She said she'd been looking to get rid of it forever and that I'd be doing her a favour. So I'm going to drive it across to Baja California (check it on the map) and then up to Tijuana. Bit of an epic trip, but I could do with some proper time by myself.

About the 15th, Mum, just to say, it's not necessary to call me or anything like that. I mean, you won't be able to anyway, but just in case you feel like you need to mark it in some way, don't worry. I'll be alright. Like I said, I'm going through a bit of a tricky patch, but there'll be a way out. There has to be a way out, right? I mean, there always is. And however it happens – whatever that route out is – there'll be something better waiting for me on the other side. Everything will be better.

I just want you to know that I love you both more than I can say – more than I've ever said. Just remember that. I am thinking about you and I miss you a lot. I know I've probably been a bit of a disappointment to you both over the years, so I'm sorry about that. We all know you deserve better.

I've got to get going, Mum. There are some pretty mean-looking clouds forming overhead. They reckon a big storm's coming in, so I better try and make up as much ground as possible before it hits.

Love you guys. Keep on smiling.

Si

42

I was dreaming again, or at least I thought I was. It was getting harder and harder to tell. It all looked the same, felt the same. I, the burned tongue, was trapped in a bubble of my own making. There was no escape. If I was dreaming, I'd awake to find myself in a dream and if I was awake, my dreams would provide no respite from reality.

I was on a never-ending road, ploughing on and on and on through the withering desert of North Mexico, the sky observing a deep, ominous grey. It hadn't seen rain for some time, the rough, brittle soil testament to the prolonged absence of nourishment. It was dour, it was numb, far from life or the living. The mountains, either side of the ever-darkening track beneath my wheels, imprisoned me to the futility of escape. If I had wanted to run off, I couldn't. My only option was to keep moving, to venture further down a straight and sinister road to which I could see no end.

I drove slowly, cautiously, trying to ignore the ever-present vultures circling to the edge of my vision that took me back to darker places, to the fierce and ruthless nature of life and death. There, in the desert, I was witness to the brutal, slow murder of life. Death rained down, waging a one-sided battle it knew it would win. There was no let up, no escape, no trick, no way out. It was the desert after all.

A dog bolted out in front of me and went straight under the front left wheel of my car. I screeched to a halt, hearing a haunting thud and a yelp, throwing mountains of dust and rubble into the air. I sprinted back to pick up the mutt, its limp body a sickening reminder of the finality of my touch.

'Where did you come from?! Come on! Give me a break!' I yelled.

I ran back to my car, the engine still running.

I tried to resuscitate it somehow, though I had no idea what I was doing. My hands pumped down like a sledge hammer on where I believed its heart to be, its still, cold tongue hanging loose to one side of its mouth.

'Give it up, Simon,' came a voice from above.

'No! Why?!'

I bundled the corpse into the car and sped off in search of help, one hand on the steering wheel, the other stroking the dog's flea-ridden head.

'Even the fucking ticks are relentless.'

I drove for mile after mile, the vultures still circling overhead, their hungry eyes trained on the carcass of the dead animal, just waiting, knowing that eventually it would come good for them. Eventually, they would win. Inevitably, I would lose.

'No, you won't!' I cried out.

I prayed, honestly I prayed. I listed every god I knew of, every deity that had ever crossed my path. I begged, pleaded and reasoned. I threatened even. I reprimanded. 'Come on, this just isn't fair!'

But no help came. No saviour appeared.

Decrepit, ruined buildings passed us by, their walls ravaged by worms, bullets, rot; their roofs cracked and caved under the constant heat of the sun. Life had upped and left. It had tried but ultimately it had lost. The only showers had come in lead, fired from the guns of those who saw opportunity in vulnerability – narcos who wanted to prove how little life was worth. All poor remaining souls – surrounded by the jangling bones of chattering skeletons – had given up and fled.

'But what about the dog? We can save him! Come on!'

I tried to move my mind on, to lead it away from darker reaches, from the spiralling, growing sadness, from chewing over the unanswerable questions that wanted to hold me hostage. I tried to keep my eyes on the snakeskin road in the hope that I might somehow find an exit.

Other people had dealt with death, why couldn't I? Of course it was fair. We all get the same shot at tragedy. Life didn't discriminated against me. Life doesn't discriminate. We are all in this mess and we all have to find our way out, or at least through. Sometimes the escape is found for you. Sometimes you find the escape for others. We're all in the mess together.

'But ...'

Yes it was your fault. Of course it was your fault. Everything was your fault and had you done things differently, you might be with her right now. She didn't deserve this and that's what hurts you the most. You let her down when she needed you. She needed you and you – selfish, worthless you – fucked it up. You did what was best for you and that's why it happened. You took a decision, a selfish decision and you'll never get over that. Never. You'll be on this road for the rest of your life, your self-imposed prison, the time you have to pay.

'Fuck off, fuck off, fuck off, FUCK OFF!' I screamed repeatedly, staining the inside of the car with the blood of my words. 'Will you never leave me in peace?!'

The mountains loomed higher and higher, stretching further and further towards the sky, forming a long tunnel, bouncing terrifying moments around, repeatedly opening wounds that I knew would never heal.

And suddenly the clouds cracked and it began to rain. It started with just a few drops the clouds had been trying to hold back, but suddenly the weight became too much and furious oceans descended, smashing into the rocks and earth below.

The deluge forced me to pull over. There was no let up, no escape. I could no longer see. I was a wreck roughly bobbing through a great sea storm, just wishing to sink somewhere beneath the surface.

I pulled a map out of the glovebox. It told me there was a hotel about a kilometre up the road. I decided to make a dash for it.

'It's OK, dog, we're going to find some help for you.'

The rain continued to hammer down as I reached the Hotel Oasis.

'I've never known it to rain like this,' the owner said. 'Do you need a hand with your things?'

He walked with me – a fast staccato walk – to my car.

'Oh God, what's that smell?' he shouted at me.

'I think we can still save him.'

'Keep that thing out of my hotel. You should have left it by the side of the road.'

'You think it deserved that?' I shouted.

'Who cares? Listen, you want my help or what?'

He took my bag in his filthy hands and rushed off to the safety of the hotel.

If only I had that gun, now.

'You shouldn't think that.'

I know.

I carried the dog to the cover of an abandoned stables off to one side of the car park.

'Stay here,' I said. 'I'll see you in a bit.'

I made my way back to the hotel.

'Give me a single,' I said, snatching the keys from the owner's grasp and throwing him enough money for a couple of nights.

I lugged my bag up to my room and booted the door open. It was spartan and dank, a crude smell of sewage emanating from the bathroom in the back-right corner of the room.

It'll do, I thought.

I lay down on the bed in the centre of the room, listening to the river of rain pound the hotel's thin roof, invigorated by the occasional flash of lightning and the foreboding sound of thunder crashing outside. The noise of the storm could have concealed the most determined of crimes. The electricity had long since fled.

Long since fled.

I get up and look out the window across an empty car park. The vast expanse of the desert offers no shelter.

I make my way to the bathroom. Grey-blue tiles stretch from ceiling to floor; a dirty towel and a bar of soap lie by the shower.

I look deep into the mirror and can see nothing but infinite darkness and the face of someone who is already half-way dead, the deep lines of regret in his face exposed by the streaks of lightning coming in through the window behind him.

He reaches down, plugs the sink and runs the taps, filling it to the brim with brownish water. He stands for a while looking at the islands of dirt and scum floating on its surface. He reaches into the water, cupping it in his hands, and brings it up to his face, allowing it to drip down and back into the basin, even dirtier than when it left the taps.

He looks up again into the mirror and this time there is nobody there, just an empty space. He opens an unmarked bottle of pills and drinks them down before making his way back to the bedroom and sitting back down on the bed. He sits resting against the damp hotel wall to begin with, his legs outstretched and his toes pointing directly up, perpendicular to his ankles. He sits there for some time, listening to the storm outside growing in strength. A fierce wind begins to rattle the roof, trying to tear it off and throw it away, pulling ceaselessly at its flimsy sheets of corrugated iron. The lightning is more frequent now. The roof has started leaking – drip drops to begin with, but as the hydraulic arms of the wind do their best to wrestle the roof from its frame, the water starts to pour in, moving like mercury across the chipped floorboards and towards the bed. He lowers his body down into a lying position and crosses his arms across his chest in an X formation. The storm continues to rage around him, but finally he has found some shelter, escape from the fury – a sedative – a place to rest. He's spent the past few years wondering if it might happen and how it might happen. Now it's just a question of waiting.

43

Dear Dr Jayawardene,

It's Jill, Simon's mum. I'm just writing to you for a bit of reassurance really. Jeff and I are terribly worried about Simon. He ran off to Mexico some months back and has been travelling there ever since. At first we thought it would do him some good to have some space and get out of the country for a bit – he was definitely showing some signs of having turned a corner – but now I'm starting to think he might be in trouble.

He's started to sound very down in the emails he's sending us. He's talking about going through a bit of a dark patch. He says not to worry, but, should we be worried? He's still taking the medication you prescribed him, as far as I know. He's always been such a sensible boy, but I do worry about him. It's getting close to the date of the accident.

Do you think we should try and get him to come home? Or is this all part of the process? Are ups and downs normal?

We really hope to hear back from you soon. I know I might just be worrying for no reason, but, I don't know, I've just got a bad feeling this time.

Jill

44

When I awoke, the storm had stopped and all I could see was black. An unnerving, eternal silence filled the air. I wondered if I'd finally done it, if I'd finally managed to do it. But then I got the smell, the smell of rain-soaked land, the smell of life flooding into empty space. I began to feel the bed around me: the rough cotton of the cheap-hotel sheets, the splintered woodwork of the bed frame and the empty bottle of tablets.

...

I couldn't tell if I was relieved or angry – whether I just felt nothing at all.

My eyes opened slowly, absorbing the stale air of a scene that had remained undisturbed for some time. Everything was exactly as I had left it.

I lowered my frail legs gradually to the floor, the tips of my toes making out the detailed grain of the wooden boards. They didn't feel like my toes to begin with, but they slowly gathered strength, the blood returning to my heart with news of life.

I sat there motionless, my expressionless face buried in my chest, contemplating the next minutes and hours, wondering how I could possibly continue.

I didn't really have much choice.

I went to my bag and pulled out my diary, running my hand gently over its fraying cover and as I opened it up, the letter my grandma had given me just before she passed away landed defiantly on the floor. I'd put off reading it until then. I thought it might have brought up too many dangerous memories. I wasn't sure if I was ready for it. But there, in the cold wake of my absolute failure, there was little else that could go wrong.

I took the letter in my hands and settled myself back on the bed. I took a deep breath, composed myself and opened it up.

It was incredible to see my abuela's handwriting again – every flick and curl carrying with it a slide show of golden memories. I traced her words with my fingers and brought her back to life.

Dear Simon,

If you're reading this letter, it's because I have left you for a while. I wish I could tell you now how much it means to me to have share my life with you, all those secrets we kept within us, the secrets I could tell to no one else but you, all those many things that I leave behind with you now, Simon.

You hopefully will read this when – and only when – you are ready. It's ironic that the closer we move to the end of our time, the more easy it is for us to understand what we're supposed to do.

I always was scared of death, Simon. I know, that is probably hard for you to believe now, but is true. As a young girl, I always say I want to live forever. I use to have nightmares about a dark curtain that came and wrap itself around my head, slowly stopping me from breathing.

And now I see the curtain, now I see it flutter and move in the wind, it makes me laugh. I use to tell your mother when she broke up with a boyfriend, or whenever she was really sad, that nothing last forever, and in some ways is true – sometimes things they disappear for a while, sometimes you don't see it anymore – but this, Simon, this is not the end.

And here's the secret: everything last forever.

Whatever happen in life, whatever come your way, good things or bad things, we will always be together. I will always be sharing stories with you, laughing with you and crying with you. And Carla, the love of your life (I never seen anyone look at someone as she looks at you), she will always be with you – no one can take away what you two feel, the memories you have share. Whatever happens in life, you will always be together, in one way or another.

I am just a humble old lady, but now, as I say goodbye to the world and I think about all the peoples that have pass before me, I realise that you never truly leave. One thing just turn into another. We will all still be here in one way or another. You just have to look sometime.

I'll miss you, of course, even though I will be with you the whole time really. Take care of Carla, my dear. She's an absolute keeper.

So be good, Simon. Enjoy life, but most important of all: explore. Explore, Simon. Never get tired of searching. And carry me with you every step that you take.

All my love,

Abue

As I wiped away the tears cascading over my cheeks, a sweet melody flooded into the cold depths of my room – a thin tunnel of refreshing light, drawing me to the surface. I'd heard it somewhere before. It floated up from downstairs, bringing words that I knew, a familiar melody.

Tendré que volar,

Para poderte encontrar,
Buscarte entre las nubes,
Y el inmenso azul del mar.

Hasta el fondo de mis recuerdos,
Tendré que bucear,
Nadando por la noche,
Para poderte encontrar.

Y así siempre te buscaré,
Así te voy a conmemorar,
Y con la luz de nuevo día,
Volver a empezar.

My heart fluttered into life like a caged bird trying to escape to freedom, sending joyous, potent blood racing around my body. I staggered, half-naked, out of the bedroom, grabbing a hold of the stained hotel walls for support, and made my way downstairs, drawn by the words of a song I had lost and found. I let my mind dance across the notes as I walked slowly, one step at a time, towards the source of the music. And there I stood, transfixed, mouthing every letter and word, a big smile spread across my face. I'd found them. I'd found both of them! That song – Carla had chosen it for my grandma's funeral. She'd chosen that song for my grandma and for us.

I reached for a pen and paper resting on the receptionist's desk and dragged myself back up to my room, sitting myself at an unpainted desk, staring out the window as the night drew to a close, my hand shaking under the weight of the words it needed to pass to paper.

To the one person I never wanted to hurt,

These tears don't do justice to the grief that I've lived. You were everything to me, a way of making sense of the world. And ever since you left, I've been crushed by an infinite sadness, by the weight of guilt and the insufferable pain of being unable to forgive myself. You can never know how sorry I am. You can never know. I dream of turning back and stopping it all from happening, but I can't. I just can't. We believe everything is possible until the clock stops and then those that are left are reminded of just how powerless they are, of how redundant they are. And now I'm left to put these pieces back together, alone. There exists no moment of my life when you aren't there, when I'm not thinking about you. I need you to know these things. I need you to know our love still exists, that you're still in my heart and that one day I hope to find you somewhere, at peace and happy. I'll keep searching for as long as it takes.

Your forever love,

Simon

As I crumpled the note under my tear-stained fingers, the sun began to shine in, a thin red line encroaching upon an eternal darkness. The clouds that had caused such destruction for so long started to float off into the distance. A new day crept in around me; from somewhere deep within I began to feel like I could do it, like I could carry on.

I thought about my abuela's message and suddenly it all started to make sense. Her, Carla, all of us – life – we're infinite. We're everywhere we've ever set foot. We're in every place we've ever been to, every meal we've ever enjoyed, every relationship we've ever poured ourselves into, every song we've ever loved.

We're infinite.

I raced to pack my things, ran outside and jumped into the car, firing it up and racing away.

Remnants of the storm were strewn by the side of the road; great rivers flowed where once there was nothing. A powerful, nourishing sun took centre stage, begging me to travel on. I wound down my window and fresh oxygen flew into the car. I could smell the salt and humidity in the air.

45

Police Report:

Time of incident – 22:03, 15th December, 2012

Place of incident – Boxtrot Corner

Vehicle – Citröen Saxo registration number PS889YAG

Officer in charge – Detective Steve Barrow

Details – A royal blue Citroen Saxo was found at approximately 22:03 at Boxtrot Corner, Gloucestershire, having left the road and collided with a tree. The incident inflicted severe damage to the passenger's side of the car. The driver managed to exit the vehicle and was found disorientated and confused by the side of the road. The passenger was cut free from the vehicle and taken to the John Radcliffe Hospital, Oxford, where she later passed away from the injuries sustained. The driver was found to have consumed alcohol, but was under the legal limit.

Statements – Driver: 'We left the Royal Oak pub at around 21:45, where we had been to celebrate a friend's birthday. Carla was drinking, but I wasn't – I only had one. I can't remember exactly what happened, but it was wet on the road. I think I swerved to miss an animal. The last thing I remember is hearing her screaming.

The family of the deceased do not wish to press charges.

1

It's been two weeks since I nearly died in the desert. Two peaceful, silent weeks full of beautiful, forgiving space and time. I've been writing non-stop and gathering emails, committing the last few months to page. I've laughed and, yes, I've cried. It's a story I had to tell.

And now that I have, I feel it can fend for itself. It can shout all it wants now. It's time to put it to one side. I think it's time for a new chapter.

I pull over to a dirt track and let it take me down to a narrow spit of sand leading out from a cove. I throw open the car door and without really knowing why, kick off my clothes and run straight into the sea, diving my body under the still water, wrapping myself in the bounteous, turquoise, infinite and forgiving ocean, staying under the water with my eyes closed until I let myself drift slowly back to the surface. And there I just lie on my back, gently floating, looking up at the playful white clouds spread out over the world's ceiling. I lie, in total isolation. Here is a different type of eternity – an eternity of space, both liberating and tranquilizing. Here is a sea and a sky that connects wandering parts. Here is a sea that can wash me of my worries. I can stay afloat or sink to the bottom, it's my call. I can take as long as I want. This is nature and this is man and here am I, without a plan. So insignificant. So small among this immense beauty.

Suddenly the fragility of life strikes me as the essence of that beauty – the very thing that drives us to learn from our mistakes and cross borders. Our time is ours to do the best we can with.

For the first time in an age I feel completely at peace, my body empty as it floats on the wide, wide sea. That peace won't last, I know that, but it doesn't need to.

I can do this.

I return to the sand and pick up a large bottle from beneath my clothes. I can hear the slow, regular beat of the breathing water, of the gentle waves carrying other stories and tales to new shores to be greeted by the timeless sand beneath our feet. I look at the bottle in my hands, stuffed full of precious memories. I move forwards, look out to sea and release it into the blanket of the water.

2

There's something supremely magical about feeling the wind sweep across your face and through your hair. I haven't always thought that, of course, but then I haven't always been in lands so cherished by the sun. The air here grabs all my redundant worries and lifts them effortlessly from my shoulders before leaving them frozen in time, available for others if they wish to learn. And do you know what? Even better still is that this breeze is fabricated – a product of my liberated soul. It's not nature, nor divine intervention, nor any other inexplicable force – it's me.

Life, that's what this is all about – beautiful, perplexing life, eternal life, far greater than you or I, irreverent and ultimately indifferent. After I'm gone, what will be left of this world? The oceans will remain, their waters gently lapping at land's edge, the sun arriving and leaving again, but not before getting a few billion people out of bed. There comes a time when we are summoned, perhaps to a greater cause or maybe just to come and rest awhile. Like the crisp, radiant evening light, we are here just a moment, our presence little felt beyond the most immediate circles – a drop in the water, whose ripples and actions will spread beyond their initial reach, but which ultimately becomes part of a greater whole, a giant, breathing body of history and time, contained within its limits. And beyond this great ocean, a museum of triumph and despair, a vast world of which we know so little, there's a far greater space, whose borders we struggle to comprehend.

And here I am, at 23 years old, with the distinct sensation that my journey is only just beginning. My life has been marked in many ways up until now by the things that I haven't done, by the opportunities I've missed and the regrets that I've carried upon my back. You know what I'd like now? To live by my achievements, to remember the things that I *have* done, no matter how big or small. To continue my journey. I have few possessions and little money, but I'm doing what I can to live beyond survival. I'm on my journey – a journey without direction that promises to take me far, further than I have ever dared to dream. I still carry my burdens, but I'll try not to let them define who I am. No *what ifs*, no *buts*, I *just am*, transient and carried by the waves, living my life as if it were my own, my only.

I reach the border and here it is that I was meant to stop, but now I know that no journey ever really meets its end. It might veer off on another course, but it never actually ends. One horizon merges into another, the sun rising not long after it has set. This journey is me and I am my journey. My destiny is to keep going along this road, for now.

I stand opposite the border guard. I stare at her, she stares at me. I smile.

'Where've you come from, mister?'

'Oh, I've been travelling for a while.'

'You're on a journey then?'

'Something like that.'

'Where you off to next?'

'Anywhere at all.'

'OK, sir, well, I hope you enjoy your trip.'

'Thank you, I will.'

Adiós México y gracias. And with that, I'm gone – at least for now.

Y con la luz de nuevo día, volver a empezar.

ABOUT THE AUTHOR

I always wanted to write a novel. So I did.

8528795R00112

Printed in Germany
by Amazon Distribution
GmbH, Leipzig